NECROMANCER

Sequel to NiDemon

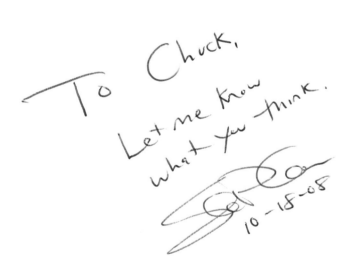

Books by Shawn P. Cormier
Published by Pine View Press

Nomadin

NiDemon

Necromancer

Night in the Desecration

"I don't know," answered Kale. His facial deformities pooled with shadows. "We should have been there by now. I think we passed it."

"Passed it?" cried Rose, straightening. "How?"

Kale looked desperately around, then hung his head.

"What's the big deal?" said Ilien. "We'll turn around and go back."

Rose took a deep breath to calm herself. "Okay. How far back is it?" she asked, her face strained in the wavering light of her magical flame.

"Too far, I think," said Kale.

Rose clenched her hands into fists, eyes wide.

"What's wrong?" asked Ilien, a growing panic building in his chest. "Can't we camp right here?"

"Night in the Desecration is complete," whispered Kale.

"That's good," said Ilien, looking from Rose to Kale. "It'll cover our tracks. Right?"

Rose's magical light flickered then dimmed. "Night in the Desecration is a death sentence." She placed a trembling hand on Kale's shoulder. "Unlike the Cyclops, the Onegod will not protect us." She lifted Kale's chin and stroked his malformed face, her eyes filled with sudden forgiveness. "It's not your fault. I do not blame you."

The air grew quickly darker, bringing with it a suffocating pressure. Ilien grabbed his chest. He looked around desperately. There was nowhere to escape.

Kale threw his arms around Rose as she gazed into her wavering flame. "No one has ever survived a night in the Desecration, Ilien. No one." The flame flickered once, then went out.

NECROMANCER

Sequel to NiDemon

Shawn P. Cormier

Pine View Press

Necromancer

Visit us on the Web! www.pineviewpress.com

ISBN: 978-0-9740151-4-9

Published by:

**Pine View Press
42 Central Street
Southbridge, Ma 01550
USA**

Printed in Canada

Acknowledgments

Thanks go out to all the wonderful readers who wanted me to keep writing, even when I didn't. You reminded me to Be, then Do, then Have.

This book is dedicated to you.

You know who you are.

To the
Eastland →

Evendolen

Greattower mountain

To the Westland
and the Giants

Berkhelven

Bamber

NEAR PLAINS

Quinnebog River

Far-Hills River

FEN LAND FOREST

FAR PLAINS

N

MIDLAND MOUNTAINS

Glen Hollow

Warren

Evernden

Southford

Spence

Dell

To Kingsend
in the south

The Three Lakes

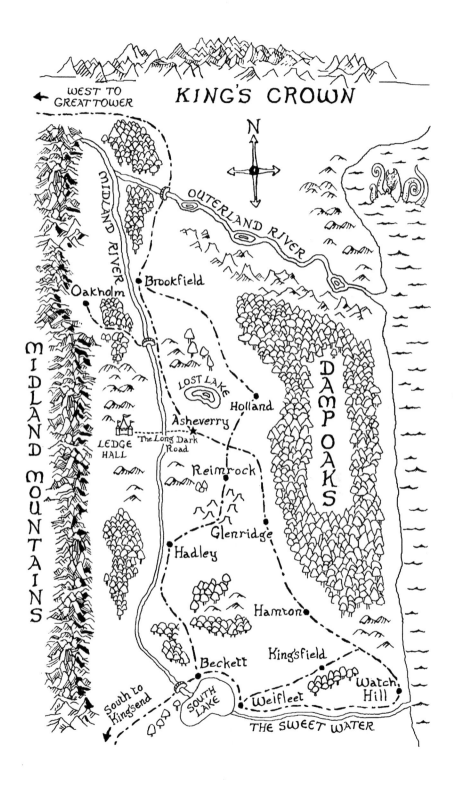

CONTENTS

Chapter I

Evil Sown

He didn't remember the Long Dark Road ever being so cold.

The tall man ran through the darkness, his long cloak billowing out behind. The echo of his boots upon the cold, stone floor rang in the gloom, reverberating the length of the tunnel. The musty air tasted of dirt, and he swallowed hard. Necessity drove him onward. Rage hastened his progress. His shirt and cloak were soaked with perspiration, and the frigid tunnel air sucked the last vestiges of warmth from his body. Only his reckless flight kept him from succumbing to the cold completely.

He settled into an easier gait. After all, he had more than a few miles to go. He cruised through the blinding darkness with the surety of a man who knew the way without fail. Truth be told, he did know the way without fail, but truer still he had no need for light or guidance. He could see through the gloom like a bat in the night. All NiDemon could.

Bulcrist smiled through his rage. Perhaps there was still hope. He was not powerless. Despite his defeat, he could still wield magic as before. The boy was stronger but he would not come into his full power so quickly. Perhaps there was still time to make sure that he never would. What he needed was an ally.

Or allies.

Bulcrist quickened his pace. His mind raced. Yes! Of course! The Nomadin!

The Nomadin would not need convincing. They truly believed that the boy was the Prophesied One, the forbidden child of Nomadin heritage who was destined to release the Necromancer from his prison. Fools! They did not know the boy's true identity. Ilien Woodhill was the Necromancer himself.

Bulcrist spat. It did not matter. The Nomadin desired the boy dead and he could use that in his favor. Their plan to use the Witch Queen to do their dirty work had failed. What they needed now was a new plan. He could give it to them. He knew the boy better than any of the Nomadin. He knew the boy's strengths and weaknesses. Together they could destroy him before he grew too powerful.

Bulcrist lurched to a stop in the darkness. He stood for a moment to catch his breath, a sudden doubt settling upon him. The boy's words came back to him.

You will return to Ledge Hall and live out the rest of your days alone. If ever you set foot outside its gates, the rune I placed upon you will strike you dead.

The boy was powerful indeed. But was he truly that powerful? And what of the Nomadin? They might think otherwise of his plan. After all, he was a NiDemon. He was their enemy. Why would they listen to him? Why would they need to? They had the boy's mother. Ilien would go to them. With their combined might they could easily destroy the boy.

A smile stole over Bulcrist as he panted in the darkness. The boy would be destroyed. That was all the mattered. As long as the boy died for what he'd done, he would rest easy. As long as he died.

2

Bulcrist frowned suddenly, recalling Ilien's final words. *Do not linger. You have until nightfall to make it back home.*

With a curse Bulcrist shook off the cold and started forward once more.

Without warning, a writhing black shadow detached itself from the tunnel wall. Like a net of darkness, it dropped to the floor before the NiDemon and flew up to block his way.

Bulcrist drew back, his hand before his eyes. The creature pained his vision, as if it leached the very sight from his mind. A stab of fear drew the breath from Bulcrist's body. The Nothingness exuded an unwholesome power he had never experienced before, an overwhelming dismay, a senseless brutality that oozed from it like blood from a wound. In defense, his fingers traced the Light rune.

There was a brief flash of brilliant, yellow light in which the Nothingness shone like a column of smoke, a brown illusion that sickened the eye. Quickly the light dimmed, cowered to a dingy glow, then died completely.

Do not be afraid, said the Nothing.

Bulcrist stumbled back, clutching at his ears. The words deafened him though he could hear them plainly in his mind.

"What are you?" he asked, his own voice stabbing the silence.

The Nothing advanced upon him.

I am friend and brother. I am aid and ally. Do not be afraid.

Bulcrist retreated, feeling the wall with one hand as he went. The creature was no ally, that much he knew. Whatever it was, it was powerful enough to steal his NiDemon sight and break his Nihilic spell. But what was it doing here? And what did it want of him?

3

I want what you want, Tannon Bulcrisst.

The Nothing expanded as it hissed his name, as if saying it gave it power over him.

Bulcrist froze, paralyzed, unable to retreat from the growing void before him. His mind filled with panic as an icy finger prodded his thoughts.

Yess.

The word lanced like a sliver of ice through Bulcrist's consciousness.

The boy musst die.

Bulcrist stiffened against the Nothing's touch, fighting to stave off the incorporeal assault. But the power of the Void was overwhelming. Slowly his mind gave way. By degrees the Nothing gained control over him.

Yess!

Bulcrist's body spasmed as the word ripped through the remnants of his mind. He moaned as the Nothing leaped upon him. Blackness enveloped him, condensing into an impenetrable, suffocating shroud. Bulcrist remained rigid, silent, as the blackness seeped into his skin. A moment later he stood alone in the tunnel once more.

"Yess," he whispered.

The Nothing opened its new eyes and surveyed the darkness in silence. *Yess indeed*, it thought. Now the boy's death was all but assured. There was power in this new body. Power to add to its own. Power to destroy the boy once and for all!

It raised its new hands and marveled at the glowing runes they drew. A geyser of white-hot fire erupted from its fingers and raced to the ceiling. The pressure-heated air exploded, cracking the walls and raining debris to the floor. The torrent of blinding magic smote the stone above in a glut of white sparks, turning it instantly to liquid glass. The molten rock poured from the blasted ceiling and pooled upon the ground. Soon the entire tunnel raged like a blast furnace. Still the Nothing stood, unharmed, impervious to the power it wielded, and leveled its rage upon the earth around him. *Yess! I will kill the boy! Ilien Woodhill will die!*

Chapter II

A Gift For Windy

Am I the Creator? Is it true? Can I really be what everyone tells me I am? And if it is true, what then? I am still a boy. I am still encased in this body, this undersized, weak little body. I can't even beat up Stanley Coothner, and he's encased in an oversized, pudgy little body. And if I can't beat up Stanley Coothner, then how can I possibly be the Creator?

Then there's my magic. How pathetic. Can't control it. Can't even find it when I need to half the time. Sure, with it I can fly. With it I can disappear, shoot fire from my fingertips and even come back from the dead. But that doesn't make me God. Every Nomadin can do what I do. And they can do it better. So what makes everyone think that I'm the one?

What makes me *think I'm the one?*

A cool mist hung beneath the trees, and the smell of damp earth lingered in the early morning air. Bright beads of sunlight dappled the forest floor and played upon the broad leaves of the young oaks that grew beneath their taller, straighter-trunked elders. The new day held the promise of warmer, dryer things to come, but for the moment the early morning still held remnants of a cold, dark night.

Ilien shouldered his pack, testing its weight as he adjusted it upon his back. It felt light—too light—and he wondered what was in it. Anselm had packed it for him so there should be plenty of food, knowing the Giant. Yet from the feel of it, there wasn't much more than a few days rations. Surely he'd need more than that. Unless . . .

Ilien shrugged the pack to the ground and quickly checked its contents. The first item he came across was his pencil, stashed within his blanket. He'd put it there earlier for safe keeping. He pulled it out and fixed it with an accusing look.

"Is there something about the contents of this pack that I should know about?" he asked. The pencil remained silent, highly unusual as the mischievous wand always had plenty to say, primarily at the most inopportune of times. He gave it a sharp pinch and stashed it in his tunic pocket.

He speared an arm into the pack and rummaged blindly about, assessing what he came across by its feel. There was a small coil of rope, his blanket, something round and hard—an apple perhaps. He fished deeper, pushing aside what felt like a tinder box for making fires. *No fireflies where we're going*, he thought, lamenting the absence of the magical fire-producing bugs. He groped about until he found something solid at the bottom of the pack.

"No!" he cried aloud as he finally came across what he feared would be there. "No no no no no!" Dense yet yielding, rectangular in shape. Quickly he speared a finger beneath the paper wrapping. Damp! It was damp, spongy and sticky!

Ilien eased out the loaf of Awefull and held it at arm's length, eyeing it with dismay. No wonder his pack was so light. It looked like he'd be eating Awefull for breakfast, lunch and dinner!

"A little gift from me," came a booming voice behind him. "I thought you might like some comfort food.

7

Something to remind you of home."

Ilien dropped the smelly, wet loaf back into his pack. "It will definitely remind me of you," he said, turning to grin in Anselm's direction. "You know, just because you think it's delicious doesn't mean everyone else does."

The Giant pushed Ilien an incredulous look. "It's not just delicious, it gives you energy. Why, you could run for four days straight with only a slice a day to eat. And healthy? I never had a lick of hair before I started eating Awefull. And now look at me." He puffed out his chest. As if to prove his point, an unruly thicket of gnarled chest hair sprouted from the collar of his animal skin shirt. "You're just not old enough to like it," he added.

Ilien cinched his pack shut and hoisted it back onto his shoulders. "Maybe when I turn two-hundred-and-sixteen I'll like it, too."

"Two-hundred-and-fifteen," corrected Anselm, frowning.

Ilien wiped his hands on his pants to rid himself of any Awefull residue. "I wish you were going with us," he said, turning serious. "I'll miss you, you know."

The Giant's frown faded to a thin smile as he looked over the boy before him. There was a gentle light in his eyes, the soft glow of a fondness born out of kinship and adversity shared. "I will miss you more," he said, kneeling and opening his arms wide.

Ilien rushed into Anselm's crushing embrace, squeezing his own arms as tightly as he could around the Giant. It was like hugging a boulder.

"I'll be back before I know it," he said, as if reassuring himself that he would. "And I'll bring the wizardesses back with me."

"And I will go west to the Giants and bring my son back to his senses. For too long he has clung to the old ways of ruling. The Giants will redeem themselves. They will stand ready to help you rescue your mother from the Nomadin when you return. And I will have a son again."

Ilien pulled away and leveled his gaze upon the Giant. "I know you will. Together we'll make the them pay for what they've done."

Anselm ruffled Ilien's long, unkempt hair with a massive hand. "You remind me of him. Strong and willful."

"Oh, he's willful alright," said Windy, suddenly appearing from behind a tree. She wore a dark green tunic that was a bit too large for her. He hands were buried in its pockets and she hugged the excess cloth around her body to fend off the morning's damp chill. The knees of her pants were stained with mud and her pack, also looking light, rode low upon her back. She smiled half-heartedly as she approached. "Gallund says it's time. Says he wants to talk to everyone before we go."

Anselm nodded and rose to his feet with a groan. "Don't ever grow old," he said, rubbing one knee. He turned to lead the way, but stopped as he saw that Ilien and Windy weren't following. He seemed about to say something, but thought better of it and smiled instead.

"I'll tell Gallund you'll be along shortly," he said after a moment, and he turned and lumbered away through the trees.

Ilien and Windy stared at each other as the morning breeze ruffled the leaves above them. The silence felt awkward to Ilien. He had always known what to say to Windy, and when to say it. They had been through much together, but their adventures had changed them. Now they would soon be embarking on another, even more dangerous adventure, an adventure that would bring even more changes, for both of them would finally meet the mothers they had never known. For Windy, it meant finally knowing what having a mother was like. For Ilien, it was more complicated. He had a mother, and loved her very much. But his mother back in Southford was his adoptive mother. Now she was a captive of the Nomadin. His birth mother, on the other hand, was a wizardess, and though he wanted to meet her, it wasn't for the reason one might expect. There was no bond between them. She had never tucked him into bed, or hugged him after a nightmare. She had never baked him a birthday cake, or washed behind his ears. But she had power, power that could help him save the one who had done all those things.

"Are you ready?" asked Windy. She shivered in the cool, damp breeze that moved beneath the trees.

Ilien knew what was going through her mind. "We'll be fine. We'll be back before you know it. And we'll bring back the wizardesses." He smiled at her. "Your mom, too."

Windy smiled back, but it was a different kind of smile. She moved closer to Ilien and reached for his hand. "I wanted to tell you something before we left," she said, capturing his hand in hers.

Ilien froze. His hand suddenly felt sweaty. His heartbeat quickened. He stared at his feet in sudden embarrassment.

"Hey look!" he cried. He stooped and quickly came back up with something concealed in his palm. "You'll never guess what I have in my hand," he blurted out. It was only a small, reddish stone he had discovered on the ground when he stared at his feet, but it seemed a good enough distraction from whatever Windy was going to say, and he thought he knew what Windy was going to say. It wasn't that he didn't like Windy that way, it was just . . .

"What is it?" asked Windy, the hint of a smile on her lips.

Ilien felt suddenly very hot. A surge of energy rushed through him, as if he had conjured a spell without knowing it. He had unknowingly conjured spells before, but this felt different. He opened his hand with a grimace.

"Ilien, it's beautiful! For me?"

Ilien stared in amazement at his open hand. There, sparkling even in the dim shadows beneath the trees, rested a brilliant, red gemstone that fit perfectly in his palm.

"How—" He stopped and looked sheepishly at Windy. "For you," he said.

Windy held it up and peered into its ruby depths. "It's amazing! It's like a crystal rose. Where did you find it? No. I don't want to know." She clutched it to her chest. "No one has ever given me a rose before."

Another awkward moment of silence fell between them. Windy broke the tension. "So how does it feel?"

Ilien blushed a deeper shade of red. "How does what feel?"

"How does it feel knowing you're the Creator reborn? What did you think I was going to say?"

Ilien wanted to laugh, but the question had hit a nerve. "How do *you* feel, knowing I'm not just some boy?" he asked. "That I'm not even human?"

Windy's smile faded. "I didn't mean to—"

"It's okay," said Ilien. He took a deep breath and let it out slowly. "I'm not sure how to feel, to tell you the truth. I'm not sure I believe it yet."

Windy grabbed his hand once more. She turned it over and studied his palm. "This looks like a boy's hand to me," she said, looking up. "You'll always be Ilien Woodhill to me, the boy I single-handedly saved from the wolves."

Ilien did laugh this time. "I guess that makes us even."

"Come on," said Windy. "I don't think we should keep Gallund waiting, even if you are the creator of the universe."

Chapter III

The Crossing

"It's about time!" called Gallund as he saw them through the trees. "Where have you been, Ilien? We've been waiting for you." The wizard turned and threw a handful of peanut shells onto the coals of the morning's fire. "Come. Sit. We have a few things to go over before we leave."

Beside Gallund stood Thessien, his weather-beaten countenance grimmer than usual, his arms folded across his chest. The Eastland soldier's bedraggled clothing, weeks-old beard and brooding look did nothing to mask the mettle of the man beneath—the air of a king.

The Swan rose to her feet behind him as they entered the campsite. A look of annoyance creased her feathered face as Gallund cleared his throat to speak. It was evident to Ilien that the two of them had not been getting along, as usual. The Swan ruffled her tail feathers and fixed Ilien with a light-hearted smile.

"Where's Pedustil?" asked Ilien suddenly, looking around.

The wizard cleared his throat once more. "As you know," he said, ignoring Ilien's question, "we will be traveling via a Crossing. There are a few rules we need to go over before we go. Some dos and don'ts."

Gallund fell silent and looked at each one in turn.

"Quit the dramatics and get on with it!" cried the Swan,

rattling her wings. "There are a few things I'd like to go over as well."

The wizard frowned and plucked a peanut from his pocket. He weighed it in his palm. "Patience is a virtue, my dear. You will have your chance to speak, but first I must warn my traveling companions about the dangers of Crossings." He regarded the peanut in his hand, decided against eating it, and returned it to his pocket. Looking up he said, "You may not know that the Crossings were meant for the Nomadin alone. They are deadly to all else, and dangerous even for those they were meant for."

Ilien began to say something but Gallund cut him off.

"Yes. It's true that many spirit creatures used them in the War of the Crossings. But spirit creatures are more akin to Nomadin than humans are." He glanced meaningfully at Windy. "Even half-humans."

"Are you saying that Windy shouldn't go because she's only half Nomadin?" asked Ilien. "Because that's not an option. She has to go."

Windy seemed to shrink, as if the air was being squeezed out of her.

"I'm not saying she shouldn't go," answered Gallund. "I'm saying that it will be risky."

"What do you mean, risky?" asked the Swan, stepping forward. "Can she die?"

Gallund chewed on her question for a moment. His hand strayed back to his pocket. He furrowed his brow. "Probably not."

Anselm grunted and moved a protective step toward the princess. Thessien eyed the wizard in silence.

"That's little comfort!" cried the Swan. "Probably not?"

"Hold on," said Ilien. "If Windy's not in probable danger of dying, what is she in probable danger of?"

Ilien's pencil wriggled in his pocket, but before it could comment he pinched it quiet.

"Crossing between worlds is tricky," replied Gallund. "All sorts of problems can arise if you're not . . . well . . ." He looked apologetically at Windy. "Made of the right stuff, so to speak."

"But I am half Nomadin," countered the princess.

"Yeah, she's half Nomadin," said Anselm.

"All I'm saying is that she's half human and that could be a problem," explained the wizard.

"What kind of problem?" persisted Ilien.

"She could get lost." Gallund turned and began to pace. "She might end up somewhere else."

"But I thought every Crossing lead to a definite destination," said Ilien. "Like a road."

"Or a tunnel," added the Giant. "Like the Long Dark Road."

"Yes, of course," said the wizard. "But like a road that has side streets, or a tunnel that has intersecting ways. Most Crossings are passages with many diverging paths. Even a Nomadin can get lost and end up somewhere else if not careful. To travel by Crossing takes a certain feel, like finding your way through a darkened room. If the house is yours, you're less apt to bump your shins on the coffee table, that's all. A Nomadin has a much easier time. But there are other risks."

"Like what?" asked Windy, her defiant chin in full gear.

"Like being talked to death," blurted Ilien's pencil before Ilien could silence it.

Gallund ignored the outburst. He looked about for a place to sit and rested himself on a large rock that jutted from the earth beside a tree. "I'm not exactly sure. You'll be the first half-blood to ever use a Crossing." He bent his head in thought. "Still . . . "

"What?" pressed Windy.

"Well, you could possibly turn into something."

"Turn into something?" said Ilien, squeezing his pencil in anticipation of a smart remark. "Like what?"

Gallund looked at Windy and smiled weakly. "Something else. Something not you."

"Anything else I should know about?" asked the princess, her face rigid.

"You could theoretically cease to be," squeaked Ilien's pencil.

"Enough!" yelled the Swan. "That's it! She's not going! It's too dangerous!" The great bird wrapped a wing around Windy.

"But I have to go," said Windy, pulling away from the Swan's feathery grip. "I won't let Ilien go alone."

"First of all, my dear," interjected Gallund, "he's not going alone. He is going with me." The wizard held out his hand to Ilien. "Second of all, I'll take your pencil, please."

Ilien reluctantly handed it over. "When will you learn to keep quiet?" he mumbled as Gallund snatched it away and tucked it under his robes.

"Now," continued the wizard, "the choice is yours, Windy. I will not stop you from going. But you have been warned."

Silence fell in the clearing. Thessien eyed Gallund. Gallund scowled at the Swan. The Swan raised an eyebrow at Anselm.

Ilien turned to Windy. "Maybe she's right. Maybe it's too dangerous."

The princess shook her head and turned away.

"I don't want anything bad to happen to you," said Ilien. Windy spun back to face him. "And you think I want

15

anything bad to happen to you? We've been in this whole
thing from the start. You have no right to tell me I can't go."
She regarded the others angrily. "None of you do."

Again there was silence—the kind of silence that
precedes the lightning.

"You're right," said Ilien. He stepped forward and put an
arm around her shoulder. "She's coming with me, like it or
not."

The Swan grunted her dissatisfaction and fanned out her
tail feathers. "Kids! They'll be the death of me."

"If we're all finished griping," said Gallund, "may I
suggest we get back to the dos and don'ts?" The wizard
stood once more, peanut shells cascading from his lap.

"First the dos. *Do* not resist the pull of the Crossing.
You will feel as if you are being pulled in several directions
at once. This pulling sensation will at times be very strong,
even violent. Do not fight it. Do not pull in the opposite
direction. To do so may get you lost."

Gallund strode to Windy and held out his hands. "Give
me your hands. Quickly now!"

Windy reluctantly put her hands in his, a questioning
look in her eyes. Without warning, Gallund yanked her
forward. Immediately the princess resisted him and pulled in
the opposite direction to regain her balance.

"That is precisely what I'm talking about," he said. "Just
there. What you did. Do not resist the pull of the Crossing!"

"Why? What happens if we do resist the pull of the
Crossing?" asked Ilien.

"You'll end up somewhere else, that's what," replied
Gallund. "Remember, most Crossings are like tunnels with
intersecting ways. There are only a few with no crossroads
at all, and this is not one of them. No resisting!"

"What's it like?" asked Anselm. The Giant's stony face

was creased with worry. "Does it hurt? Will it hurt them?" All eyes fell on the wizard.

"Have you ever jumped off a cliff?" he asked.

The Swan snapped her beak in dismay. "That's it! She's not going! It's too dangerous!"

"No, no," replied Gallund. "You've misunderstood, Penelope. You've got it all wrong. Just calm down."

The Swan pushed her way forward and stretched out her long, feathered neck toward the wizard. "Listen, old man!" she cried. "All this thrill seeking might be fun for you, but it's no laughing matter to me! If something bad happens to either of these children, I will personally hold you responsible."

"Put your neck away, Penelope. I didn't say it was as dangerous as jumping off a cliff. I said it was *like* jumping off a cliff."

"As if they know what that's like," she replied.

"Actually, we do," said Ilien, remembering their flight over the Midland Mountains. "We were on your back at the time, if you recall."

The Swan lowered her head and pushed a weak smile at Gallund. "Continue," she said.

"Crossing is like jumping off a cliff because that's exactly what it feels like. Except for the sudden stop at the end."

Again the Swan looked startled.

The wizard continued. "It will feel like you're falling. Your stomach will launch into your throat."

Ilien swallowed hard.

"This feeling will intensify, then lessen, then disappear completely. And that's when the fun begins. You will feel like you're floating in space, which of course is absurd because you'll actually be hurtling through it at incredible speed. At this point you'll have some freedom to move, but I must warn you not to." He eyed Windy. "Keep as still as possible."

The princess scowled at being singled out again by the wizard.

"How long will all this last?" asked Thessien. He regarded Ilien and Windy as if sizing them up for the task. "I always assumed that crossing was instantaneous."

"Yes. Most people do," said Gallund, returning to his stone seat once more. "But time is a curious thing. What might seem a few moments to one may be a week to another, or vise versa. It's enough to say that to those crossing it will take only a few minutes to reach their destination."

A giant hand closed on Ilien's shoulder. "Then you will find the wizardesses. They will teach you all they know and you will return back here to defeat the Nomadin."

"And rescue my mother," added Ilien, his face suddenly grim.

"And deal with the Evil," said the Swan, her feathery brows knitted with determination.

"And I will finally meet my mom," whispered Windy.

"Yes, yes," said Gallund, pinching the bridge of his nose. "You'll do all those things and more, but not before we get there, so can we please get going?"

Ilien adjusted his backpack and looked around. Trees. Everywhere he turned he saw only trees. "So where is this Crossing you're talking about?"

The wizard reached beneath his robes and drew out his leather pouch. "It is near. Very near," he said, opening the pouch and pulling forth a frayed patch of cloth embroidered with thick, yellow thread. He held it up for all to see.

"The witch's scroll," said Ilien. "The one we found when you turned those witches into toads." *The one I thought was a large hairy spider,* thought Ilien, remembering his embarrassment. "Wait! That's the Map of the Crossings!"

A collective shudder passed through the group as each beheld the prize the Witch Queen had so desperately wanted, the prize she would have used to release the unstoppable hordes of spirit creatures upon Nadae, the same prize Bulcrist would have used to release his NiDemon compatriots.

"Don't look so grim," said Gallund as he studied the frayed cloth scroll. "This will soon be in safe hands. We're taking it to the wizardesses. But first—" He raised a hand over the scroll and announced, "Ilustus bregun, ilustus bregar." The cloth began to shimmer, and the yellow thread disappeared. The scroll grew larger as its frayed outline knitted into a hard, straight line. Soon the small piece of cloth was gone, replace by a folded parchment map. Gallund gently unfolded the Map of the Crossings, holding it at arms length. He pored over it in silence, then looked up at Ilien. "As for the Crossing, I do believe you're standing on it."

Ilien jumped back, and all eyes fell to the ground at his feet.

"But there's nothing there," said Anselm.

"It's hidden," interjected Thessien.

Gallund gave the Eastlander an approving look. "That's quite correct. It's closed at the moment. Closed and hidden. But I can reveal it. More importantly, I can open it." At that he refolded the Map and everyone watched as it morphed back into a frayed piece of cloth. The wizard stashed it into his pouch. "Very nice trick, isn't it?"

"Get on with it!" said the Swan, her patience for the wizard waning.

"Fine, fine," said Gallund. He strode forward and waved everyone back. "Clear the area, please. You, too, Ilien.

That's a good boy. No. No. To the left. Everyone move left."

The party scrambled to get in their proper positions while the wizard circled around to the right. "Farther back, if you don't mind," he called. "That's it. Keep going."

Soon everyone stood opposite Gallund with thirty feet between them and the wizard. It was then that they noticed that the ground within those thirty feet was unusually level and devoid of trees and underbrush. In fact, most of the dead leaves and stones that littered the forest floor were missing as well. It became obvious they stood on the outskirts of a small, circular clearing forming a small depression in the ground.

"How peculiar," remarked the Swan.

"Here rests the Crossing," said Gallund. "Hidden and closed for many long years."

He made his way across the clearing toward the others. Halfway there he stopped, and Ilien jumped, expecting him to disappear. But the wizard kept walking. Soon he stood before Ilien and turned to face the clearing once more.

"Stay behind me. I will now invoke the words of Revealing in the True Language. Behold!"

The wizard raised his hands high above his head. "Revel bevel metor annoy!" he shouted.

"You can say that again," said the Swan as she shook her head at the wizard's theatrics.

Gallund slowly lowered his arms, tracing a wide arch in the air. In the center of the clearing, hovering in the air, a circular black hole appeared. Tiny a first, it quickly grew, like a drop of ink splashed upon white parchment. It spread outward, blotting out the trees behind it. It formed a pitch-black entryway, flat, solid, opaque, a closed door filled with night suspended just inches above the forest floor.

Ilien stepped forward but the wizard stopped him.

"No, Ilien. Wait."

The Crossing continued to expand until what stood before them became a gaping, black entrance capable of swallowing a dragon.

Or a Gorgul, thought Ilien.

Gallund grabbed Ilien's shoulder. "It is here, but it is not open yet. Please, everyone remain where you are as I speak the words of Opening." He eyed Thessien uneasily. "Remain at your guard. You, too, Anselm."

Thessien's hand strayed to his sword. Anselm's stony visage knotted in apprehension.

"Why?" asked Windy. "What's going to happen?"

The wizard studied the flat, black patch of night with a brooding look in his eyes. Everyone fell silent, including the Swan.

"Nothing, I hope," said Gallund. "But you cannot be too careful when opening a Crossing. One never knows what waits on the other side, eager to enter our world."

"Opening a Crossing here also opens a Crossing there?" asked Windy.

"Precisely," replied Gallund, eyeing Thessien's sword.

"But you said that the wizardesses crossed here," continued the princess. "Why would there be anything dangerous waiting on the other side?"

Ilien thought he knew the answer before Gallund even spoke it. The wizardesses had long since left Nadae through this Crossing, and none had ever returned. *Why was that?* he wondered. Could it be that Gallund was wondering the very same thing? Could it be that something had befallen them on the world where this Crossing led?

"It's best to be cautious," said Gallund. "A closed door at night is never something one should open carelessly, even if it's the one to your very own house."

The wizard nodded to Anselm and raised his hands once more. "Now for the words of Opening."

"Wait," said Ilien. "Why did the wizardesses leave Nadae, anyhow?"

Gallund left his hands suspended in mid-air, and winced. "What?" asked Ilien. He looked around at the others. Thessien tightened his grip on his sword. The Swan grimaced, and the feathers upon her neck bristled. Anselm looked puzzled.

"It's them you're afraid of," concluded Ilien, "not some foul creature from another world. It's them. I don't believe it!"

Windy put her hands to her hips. "You did something to make them leave, didn't you? Didn't you!"

Gallund lowered his hands, a grimace upon his face. "Nonsense. The wizardesses left Nadae of their own accord. They understood the dangers of Reknamarken's prophesy. They knew it was the only way to prevent it from coming true."

Ilien shook his head in disbelief. "You forced them to go. You were so afraid of fulfilling the Prophesy that you made them leave."

Windy could hardly contain herself. She stormed about between the trees, throwing her hands in the air. "You men are unbelievable!"

"Now hold on there," said Gallund.

The princess spun on him. "It takes two to tango, you know. Why do men think they're so high and mighty that they can throw their weight around and make women do whatever they wish? So the Necromancer prophesied that a Nomadin child would free him from his prison. So what! So what if having a child would doom the world to destruction. Why condemn the women to exile? Why force the

22

wizardesses to leave? If you were all such tough men then it should have been you, not them, that left. It's just so typical!"

"The wizardesses abandoned the wizards," said the Swan. "Not the other way around."

Silence fell about the small clearing.

"I don't believe you," said Windy. Her voice sounded small.

The Swan sat down, her feet disappearing beneath her feathery body. "It's true. They left on their own accord, as Gallund says. It was their idea."

Windy turned to Gallund.

"We didn't want them to go," said the wizard. "But they insisted it was the only way. So they left." He gazed at the black entryway of the Crossing, the closed door behind which the wizardesses could be found. "They just left."

Thessien lifted his head suddenly and searched the woods with his eyes.

"What is it?" asked Gallund.

"Where is Pedustil?"

Gallund shook his head in annoyance. "How should I know? Now stand back. Stand back everyone. I'm opening the Crossing."

The wizard raised his hands once more. "Pentar, entar, figaru, pari!"

The darkness of the Crossing paled. A grey pall spread from its center, pressing back the black void. Like a swirling whirlpool, the Crossing began to roil, fast and faster, casting out dizzying eddies of rippling magic. Ilien found himself strangely drawn to it, as if the Crossing was truly a whirlpool seeking to drag him forward, pulling at his mind and body.

"Ilien will go first," said Gallund. "Then you, Windy. In quick succession. I will bring up the rear."

Ilien adjusted the pack upon his back and stepped a pace forward.

"Get ready, Ilien," warned the wizard. "Follow him quickly, Windy. Ready! Now go!"

Ilien felt the world drop from beneath him.

"No! Stop!"

He heard the startled cry, but it was too late. Blackness descended upon him like a net and yanked him off his feet. He remembered Gallund's words and did not fight the pull of the Crossing. He turned in somersaults as an invisible hand flung him down and around, down and around. He couldn't see. He couldn't hear. Nauseating vertigo overwhelmed him. Then came a jerk so violent that his very thoughts went blank, as if they were knocked from his mind by the force of the blow. Specks of light filled his vision, phantom stars that told him he was close to blacking out. He sped through the nothing around him like an arrow from a string. The startled cry returned.

"No! Stop!"

It sounded like his own voice ringing in his ears. Lightning crashed over him and he knew no more.

Chapter IV

The Boy and the Beasts

Ilien awoke with a gasp. He opened his eyes to the grey and dingy sky above him. With a moan, he rolled to his side. He lay on a large, flat stone, the ground around him a mirror image of the sky, flat, barren, devoid of life. He sat up, and quickly fell back down. His hands and feet were bound with frayed rope.

"It's awake," came a stony voice behind him. Ilien craned his neck to see who had spoken. Two massive feet, shod in worn, leather boots, shuffled forward. Thick, hairy legs towered over him.

"Anselm?" said Ilien, squinting upward.

The creature came into view, and Ilien gasped.

A single watery eye dominated a wide, craggy face. Off-center, as large as dinner plate, the eye blinked with a moist, sticky slap. Two gaping, hairy holes flared open where a nose should have been. A lipless mouth split into a grin showing sporadic, jagged teeth. The skin of the creature's face lay pulled and smeared like batter in a bowl, stirred with a knife then cooked into place. Tufts of coarse, black hair grew from its oversized head. The monstrosity stood straight and towered fifteen feet in the air.

"Leave it be," came another voice, a snarl and a bark at once, higher pitched but more commanding. "Our orders are to take it to Shrieve. Then it's on to the west for this one. So don't go exciting it and making it difficult."

25

"It's going west?" asked the other, looking suddenly frightened. Its single eye rolled in its head and it gnashed crooked teeth. "To the ungod?"

"It's not the ungod. It's the Onegod, you overcooked Giant!"

"Don't call me a Giant," whined the other. "I'm not a Giant."

"Just leave it alone! Get back here and stow your gear. It's time to go."

Ilien struggled against his bonds, but it was no use. He felt weak and lightheaded as if he hadn't eaten in days.

"How much farther until we meet Shrieve?" asked the one nearest him.

"You mean how much farther do you have to carry it," snarled the other. "A few days and you're tired already? I'll tell Shrieve how lazy you are, that's what I'll do."

A few days? thought Ilien. What happened? The last thing he remembered was stepping into the Crossing, then a voice, a voice that had sounded like his own, shouting for him to stop. No, not his own voice. That was impossible. It had been Gallund's. Something had gone wrong back at the clearing. Something had gone horribly wrong. And he had crossed to this horrible place . . . alone.

"I'm not lazy," said the first. "It's awake now, that's all." Again its eye rolled in its head. "Is it really the Necromancer? What if it can do magic?"

The Necromancer? thought Ilien. *Did that thing just call me the Necromancer?*

Ilien heard the scuffle of boots as the other creature rushed over and grabbed its companion by the neck. "Better lazy than a coward!" it shouted. Its eye glared into the eye of the other. "Cowards are punished with death!"

It threw the other to the ground and yanked forth a long

knife from beneath its dirty shirt. "Of course it's the Necromancer! Why do you think we're bringing it to Shrieve. The Onegod wants it alive!"

The other began to shiver, eye jiggling like a plate of runny eggs. "But the Necromancer can turn us into toads."

"You're a disgrace to the Cyclops people!" spat the leader. "I ought to slay you myself." It kicked its companion in the stomach. The sound made Ilien wince. "But I need you to help bring it back to Shrieve. So get up and grab your gear."

Ilien watched the two creatures, unsure of what would happen next.

"I'm sorry, Jann," said the one, holding its wounded ribs as it lumbered to its feet. "I'll carry it. I will. I'll carry it."

Jann stashed his knife beneath his shirt once more and hoisted Ilien's pack. He turned to face his companion. "No more out of you. Understand? No more. Now grab that boy and let's go."

He turned to leave, and stopped.

Before him stood a small, lone figure. Ilien craned his neck and tried to sit up. It was a boy a few years younger than him. But this boy was as horribly deformed as the two Cyclops he faced. His bald head was lumpy and misshapen, like a runted potato. Oversized eyes set too far apart peered unevenly at him from a malformed face. Swollen, blood-red lips pulled back to reveal shiny white teeth filed to points. The boy's clothes were little more than dirty rags draped across his torso and hung from his waist, but the body beneath them bore the signs of rigid training. His arms were lean and muscular. Though repulsive to behold, the boy's bent face held a look of such bravery and determination that all his deformities seemed to disappear. In his right hand he clutched a simple, bone-colored staff, straight and smooth.

"Leave him," commanded the boy. His voice, like his body, was lean and hard.

Three steps carried Jann to the child. He aimed a crushing blow at his oversized head, intent on crushing the life from him. But the boy raised his staff and side stepped his attacker. The Cyclops stumbled forward, his hands grasping empty air. He spun back around, maddened by the boy's quickness.

"Your Breaching Arts will not save you this time," he spat. A flick of his wrist and he suddenly held his knife again. He signaled to his companion, who circled around behind the boy, his own knife at the ready. "Can you defend against two, I wonder?"

Ilien watched from the ground as the boy held his position, the staff gripped firmly in both hands. He had to help him.

"Mitra mitari mitara miru!" he shouted, wishing his hands were free so he could add Nihilic power to his spell.

Nothing happened. The boy looked at him, quizzically.

The Cyclops attacked.

This time the boy did not dodge the blows. He blocked them. Front and back, side to side, the two one-eyed marauders hacked and slashed at him, and over and over the boy parried with his staff, leaping to avoid a strike he could not counter. The Cyclops' knives whistled the air around him, but the boy never faltered. Tirelessly, he beat back their assaults, dodging and blocking. They could not breach his defenses.

Back and forth the three fought upon the hard-packed earth. Twice the Cyclops stumbled upon the rocky ground, but the boy kept his footing, neatly parrying without effort. The Cyclops began to tire. Their blows became unwieldy, their breathing labored. Soon they lumbered about, their knives held at their sides in utter exhaustion.

Still the boy pressed them, drawing more ungainly strikes, blocking them all. Never once did he himself attack. Not once did his staff inflict a wound. Yet, nevertheless, the two Cyclops collapsed to the ground defeated.

The boy sprang upon a rock and leaped in the air above his fallen enemies. He landed before Ilien, his back to the two spent attackers. He touched his staff to Ilien's ropes and closed his crooked eyes. The twisted features of his deformed face contorted in pain. The ropes slid to the ground, sliced neatly through.

The boy opened his eyes and smiled a mouthful of pointed teeth. "Ilien Woodhill, you must come with me."

"How do you know me?" Ilien climbed to his feet and kicked the ropes away. "Who are you?"

The boy glanced back at his defeated enemies, who were just beginning to stir again. Ilien looked the boy up and down.

"How did you do that?"

"Who I am is unimportant. I've been sent by the girl. Will you come with me?"

The girl? Could it be? He assumed Windy hadn't crossed with him, but perhaps she had.

The boy saw his confusion. "She told me where you'd be. She knew where to find you. She sent me to get you, but they got to you first."

Ilien shook his head. "Wait. Who told you where I was?"

The boy's malformed face twisted grotesquely. "The girl." He hung his head and touched his swollen cheek. "The pretty girl."

"Windy?" asked Ilien in disbelief.

The boy looked up. "She came here just like you."

It *was* Windy. She had crossed after all. And if she had

crossed then perhaps Gallund had crossed as well.

"Did you see an old man? Was there an old man with her?"

"No man," replied the boy. "No old man."

There came a moan from one of the Cyclops.

"Come," said the boy, his twisted features suddenly set in grim determination. "They will be well enough to attack again soon."

"My pack," said Ilien suddenly, realizing that the Cyclops leader still wore it. "There's food and water inside. We'll need it."

"You must leave it. Come."

With staff in hand, the boy turned and led the way. As Ilien passed the two unconscious Cyclops, he still couldn't believe that the boy had defeated them only by defending himself. It was the Breaching Arts, the mysterious ability he had overheard in a dream. Ilien had always assumed that the Breaching Arts was a magical ability, not a physical one, but magical or not it was more powerful than he had imagined.

Ilien studied the boy who ran before him, and wondered how his face had become so deformed while the rest of him remained so sculpted and agile—so seemingly perfect in form. He let his eyes wander from the boy to the landscape around them. So desolate. So barren. Devoid of color and life. It made Ilien feel ill, like the land itself. As he ran he felt the sickness beneath his feet, as if he were traversing an open sore, scabbed over and infected with disease. It sucked the energy from him, sapped his well-being. In every direction he saw more of the same. The sky lay low and smothering above him, like a blanket of despair, and he felt suddenly entrapped, encased in a festering wound with no way out. His head began to swim and he called out to the boy, who by now was far ahead of him.

"Wait! I need to stop!" He lurched to a halt and fell to his knees, holding his head in both hands. "I don't feel well." The boy returned to him, light on his feet. "Ilien, we need to go. We must not stop. The Onegod seeks your life. Those Cyclops are on their feet by now. We must go."

The Onegod? What was happening? Where did that Crossing take him? Where were the wizardesses?

"I don't think I can," he said, fighting off nausea. "Something's wrong. Everything's wrong."

In frustration, the boy bared his jagged little cat's teeth. "The girl will make it better. She can take away your sickness. Now come. The Cyclops have roused themselves by now. They'll be after us. We must go now!"

Ilien lurched to his feet and the boy urged him forward. One foot, then another, Ilien willed himself to follow. A dozen paces later he collapsed again.

"I feel so weak," he said. Why was this place so blasted and lifeless, so cursed? What was this power it had over him that stole his magic and sickened him to his very core? "What's happening to me?"

The boy cast a worried look behind them. He reached a lean hand beneath his dirty rags and drew forth a small piece of bread. "Here. Eat this. It will give you strength." He placed it in Ilien's trembling hand.

Damp, slick and grey, it felt and looked like Awefull. Without question, Ilien slipped it into his mouth. It tasted like Awefull, too, but saltier, and he nearly gagged. But it did give him strength. Instant strength. He felt energized, invigorated. It was like eating concentrated Awefull!

He rose and nodded. Though the overwhelming weariness had left him, his head and stomach still waged war with nausea, and the sour taste in his mouth didn't help. "I can run now."

31

"Good," said the boy, his swollen face contorting into a broken smile. "Come."

They loped through the lifeless landscape for hours, but not once did Ilien tire. Whatever he had eaten, wether it was Awefull or not, it sustained him like nothing he had ever known. His legs carried him as if his body had no weight at all. His breath came slow and easy. Even his head cleared a bit, though a touch of nausea still squirmed in his stomach.

He still couldn't summon his magic, though. Twice he had tried to conjure Globe, and twice he had failed. He longed for the company of that pesky little sphere of light. It seemed years ago that he first brought her to life in his study back home. Now even such a simple spell as that was impossible. He could recite the proper words, but somehow they lacked meaning. It was as if some invisible hand was covering his mouth, or pressing on his thoughts, impeding his connection with the True Language. His Nihilic magic proved just as unreachable. His fingers felt stiff, unwieldy. The runes seemed no more than silly gestures. He wished he had his pencil, though he doubted it would help.

It bothered him greatly, not being able to conjure magic. He was powerless here, wherever here was, with only a small boy between him and impending danger at the hands of those one-eyed behemoths.

The boy stopped suddenly and dropped to his knees, weariness finally showing on his misshapen face. "We'll rest here for a little while."

Here was little more than a shallow depression in the hard packed dirt. There were no trees, no vegetation at all, only dirt and rocks and the endless grey-brown sky.

"Why here?" asked Ilien. Though the full effects of the bread he'd eaten had worn off some time ago, he still felt as if he could run a while longer. He looked back along the way they had come. Their footprints in the hard dirt stretched into the grey distance. "What if they're still following us?"

"They're not," replied the boy, rubbing his lumpy face as if it were sore.

"How do you know? Just because we can't see them doesn't mean they're still not back there, gaining on us even as we sit here."

The boy sat down on a flat rock that jutted out of the ground. He set his long staff on his lap. "We've covered more ground than you realize," he said, reaching beneath his ragged clothing and retrieving two more pieces of the sticky, grey bread. He tossed one to Ilien. "We've run nearly fifty miles. There is no pursuit."

"Fifty miles!" Ilien gazed in wonder at the hunk of bread in his hand. "What's in this stuff?"

The boy smiled his jagged smile and popped a piece into his mouth. As he chewed, the misshapen features of his face contorted even more. His swollen lips smacked together and spittle escaped the corner of his mouth. His hand flew up to hide his embarrassment, and he looked away suddenly, his light-hearted mood gone.

Ilien felt bad for the boy, and again he wondered what had happened to him. "I could have used this stuff in gym class," he quipped.

The boy perked up at that. He turned to Ilien, his crooked eyes sharp and focused. "What is gym class?"

Ilien laughed and sat down beside him. "It's nothing important. Just something we're forced to do where I come from." Ilien raised his hunk of bread to his mouth.

"Careful," said the boy. "Nibble it slowly."

"Why?" said Ilien, lifting an eyebrow. "This stuff is so much better than Awefull."

"Because Manna is very nourishing."

33

"You can say that again," replied Ilien.

"The arrow that flies the highest also falls down the fastest," said the boy. "I think you've eaten enough."

Ilien stared at the Manna in his hand, thought better of it, and stashed it in his pocket.

The boy sat cross-legged, cradling his staff on his lap and absently stroking its smooth surface with one hand.

"How far until we reach Windy?" asked Ilien.

"The girl? Not far."

Ilien's eyes fell to the bone-colored staff. "What happened?" he said, suddenly. The boy turned and glared at him. "When you cut my ropes with your staff," continued Ilien. "Somehow it hurt you. What happened?"

The anger in the boy's eyes faded, and he regarded the staff in his lap. "It's not a staff," he said. "It's a Breach. And it shouldn't be used to cut rope. It shouldn't be used to cut anything."

"You mean you can't use it to fight? But I saw what you did to those two creatures."

"Of course I can fight with my Breach," said the boy, his jagged little teeth bared by a grin.

Ilien remembered how the boy defeated the Cyclops only by defending himself. "You can't use it offensively."

"Of course I can," stated the boy, "but it hurts me to break the Vow."

"The Vow?" Ilien was glad to have struck up a conversation that brightened the boy's mood.

"To practice the Breaching Arts is to pledge fealty to nonviolence, to vow to never intentionally inflict harm."

"Even to rope?" said Ilien, scratching his chin.

"Yes. To anything and anyone." The boy held his Breach above his head. "This is my vow, to never kill, never wound, never maim, never breach another, be it living or dead."

34

"What if someone breaches you?"

"It is said that those who uphold their vow and devote themselves to the Breaching Arts can never be breached."

Ilien looked skeptical. "Never? You mean no one can hurt you?"

"Do I look hurt?" asked the boy. His swollen lips parted in a smile to reveal his jagged teeth.

"But you hurt yourself when you used your Breach to cut my ropes."

The boy's twisted smile remained, but he kept silent.

"If cutting rope hurt you that much," continued Ilien, "then what would happen if you cut a person?"

The boy's misshapen features grew serious. "The more grievous the harm I cause, the more dire the consequences. What I cause to happen will happen to me."

Ilien looked dumbfounded. "If you kill then you die?"

"Yes," answered the boy, flatly.

"What kind of twisted magic is that? That isn't very fair."

"It is perfectly fair, Ilien Woodhill. If everyone practiced the Breaching Arts, there would be no killing."

"But everyone doesn't practice the Breaching Arts. Unlike you, others can kill without consequence."

The boy glided his hand along the length of his Breach. "Don't look so glum. I'm skilled enough to save your skin again." He grinned his cat's grin, and glanced around their barren campsite. The chalky sky was darkening to deeper shades of grey. "You should prepare yourself."

Ilien followed the boy's gaze, still amazed at the utter desolation of the land. Where were all the trees? Where were the shrubs and grasses? The world lay still and lifeless around them, the sky bleak and empty. There were no birds or buzzing insects.

"What happened?" he asked, his heart suddenly filled with anguish. "Why is your world so dead? Who did this?" The boy's deformities softened as he looked at Ilien, and for a moment he almost looked normal. "You did this," he said. "Though you didn't mean to."

Ilien shot to his feet. "What are you talking about? I just got here. I didn't do any of this!" He was surprised by his own outburst. Of course he didn't do any of this. Why was he getting so defensive? "Listen, kid, I'm grateful that you saved me, but I think you've mixed me up with someone else. I crossed to this world with my friend, Windy, to find the Nomadin wizardesses and bring them back to my world. Beyond that, I assure you that I have nothing to do with any of this."

The boy's swollen features sagged, and he hung his head. "I have offended you. I was wrong to have said what I said. Forgive me."

Ilien stood glaring at the boy. Finally, he shook his head and sat down beside him again. "There's nothing to be sorry about. Let's just forget I ever asked you about this place and get going. I'd like to find Windy as soon as possible."

Ignoring him, the boy laid himself on the ground and curled up around his Breach. "You should prepare yourself."

Ilien became annoyed again. "Prepare myself for what?"

"For the Consumption," said the boy.

"The what?"

The boy closed his eyes. "You've run fifty miles in four hours. Manna imparts tremendous energy, but there is a price to pay. The Manna will wear off soon. When it does, you'll black out."

Ilien stared at him in confusion.

"Lay down!" shouted the boy. "Lay down before you—"

Chapter V

Desecration

Ilien awoke with a start, snapping out of the blackness that had overwhelmed him so quickly and thoroughly. His head swam as he rolled to his side. The boy sat beside him, his Breach balanced across his knees. His deformed face was hunched with worry.

"How do you feel?" he asked.

Ilien sat up and grabbed his head. He lay back down with a moan.

"You have been unwakeable for hours," said the boy, frowning.

Ilien tried to rise. Dizziness overwhelmed him and he sank to the ground once more. He began to shiver.

The boy leaned over him and felt his forehead. "You're burning with fever."

Ilien's stomach seized with cramps. He curled into a ball and closed his eyes against the pain and nausea.

"You cannot travel," said the boy.

"But we have to find Windy," moaned Ilien. He managed to roll onto his back without getting sick. "Just give me some more Manna and I'll be fine. We have to keep going. What if something happens to her?"

"Nothing will happen to her," said the boy as he rose to his feet. He surveyed their surroundings and nodded to himself. "I will bring her here."

"You're leaving me?"

37

"It cannot be helped. I was told to bring you to her, but I fear you are dying."

The shock of what the boy said drove the nausea and weakness from Ilien's body. "Dying? I'm not dying! I'm just sick!"

The boy knelt beside Ilien again, his oversized eyes filled with worry. His brow knotted and his swollen lips parted in a twisted grimace. "There is a curse upon the land. You feel it even as we speak. It drains you. It weakens you. It leaches your very life away and gives it to the Onegod. This is the Desecration, a curse against you, Ilien Woodhill. I am afraid we tarried too long."

Ilien felt a spear of pain lance through him and he huddled into a knot again.

"Get up," bade the boy. He grabbed Ilien's arm. "Get up and sit over here on this rock. It will help. It will slow the curse."

Ilien crawled to the large, flat rock that jutted out of the ground. "But how?" he managed to croak.

"Take this," said the boy, an urgency in his voice. He handed Ilien another piece of Manna. "Nibble it. It will sustain you until I bring the girl back here. She will be able to save you."

Ilien took the proffered bread, feeling suddenly better as he sat upon the rock. "But what can Windy do? What do you mean, she can save me?"

"She can carry you."

"She can't carry me!" The boy turned to leave. "Wait!" cried Ilien. "What if those two creatures come back?"

"Pray they don't," answered the boy as he jogged off. "Stay here. Do not leave. I will return."

Ilien watched the boy disappear in the flat, grey blur of the land. He nibbled at his Manna bread, and patted the rock beneath him. It jutted from the ground only a foot or so, but somehow it protected him from the ravages of the curse placed upon the ground, the Desecration, as the boy had called it. He breathed a sigh of relief and tried to clear his mind. He took a large bite of Manna and felt a wave of energy wash away his weariness.

What kind of world was this? The wizardesses clearly did not live here. Gallund had opened the wrong Crossing. That was why he had called for him to stop. Gallund must have realized he'd made a mistake, but he realized it too late. And now here he was, stuck in this murderous place where a twisted creature called the Onegod preyed upon life itself, where somehow the land, the very earth, conspired to kill anything and everything that walked upon it. He felt the sickness all around him.

How am I ever going to get out of this one? he wondered.

As Ilien's head cleared and his strength returned, he looked around for more rocks like the one he sat on. He dreaded the idea of having to touch the ground again. If there were enough rocks, perhaps he could travel by jumping from one to another, or at least avoid treading on the ground for any length of time. But his hopes were dashed. Though there were plenty of rocks, most were too small to stand on. Once the boy returned with Windy, he'd just have to grin and bear it until he came across another rock like the one beneath him. One thing was certain. No matter what the boy said, Windy could not carry him. Going would be slow, but at least they'd be able to travel. And when it came time to stop for the night, he'd just have to make himself a bed of stones. Uncomfortable, yes, but not that bad. In fact, it would feel like paradise compared to the draining ache of the bare earth.

Ilien placed the rest of the Manna in his pocket, wrapped

his arms around his knees, and waited. The boy said he'd be back soon. Back with Windy. That thought comforted him and let him get a handle on things as his strength returned. If only he could reach his magic.

Perhaps he could, now that he no longer touched the ground. Perhaps the same twisted power that had drained him of his strength and health had also drained him of his magic.

"Kinil ubid illubid kinar," he chanted, careful not to lose his balance on the rock.

Nothing happened. He eyed the air in front of him for any signs of Globe. Not a spark of light was visible. He sighed and recited the spell again, half-closing his eyes to better concentrate. Again, nothing.

Perhaps if I sign the Nihilic Light rune while saying the spell aloud, he thought, remembering how he had miraculously combined the two magics, Nihilic and the True Language, when he fought the Gog back at Asheverry Castle. He teetered on the rock, suddenly afraid to let go of his legs for fear of falling. But he had to try. He took a deep breath, raised a hand, and drew the Nihilic Light rune.

"Kinil ubid illubid kinar!" he shouted. His cry seemed swallowed by the all-pervading grey around him. In the silence that followed, he willed Globe to appear. He held out his palm and recited the spell once more. He searched the space above his hand for signs of life, a spark, a gleam of life, anything.

Nothing. Ilien hung his head in frustration. He still couldn't reach his magic, Nomadin or NiDemon. If he couldn't use magic, how could he hope to ever get out of this god-forsaken place? Despair began to fill him again. He was powerless, helpless, besieged on all sides by the deadly power of the ground itself and hunted by the servants of the Onegod, with only a boy to aid him who literally couldn't harm a fly. And though the boy would bring back Windy, what could she do to help him? She was Nomadin, but only half so, and untrained in magic. Ilien felt his cheeks grow hot and itchy, he looked around in exasperation.

In the distance, he discerned two figures walking toward him—two, very large figures.

"The Cyclops," he cried. "They're following our trail." He almost ran for it, but knew he wouldn't get far before the vile power of the ground overwhelmed him. Besides, he couldn't possibly outrun those two beasts, even if the ground wasn't cursed. If ever there was a moment when he needed to reach his magic, it was now. The Cyclops hadn't seen him yet, but they soon would. He needed to disappear, and quick.

"Inhibi inhabi hababi viru!" he said through clenched teeth, fighting off panic. He knew the spell would not work. "Inhibi inhabi hababi viru!" he cried. He peered at his hand. It was still visible. He searched the horizon for signs of the boy. He was completely alone, as usual, without even his pencil for company. This time, the bullies were far bigger than Stan and Peaty.

The Cyclops stopped in the distance, having evidently found something that caught their interest. Now was his chance. There was nothing to be done but to swallow the last of his Manna and run for it. With any luck he might catch up to the boy before the energizing effects of the bread wore off and the ground overwhelmed him. And if luck wasn't on his side, he had a date with someone or something called Shrieve.

He looked up and saw that the Cyclops were moving toward him again. One of them was pointing, directly at him. He'd been spotted.

He forced himself to move, but his legs were so cramped and numb from crouching so long in one position that he couldn't stand up. He lurched forward, grasped at the empty air, and toppled to the ground.

Jolts of nausea swept through him as the earth assaulted him as never before. His skin prickled with cold sweat as his insides roiled. His head swam. He pulled himself up and reached for the safety of the rock, but the leeching pull of the ground overwhelmed his senses. His vision receded.

Get up, Ilien! Get up! he shouted to himself. *They're coming!*

He struggled blindly to his knees. Icy numbness washed over him. He couldn't feel his legs. The earth was an abyss filled with darkness that he couldn't escape. But he had to escape. He had to get back to the rock, even if only to witness his own capture at the hands of the Cyclops. He fell forward and flung his arms out in front of him.

His right hand suddenly regained feeling. The rock! It had found the rock! Like an anchor in the abyss, it steadied him, pulled him back from the brink. Waves of feeling coursed from the rock, down his arm and crashed through his body, slamming his nerves as if he crashed into a stone wall. He forced his eyes open, saw his hand as it clutched at the rock, willed his arm to pull the rest of him forward up onto the rock and out of the abyss. His legs regained life. They burned and thrummed as if a thousand barbs pierced his flesh. He inched closer to the rock, pulling then pushing. He began to tire, and he gulped in air.

With an agonizing heave, he threw himself up and forward, landing on his chest upon the rock. Quickly he curled into a ball. Free of the painful ravages of the earth, he lay hunched in a knot, and remembered no more.

Chapter VI

Kale and Rose

"It isn't very good."

Ilien's ears were the first things to come to, and the voice he heard sounded familiar.

"It's wonderful," replied another voice, this one unfamiliar. "It's a bit stunted, and the color's a bit off, but it should still taste delicious."

Ilien struggled to open his eyes. What he just heard worried him.

"Well, it doesn't," came the familiar voice again. It was the boy's voice, the boy with the misshapen face. "You can keep it. I'll stick with Manna."

"You can't live on Manna alone, you know," countered the other voice. It was the voice of a woman, soft, soothing, yet firm in its assertions, like a teacher's voice.

"Yes. I can," claimed the boy.

Ilien opened his eyes and blinked. It was pitch black and he couldn't see a thing.

"He's waking up," said the woman, her voice like a disembodied spirit in the dark.

Ilien blinked again. There was something wrong with his eyes. He was blind! The earth had leeched his sight away!

"Relax," said the woman. "You're not blind. It's just dark, very dark."

Ilien tried to calm himself. He could feel cold stone beneath him, and he wondered where he was.

43

Wait! he thought. *How—*

"You are in a cave," answered the woman, "and yes, I can read your thoughts." A small flame jumped up in the blackness, illuminating rough stone walls all around. Ilien shielded his eyes, momentarily blinded by the dazzling light. "We have saved you from certain death," added the woman. Ilien's eyes slowly adjusted. Before him, with a candle flame suspended magically above one hand, sat a middle-aged woman. Her green eyes squinted at him, wether with mistrust or bad eyesight, he couldn't tell. Her long brown hair fell in tangled, wavy locks past her shoulders. She was pretty, or had been, but time and the cursed land had taken their toll. Care-lines marked the corners of her eyes and mouth. She wore a faded green cloak, torn at the edges, over clothes of coarse, brown material. Though dirty from head to toe, she looked somehow familiar.

Ilien stared at her, then at the magical flame in her palm. "Are you a wizardess?"

"You could say that," she answered. "Kale here might disagree. Seems my magically grown carrots have fallen short of someone's tastes." She raised an eyebrow at the boy.

"They taste like dirt," replied the boy. "And according to you, they're supposed to be orange. They're not." He raised a tufted eyebrow back at her, his lumpy face set in a defiant grin.

Ilien stared blankly at the woman, then at the boy, then at the two, small pale yellow carrots resting on a stone between them.

"It's hard enough growing them at all without soil. Now Kale wants color as well." She grinned and tossed her magical flame in the air where it floated above Ilien's head, lighting the cave with its warm glow. Ilien hunkered down where he sat, casting worried looks at the hovering fire.

"It's not a candle, Ilien," said the woman. "It's not going to drip wax on you."

Ilien tried to look more relaxed. "How do you know my name?"

"Many people know your name," said Kale, his twisted face somehow less grotesque in the magical firelight.

Ilien frowned.

"It's true," said the woman. "Your crossing has long been foretold. Children whisper your name before they go to sleep. For two thousand years they have waited and watched."

"Watched what? What are you talking about?" Ilien heard what she said, but it made no sense. "For two thousand years?"

"Yes," said Kale. He smiled and his swollen lips accentuated the effect. "You will bring an end to the Onegod's reign! You will set everything right! It has been foretold that you would come, and now you are here! She told me where to find you, but I got there too late. The Onegod's soldiers found you first. But now you are here, and everything will be better."

The woman raised her hand. "Slow down, Kale. Slow down. You don't want to frighten him off, do you?" She turned back to Ilien. "Now where was I? Oh yes, the children." She stopped to gather her thoughts, and in the brief moment of silence, Ilien was reminded of something.

"Windy?" he blurted. He turned to Kale. "Where's Windy?"

The boy looked to the woman, his swollen face a mask of light and shadow in the flickering flame-light. The woman shook her head, and the boy turned back to Ilien. "I don't know who Windy is."

"But you said she was here, that she came here like me!"

45

The boy's face dropped, and he reached up to touch the lumps on his forehead. "I'm sorry. I needed you to come with me. I didn't want to mislead you."

Ilien looked at the woman. "So this is the girl you told me about?"

"Yes."

"And she came here like I did?"

The woman answered, her voice hushed. She leaned forward and whispered, "Yes, like you did."

Ilien slumped against the cave wall. "So I'm all alone, then."

"You have us," said the boy.

Ilien sat straight. The light in the cave tilted and jumped as the magical flame bobbed in the air above him. "You're a wizardess," he said to the woman, suddenly brightening. "You're who I came to find. You must return to my world, to Nadae." He looked about. "Where are the others? Where are the rest of the wizardesses? I was told to bring them all back. We'll need all your powers if we're to defeat the Nomadin wizards and rescue my mother."

"And what of this friend of yours, this Windy?" asked the woman. "Are you no longer concerned about her?"

Ilien picked up one of the pale, yellow carrots from the rock in front of him. "She must not have crossed after all," he said. "What a relief. All things equal, I'm probably better off that she didn't."

"How do you know she didn't cross?" asked the woman, snatching the remaining carrot from the rock. "Crossings are unpredictable. She could have crossed. She could have ended up in a different place."

"Are you trying to worry me, or do you know something I don't?" asked Ilien. "Because I'm getting the feeling you aren't telling me everything."

The boy wiped at his swollen lips with his dirty sleeve. "We know nothing you don't know."

"Relax, Ilien," said the woman. "All I'm saying is that this world isn't a very safe place and we should be sure your friends aren't out there, that's all."

"My friends?"

"Yes. Kale told me that you asked about an old man. A wizard, I imagine?"

Ilien looked to the boy. The boy looked away.

"I was supposed to cross with Gallund and Windy. But I went first and something went wrong. Someone cried out for me to stop, but it was too late. The next thing I knew, I was waking up as a captive of those one-eyed creatures."

"The Cyclops," said the boy.

"You don't really think they're out there somewhere, do you?" Ilien eyed the pressing darkness. "My friends, I mean."

The woman snapped her carrot in two. "No," she answered. "I think your friends are safe back home. I don't think they crossed with you." She leaned back and studied Ilien, as if measuring his will to do what he came to do. "I am not a wizardess," she said.

"Not a wizardess?" Ilien pinned Kale with a crushing look. "But you said—"

"Kale said what was needed to bring you here. Go easy, Ilien. Without Kale, you'd be dead."

"The truth, then," said Ilien. "Who are you? Where am I? Why is this place so lifeless? Who is this Onegod, and why does he want to kill me?"

The woman tossed Ilien a piece of carrot. "You ask many questions. I have many answers. But first we must eat. You will hear the truth better on a full stomach. Kale, fetch some water."

Kale rose silently and disappeared into the darkness. The

woman saw the look on Ilien's face.

"There is a spring farther down the tunnel. Good, clear water cleansed by the rock beneath us, made pure by the bones of the earth."

Ilien heard the scrabble of rocks from out in the blackness.

"Don't worry," said the woman. "Young Kale's eyes see straighter than they look, even in complete darkness."

Ilien suddenly realized that he had a carrot in his hand, a stunted, yellow twisted root that barely resembled the carrots he remembered from Farmer Parson's garden back home.

"What happened?" he asked. "Why is Kale like that?"

"Like what?" asked the woman.

Ilien held up the carrot. "Like this. Like everything else here that's so—"

"So abnormal? So stunted and deformed? So twisted and ugly?"

"I didn't say that," replied Ilien. "I only asked why—"

"Why Kale's not like you."

Ilien looked away, suddenly ashamed. "What happened? What happened here that made everything so . . . different."

"You happened."

Ilien spun on her in anger, but held his tongue. She studied him again, as if to gage his reaction.

"Kale said the same thing," said Ilien, evenly. "Explain what you mean. I crossed to this place only a few days ago."

The woman leaned back and sighed. "You've been here before. A long time ago." She looked off into the blackness where Kale had vanished. "A very long time ago."

"That's not true," countered Ilien. "I've never been here before. I would have remembered coming here. I've never even left my hometown until a month ago."

"Trust me. You were here." With a wave of her hand she sent the magical flame from above Ilien's head out into the darkness after Kale. "Where is that kid?"

Ilien threw his hands up in frustration. "I'm telling you, I've never been here before!"

The woman spun on him. "Keep your voice down! You were here two thousand years ago!" Her own shout echoed off the cave walls and reverberated along the tunnel.

As if in answer, they heard Kale cry, "I'm coming! For crying out loud, I'm coming!"

"This twisted land," said the woman more quietly, "that twisted kid. Me. We're all here because of you. You left and the Onegod rose to power. But it was prophesied that you were to return to overthrow the Onegod, and you were to return through the very same Crossing where you left. The Onegod blighted the land and cursed the very earth in all directions for hundreds of miles so that when you returned it would kill you. For two thousand years a secret watch has been kept upon that Crossing. Every year for the last two thousand years the people of this world have hidden away a lone scout. Generation after generation, they kept vigil so that when you returned that lone scout would find you before the Onegod did."

Ilien's anger left him. He seemed to deflate before the woman. "Kale," he said. "That lone scout is Kale."

The magical light returned to float above Ilien's head. "Yes," she replied.

"And you?" asked Ilien. "Who are you? Why are you here?"

There came a long moment of silence, then, "My name is Rose. Kale is returning." The woman looked at the pale, yellow carrot in Ilien's hand and nodded. "Some things that look twisted and deformed are still just as sweet."

Ilien stared at the gnarled and stunted root in his palm. He brought it to his lips and absently took a bite. He closed his eyes, and in the dusty darkness of the cave sanctuary, with the cold grey world pressing in from every side, he savored the sweet, earthy flavor of a carrot freshly drawn from Farmer Parson's field.

"Hey!"

The loud echo of Kale's shout snapped Ilien back to the present. The boy stood before him, a stone bowl brimming with water balanced in his hands. A grin broke across the twisted features of his lopsided face, and his jagged, little teeth gleamed in the dimness.

"That was my carrot!"

They sat and ate a cold meal of Manna and carrots, washed down with the sweetest water Ilien had ever tasted. Ilien mused that perhaps it tasted so sweet in contrast to the sour flavor of the Manna. But then he couldn't remember drinking anything since crossing to this god-forsaken land and realized the truth. He was parched. He gulped water from his stone cup until his stomach felt tight and his throat ached from the icy cold. Then he nibbled at the last of his carrot. He had decided to forgo the Manna.

"Now that you have me, what next?" he asked, to no one in particular.

Kale popped a piece of Manna between his cat-like teeth. "We need to bring you to the wizardess."

"The wizardesses?" said Ilien, sitting up. "Where are they? How do we find them?"

Kale looked at Rose, then hung his head in silence.

"There is only one wizardess, Ilien," replied Rose. "And she is difficult to find for she has concealed herself from this world."

Ilien started. "One? Where are all the others? I was sent

50

to bring them all back with me."

"The Onegod took them," answered Kale.

"Took them? Took them where?"

"To his castle, his castle in the mountains."

Rose took a sip of water and placed her stone cup on a rock beside her. "They have all perished," she said. "The Onegod killed them. All but one. It is she we must seek out."

Ilien sagged against the cave wall. "Dead? All of them?" He'd never met his birth-mother, held no more emotional bond for her than for a stranger, but he felt a sudden pang of sorrow nonetheless. "Who is she?" he asked. "The last one. What's her name?"

"What's the difference?" asked Rose, her gaze suddenly penetrating.

Ilien stared back at her, unsure if he wanted to reveal that his birth-mother was Nomadin. A moment of awkward silence fell in the cave.

"I don't know her name," said Rose finally. "But she's the last wizardess, and she's waiting for you."

"The last wizardess," repeated Ilien, as if saying the words would help him accept them. "I can't believe they're all gone. Now what am I supposed to do?"

"I just told you what we must do," said Rose.

Ilien sat up angrily. "What good is it to risk finding the last wizardess when one won't be enough?" He stood and swatted at the magical light that danced above his head. "I'm supposed to bring them all back home. All, not one! We need all their magic to save my mother."

Rose motioned for Ilien to sit. "Calm down."

"Calm down?" shouted Ilien. "Calm down? You don't understand. My mother is a prisoner of the Nomadin, and the only way to rescue her is with the help of the wizardesses. I'm supposed to bring them all back with me through that

Crossing, back to my world."

"You cannot return to that Crossing, Ilien," said Kale, straightening, his eyes wide. "You can never return to that Crossing." His sculpted, rigid body struck a sharp contrast to the puffy features of his misshapen face.

"Kale's right," said Rose. "The Onegod is hunting you. There is no going back."

"No going back?" Ilien felt his cheeks grow hot and itchy as panic flooded through him. "I must go back!"

"That is why we need to seek the wizardess," pressed Rose. "She, too, has been waiting for you. She can help you get back home. She will help you destroy the Onegod."

"I told you, I'm not who you think I am!" shouted Ilien, his panic turning to pointed anger. "I have never been here before and I didn't come here now to destroy your Onegod!"

"But you did and you have," said Kale.

Rose raised a hand to quiet him. "Regardless of what you believe, there is only one path before you. You cannot return to that Crossing. If you do, you will be killed. There is no going back. There is only going forward."

Ilien paced in anger. He knew they were right. Even if the Onegod wasn't hunting him, even if he could defeat the one-eyed beasts who had captured him, he couldn't escape the ravages of the cursed earth. The ground outside would kill him before he made it back to the Crossing. He turned to face Rose and Kale, and sat down in defeat.

"Good," said Rose. "Now that you are calm, let me tell you how it's going to be." She leaned forward to make her point. "You need to listen better and start doing what I say. You were always strong-headed and stubborn and it served you well. But not now. Not here. Whatever you've been through in the past, whatever adventures you may think you've undertaken, whatever quests you fancy you've completed, this is far more dangerous."

Ilien opened his mouth to speak.

"Trust me," she continued. "You may not know it, but you've been here before. You were here two thousand years ago. You left, and this world fell to pieces. Everything you see, all the hopelessness, all the grey, lifeless existence outside, it all came to be because of your absence. There are those who believe you are the Creator who left because your work was done. Others believe you are the Necromancer who abandoned them to Evil, for that is what the Onegod teaches. Regardless, you are back now, and it is time to set things right."

Kale rubbed at the lumps on his forehead with downcast eyes. "You should not be so harsh with him," he said, quietly. "This is not his fault. It is the fault of the Onegod."

Rose turned to Ilien with a dour expression. "Kale, here, is one of the many who believes you are a hero, Ilien. Do not let them down."

Ilien felt rebuked and admired at the same time. Whatever it was they believed, he would have to go along with them for now. He was in no position to argue. If they believed he'd been here before, two thousand years ago, then let them believe it. So what if somehow they knew his name. There could be two Ilien Woodhills in the universe.

Right?

"So what will it be?" asked Rose. "What will you do?"

"I'll go with you," said Ilien. He looked at Kale, who quickly looked away. "Under one condition," he added.

Rose regarded him suspiciously. "Which is?"

Ilien stared off into the darkness. "After I kill this Onegod for you, you help me get home."

For the first time, a genuine smile crossed Rose's face.

Chapter VII

Doubts in the Dark

The cave was steeped in darkness, and filled with the sounds of steady breathing. Rose had insisted they all get some sleep, but Ilien wasn't tired. His mind buzzed with thoughts—and Manna. The salty, slick bread imparted amazing energy, at least to him. Both Kale and Rose had eaten their fair share, with Kale eating his usual double portion, and they seemed to have no trouble falling asleep.

Ilien lay on his back, his mind turning in circles as he tried to make sense of everything that was happening. He sorted things into two categories: things he knew, and things he didn't know. The simple act of organizing his thoughts helped calm him down.

First, the things he knew for sure. Number one, he was Ilien Woodhill.

The first one stopped him, and he felt a sudden panic. *Of course I'm Ilien Woodhill,* he thought. But he was something more, wasn't he? Someone else. *Something* else. Nomadin. NiDemon. The Necromancer. The Creator who had forgotten his identity.

His identity? If he was the Creator then perhaps he wasn't even a *he.* Wouldn't he be more of an *it*?

"I *am* Ilien Woodhill," he said aloud.

Kale stirred in the darkness and Rose's breathing shifted, but no one woke.

"I am Ilien Woodhill," he whispered. "Whatever else I

may be, I am Ilien Woodhill. Let's get that one out of the way." He took a deep breath and let it out slowly.

"Other things I know are true. I crossed to this world to seek help from the wizardesses. Yes. That's true. I was supposed to cross with Gallund and Windy, but I crossed alone. Gallund tried to stop me, but it was too late."

Again he stopped. He wasn't sure if that was entirely true, either. He had heard someone shout, "Stop!" but couldn't be absolutely sure that it had been Gallund. In fact, the voice he heard had sounded like his own. That was impossible, of course, but if he was to be absolutely accurate he would have to move that one to the "things I don't know" category.

One thing I do know for certain is that I've never been here before, especially not two thousand years ago. That's just ridiculous, no matter what they say.

I need to get out of this wretched place, that's what I need to do. I have to get back to that Crossing so I can go back home.

Ilien's thoughts froze and a chill climbed his spine in the blackness.

I can't go back to the Crossing, can I?

A knot grew in the pit of his stomach.

It was prophesied that I would return, so the Onegod cursed the earth to kill me.

It nearly did. The earth didn't hurt Kale, or the Cyclops. Only him. The earth only hurt him.

He felt sick with sudden realization.

Things I know to be true. I have been here before.

The idea overwhelmed him. He felt a flutter of panic run through him. Out of habit he recited his Light spell.

"Kinil ubid illubid kinar."

Globe sprang to life above him, softly glowing yet

dazzlingly bright in the utter darkness. Ilien reached up in surprise to catch her in his palm. She dimmed until only the faintest outline could be seen, a ghostly moon that revealed the joy on his face.

"I didn't think I could reach you," he whispered, sitting up in the gloom. "I didn't think you would come." He peered at the darkness all around. Kale and Rose slept soundly not ten feet away. "It must have something to do with this cave. The rock must block the draining effects of the Desecration. It's all so strange."

Globe hovered closer, pulsating as she spoke in a hushed voice. "Remember, Ilien. Be, then do, then have."

"Be who?" he asked, turning back to her. "Ilien? The Necromancer? This world's savior? God? This one tells me I'm that one. That one tells me I'm this. Still another says I'm something else. Sometimes I wish people would just shut up and leave me alone."

Globe brightened noticeably, and Ilien cupped his hands around her, afraid the light would wake the others. "Not you. I didn't mean you. You know what I mean, don't you?"

"Be, then do, then have," she repeated, dimming again.

"I know," said Ilien. "It's my choice. I have to choose, or life will choose for me."

"Your choices in the present lead to outcomes in your future."

Ilien sighed in exasperation. "I know that, too. Tell me something I don't know."

"You don't know what you want to *have*," said Globe.

"What I want to have?"

"Be, then do, then have."

"Will you stop repeating yourself? I know all about your precious mantra. Decide who you want to be, then do what that person would do, and you'll have what you wanted all along." Ilien fell silent, fearful that his whispered outburst had woken Kale or Rose. No one stirred.

"Decide what you want to *have*," said Globe, "and you'll have decided who you want to be and what you should do. Your problem is you don't know what you want to have. What is it you want most?"

Ilien sulked in silence, all the while wishing he had never conjured Globe and trying to put her words out of his mind. But he couldn't. They began to make sense to him. He couldn't deny that she was right. If he didn't know what he wanted then he wouldn't know what to do. If he didn't know what to do, then he wouldn't know who he should *be. Be. Then do. Then have.* But first he needed to know what he wanted. That would dictate the rest.

"Right now, I want to go home," he whispered.

"That's a start," said Globe. She glittered like a pale coal cast from a fire. "You want to go home. What do you need to do to get what you want?"

Ilien peered into Globe's luminescent depths. The answer was clear. "I need to seek out the last wizardess."

"And?" Globe brightened. Ilien squinted at her.

"Destroy the Onegod." He rubbed at his eyes, suddenly tired. It made sense. It seemed so simple that he felt foolish for not realizing it sooner. He wanted to go home. He needed to destroy the Onegod to do so.

"I must choose to be the person they believe me to be," he concluded. "I must be their hero."

"Good. Now get some rest." Globed dimmed then faded to black.

Ilien fell into a fitful slumber.

Chapter VIII

Battle on the Buried Road

"**R**ise and shine!"
Ilien stirred and opened his eyes to Rose's magical flame dancing before him. He groaned and pushed the flame away.

"Ouch!" he cried, jerking back a singed hand and rolling away from the hovering flame. "I thought you said that thing wasn't real!" He jammed his burned fingers into his mouth.

Rose raised an eyebrow. "I said it wasn't a candle." She smiled and added, "Are you alright?"

Ilien sat up. "I'm fine. Why are you waking me?"

Kale emerged from the darkness holding a fresh bowl of water. "It's morning outside," he said. "We need to reach the next stonehall before nightfall."

"We're leaving?" asked Ilien. He propped himself up on one elbow. "What's a stonehall?"

Kale sat beside him and handed Ilien a stone cup. "The stonehalls were built over a thousand years ago. They are safe havens placed within a long day's walk from each other."

"It's how we're going to escape the Desecration," added Rose, filling her own stone cup with cold, clean water.

"We built them for you," said Kale.

Ilien had to hand it to the people of this world. They had thought of everything. Not only had they kept watch for two thousand years, they constructed solid stone sanctuaries to protect him from the ravages of the Desecration.

He frowned. "They're a long day's walk away from each other? How will I reach them if I can't touch the ground?"

Kale handed a piece of Manna to Rose, who broke it and gave a piece to Ilien. "We will take the Buried Road," answered Rose.

"The Buried Road? You mean a tunnel? Don't tell me they've dug tunnels from stonehall to stonehall."

Kale hurried to swallow the hunk of Manna he chewed, but Rose answered for him. "Not a tunnel. A road. A road made of stone buried beneath the ground."

Ilien looked incredulous. "If it's buried beneath the ground, what good will it do?"

"It's only a few inches beneath the ground. It will help protect you from the effects of the Desecration, and help keep your location secret from the Onegod."

Kale finally swallowed his mouthful of Manna, his swollen lips smacking together. "It's completely hidden," he added, excitedly. "Only I know where it is."

Ilien looked to Rose. "It's true," she said. "The Buried Road's location, even its existence, is a closely held secret. If the Onegod ever found it, your chances of escape would be slim. When Kale was chosen to be a Watcher, its location was revealed to Kale and Kale only. Outside of the Watchers who came before, Kale is the only person to know how to travel the Buried Road."

Ilien regarded the young boy, with his misshapen head, crooked eyes and swollen face atop his chiseled, muscular body. He felt a growing sense of both awe and sadness. The boy lived in a horrifying land of desolation and death and suffered from a birth defect so hideous that it was often hard to look upon him. He carried such overwhelming responsibility. This was his childhood. There was no chasing dogs and climbing trees for Kale. No racing go-carts down Parson's Hill. No fun. No security. No love. Only fear, anxiety, violence. Ilien felt suddenly ashamed and terribly sad.

Kale's face dropped. He reached up to touch the bumps on his forehead. "What's wrong?"

Ilien's throat ached as he fought back sudden tears. "I'm sorry," he said. He blinked hard. "Where are your parents?"

Kale's face went blank. "My parents?"

Ilien gathered himself together. "Yes, your mom and dad. Where are they? They must be worried about you."

Rose placed a hand on Kale's shoulder. "The children of this world have no parents," she said. "I am the closest thing Kale has to a mother."

"That's just crazy," said Ilien. "No parents? Why not?"

"There can be no attachments, Ilien," answered Rose. "Kale's people have been awaiting you for a millennium. They consider you their only hope against the Onegod and the horrible life they must bear. In their single-mindedness, they gave up all attachments. Children are raised not by parents, but by everyone. In that way they can best prepare for your return. There is no one to worry about Kale, and no one for Kale to worry about."

"There is only you," said Kale, smiling his twisted smile and showing his cat-like teeth.

"No attachments," said Ilien. "You mean, no love."

"No selfish love," replied Rose.

"A parent's love is selfish?"

Rose snatched the forgotten piece of Manna from Ilien's hand. "It is the most selfish love of all."

Kale sat in silence as Ilien protested. "How can you say that? That's ridiculous!"

Rose raised and eyebrow. "Is it?" She leaned in closer

to Ilien. "Who do you love?"

Ilien drew back. "What do you mean? I love lots of people."

Kale stared at Ilien, his twisted face knotted with sudden emotion.

"Who do you love most, worry about most?" asked Rose. "Who has captured your heart? Who is in your thoughts constantly?"

Ilien thought he knew the answer immediately. He loved his mother. He thought about her often. Worried about her. But there was someone else, someone he worried about more. Someone who, he suddenly realized, might have captured his heart.

Rose took a bite of Manna. "If you had to choose between that person's life and the lives of ten strangers, what would you choose?" She chewed thoughtfully as she awaited Ilien's answer.

"You can't ask that question," argued Ilien. "That's not a fair question."

"I'm asking it. And it is fair," said Rose. "If you had to choose who would live and who would die, what would you choose? If you could save only one or the other, would you save the one you love most, or ten complete strangers?"

"That's a ridiculous scenario," said Ilien. "No one can answer that question."

"Of course they can. In this world, people answer that question all the time."

Kale looked on intently, his misaligned face bent with sudden emotion. One hand gripped his Breach, the other his empty stone cup.

"So what would it be?" asked Rose. "Would you let the one you love most die and save ten strangers? Or would you save her and send ten innocent people to their death?"

Ilien sat quietly, mulling over the question.

"Well, who will it be?" badgered Rose.

"You're right. I'd have to save Windy," said Ilien.

Rose stared wide-eyed at Ilien, then sat back. "Of course," she said. "You'd save the one you love."

Ilien understood. "And send ten people to their death. That *is* selfish."

Kale grabbed the stone bowl. Without a word, he left to fetch more water.

Rose took a deep breath and watched Kale recede into the shadows. "A parent's love is even stronger, Ilien. It's the most selfish love of all. There isn't a loving mother alive who wouldn't sacrifice a hundred innocent people in order to save her child."

"So that's why Kale has none, so that his people would always put me first?"

Rose smiled weakly. "Your return is their only hope."

Ilien looked away. "The Buried Road," he said. "Will it take us to the Onegod?"

"No," said Rose. "The Road will lead us to the next stonehall. There we will rest before taking the Road again. That's how we'll escape the Desecration, for the Buried Road leads to the world outside."

"The world outside?" asked Ilien.

"The world outside the Desecration."

Ilien peered into the darkness where Kale had disappeared. "This Desecration," he said. "Were there people living here before the Onegod desecrated the land?"

Rose followed his gaze. "You're wondering if the desecration did that to Kale's face?" She turned back to Ilien, her own face a mask of shadows in the flickering light of her magical flame. "Few people lived in the immediate area where you left this world—where you were prophesied to return. After the Onegod blasted the land and sickened the earth, the Watchers were established. Many people have lived in hiding in the Desecration since, building the Buried Road piece by piece in secret, keeping watch, waiting. Generation after generation, the Watchers lived in this foul place. Then the deformities began—the birth deformities." Rose gazed off into the darkness to see if Kale was approaching. "The Desecration was designed to kill you, Ilien, but its twisted power has an effect on all life. Plants do not grow here. Insects cannot live. Animals avoid it at all costs. But people, people it slowly warps."

Ilien continued staring off into the darkness. "Why did I leave?" he asked.

Rose straightened suddenly, startled by the question.

"What was so important that I would just leave this world to such a horrible fate? Why would I do that? It doesn't make sense." Ilien searched the cave floor with his eyes, as if he might find the answer there written in the dust. "You say that I've been here before," he said, suddenly looking up at Rose. "That was two thousand years ago. Don't you see how crazy that is? Can't you see that it's impossible? You'd be talking about reincarnation."

Rose was silent, her eyes hard in the darkness.

"How do you know that I can defeat the Onegod?" asked Ilien in desperation. "If I was here in some past life, was I some kind of warrior or powerful wizard? Look at me now. Do I look like a warrior or powerful wizard? I have magic, but not enough to destroy a god, no matter what everyone thinks. I'm not even supposed to be here. I'm supposed to be somewhere else, doing something else. I'm supposed to be looking for the wizardesses, all of them, not one of them in hiding. I'm supposed to rescue my mother, not some wretched world."

Ilien stopped, suddenly aware that his voice carried far in the stone cave. Again he peered in the direction Kale had left, expecting to see his malformed face twisted even more with disappointment at what he'd just heard. Kale was nowhere to be seen, but Ilien felt a sharp jab of shame, nonetheless. He hung his head in silence.

The cave was hushed. Rose's magical flame cast Ilien's hunched shadow before him, a wavering pool of darkness upon the cold stone floor. An echo reverberated up the tunnel as Kale returned. When Ilien finally looked up, his face held a grim determination.

"Okay," was all he said.

Before they left, Rose and Kale took care to tidy up the stonehall. Rose made sure there was no food left behind. Kale stacked the stone bowls neatly in a corner and hid them behind a flat rock. They both set about removing any signs that they'd been there, brushing away their tracks on the dusty floor. When they finished, the stonehall looked like an ordinary cave.

"Come," said Kale, snatching up his Breach where he'd left it leaning against the wall. "We leave by the entrance, so we must be cautious. The Cyclops might still be searching the area."

"I thought you took care of them," said Ilien, hoping the boy understood what he meant.

Rose lit two more small magical flames and tossed them into the air to light their way. "Kale defeated them with the Breaching Arts," she said. "That's how we rescued you."

"Oh," said Ilien. The Breaching Arts were impressive, but not being able to kill those trying to kill you meant you were certain to meet up with them again. "Don't we need supplies?" he asked, changing the subject. "Food and water?"

"Everything we need will be found at the next stonehall," said Rose.

As they made their way back through the cave toward the entrance, Ilien wondered if all the stonehalls were so large. He'd been unconscious when they had carried him in. He didn't realize just how far underground he was. The cave floor sloped upwards and spiraled to the right. Ilien figured the stonehall corkscrewed into the ground some hundred feet or so. He trailed his hand against the damp, stone wall as he walked and Rose's magical lights danced in the gloom ahead of them. Soon the air ahead brightened. The tunnel opened into a wider cave with a low stone ceiling. Roots hung down in places, like tentacles of some giant monster attacking from above.

"The Onegod may have desecrated the land," said Rose, "but he could not destroy all life. His power is not absolute, Ilien. These roots you see will one day shoot life back into the world. When you destroy the Onegod, life will flourish here again."

Light seeped into the cave through a wide, low opening along the far wall. Only a foot or so high, the cave entrance would have been nearly invisible to anyone outside.

"I'll go first and make sure we're alone," said Kale. He quickly made his way to the entrance and crawled through, pulling his Breach behind him.

Ilien sized up Rose and said, "Are you sure you'll fit?"

Rose hit him hard in the arm.

"Ouch! I only meant that it looks awfully small," he said, rubbing his elbow.

In a short time Kale returned, his twisted features locked in a broad, apish smile. "There is no sign of the Cyclops or their tracks. It's safe to come out." He crawled back through the entrance and disappeared.

Rose motioned Ilien forward. "Brats before brains," she said, a hint of a smile on her face.

As Ilien turned to go, he thought of Windy. He hoped, once again, that she hadn't crossed to this godforsaken land.

Outside the stonehall, the world looked just as grey and lifeless as Ilien remembered. He climbed to his feet and discovered they were in a narrow gully with a low dirt rise on either side. Stones littered the ground around the entrance to the cave. A dark crack in the side of a nondescript dirt hill, no one would ever have found it if they didn't know where to look. Rose slowly emerged, huffing and puffing as she came. Ilien reached a hand out to her, but she managed to climb out unassisted.

Ilien suddenly realized that he was standing on hard, packed earth. His breath caught in his throat. He froze, not daring to take a step.

Kale came up behind him. "You're safe, Ilien. You stand upon the Buried Road built just for you and hidden a thousand years ago. The Onegod's power cannot hurt you upon the Road, nor can he detect your presence." Kale stooped and grabbed a rock in each hand. He tossed one to the right, and tossed one to the left, up onto the small dirt banks on each side of the narrow gully. "But wander a few feet to either side and you will not only feel the pain of his power, he will know where you are instantly. Then the Cyclops will return."

Rose dusted herself off. "Let's hope that's all he sends after us."

"How will I know where it is?" asked Ilien. "How wide is this Buried Road?"

"Follow behind me," answered Kale, a smile upon his swollen lips. "The Road is six feet across at its widest point, and often much narrower, so don't stray from my path."

Ilien looked up at the thick, grey sky. "Shouldn't we be traveling at night? What if we're spotted? There isn't much cover out here."

"Night in the Desecration is complete," said Rose. "The darkness is impenetrable. We travel only in the day."

"Besides," said Kale, "no cover for us means no cover for our enemies, as well."

They set off at once. Kale took the lead. Ilien followed behind, careful to stay close to Kale's footsteps. Rose brought up the rear. The going was painfully slow with both Kale and Rose looking to and fro as they went, and Ilien with his eyes trained on Kale's footfalls.

The gully offered them cover for less than a mile. Soon its low, dirt banks receded, and they emerged onto a flat sea of lifeless grey earth littered with broken stones as far as the eye could see. Ilien felt the presence of the gully behind him like a haven from an oncoming storm. In the open he was exposed, vulnerable. The desire to run back and hide in the stonehall overwhelmed him. What if they were spotted? But Kale walked assuredly out into the open, and Rose placed a hand on Ilien's shoulder, urging him forward. He scanned the unbroken horizon in the distance, lifeless, empty, safe. With a quick breath he followed after Kale.

Near midday, they stopped between two low hills—large brown humps on the ruined landscape. The hills offered a small measure of cover as they nibbled on some Manna that Kale had pulled from his pocket.

"I suppose you don't have any chicken legs in that pocket of yours," asked Ilien with a smile. "Or perhaps some boiled eggs or cheese?"

Kale shook his head. "Just Manna," he said through a mouthful. "Want some more?"

Ilien grimaced. "How about some water, then?"

"I'm sorry, Ilien," answered Rose. "You'll have to wait until we get to the next stonehall. There will be water, and perhaps something other than Manna to eat."

Kale smiled and his misshapen face hunched into a swollen knot. "Eat more Manna. It's full of moisture." A line of spittle escaped his fleshy lips and he covered his mouth with a hand. The smile receded, replaced by embarrassment. Ilien was about to say, "Don't worry. I once shot milk out my nose," when Kale leaped to his feet, his Breach held firmly in both hands, eyes ablaze. The muscles in his arms rippled as he squeezed the bone-colored staff.

"Ilien!" cried Rose as she scrambled to her feet. "Behind you!"

Ilien spun about, a spell upon his lips, his hands weaving runes on their own. No magic came.

Before him, flanked by one-eyed Cyclops, stood an old man in long crimson robes. Tall and frail, he held a long, blue wand in one bony hand. The skin of his face was white as parchment, his hair grey as smoke. His eyes, cold and pale, looked through Ilien, yet deep within there moved something else, an inner eye, a shadow of an inner power that saw the boy and knew what he was. Ilien stumbled backward, forgetting his place upon the road. A jolt of wrenching pain shot up his leg. He fell forward to his knees, onto the Road once more.

"The Onegod!" shouted Kale.

The old man raised his blue wand, but Kale was too quick. He sprang high over Ilien, his Breach a heartbeat ahead of him. Agile beyond his aged appearance, the old man withdrew his wand and retreated behind his Cyclops guard. The tip of Kale's Breach swayed in the empty air, then lanced to the left. The ring of metal split the air as he blocked a Cyclops' sword. He landed with his feet beneath him, unswaying, an unmoveable wall between him and Ilien. Rose dragged Ilien to his feet. "Come on!" She pulled him forward, but Ilien resisted.

"The Road! Where is the Road?" He feared stepping off it again, feared the pain would overwhelm him and all would be lost.

"Go!" cried Kale as he parried blow after blow. The Cyclops could not advance beyond their smaller opponent, and the strain of battle showed upon their one-eyed faces.

"Move!" commanded Rose.

"Kale! We can't leave Kale!" Ilien closed his eyes, envisioned the rune for Fire, hoping the stones of the Buried Road beneath him would help him reach his magic. His fingers began to move. In his mind's eye he saw the rune take shape. It shimmered like heated metal, then quickly faded to darkness.

"Ilien!" Rose grabbed him and yanked him backwards. He stumbled to the ground.

The old man stood before them, wand raised in his bony hand, his crimson robes flowing about his skeletal frame. The clots of darkness in his unseeing eyes gathered to form pupils as black as coal.

Ilien looked into those pupils and staggered back, blinded. He clutched at his eyes. "I can't see!"

Rose jumped in front of him, but Ilien pushed her aside. His fingers wove the air as words tumbled from his lips. He sensed power gathering to him, but was unsure if it would be enough.

"Mitra mitari mitara miru!" he shouted as he finished the rune for Fire. His vision returned as shooting stars of bright green flames erupted from his fingertips.

The old man stood rigid as the magical fire engulfed him. His mouth dropped open in a silent cry. His eyes paled as the darkness within them receded. A peal of laughter split the air. Still the flames assaulted him.

Ilien incanted the words of power again, "Mitra mitari mitara miru!" strengthening the fire's intensity—swirling green power turned blue at its edges. The laughter grew frantic as the old man began to move. He lowered his wand. His pale, white lips uttered unheard words. The wand began to glow until a black light flickered at its blue tip, a tiny flame of dark power amidst the green and blue turmoil of Ilien's magic. Ilien closed his eyes. Conjuring the rune in his mind again, he traced it once more with his free hand.

Black tongues of fire lashed out from the old man's wand, whipping Ilien's green flames into a frenzy of tumultuous magic. But the old man's assault could not break through. The blackness in his eyes returned, condensing in rage at his failure to overcome the boy before him. Aware of the blinding power of his gaze, Ilien looked away. As he did so, his foot stepped back a pace off the Buried Road.

Blue and green fire burst around Ilien as a jolt of pain raced up his leg and coursed through his body. His magic extinguished in a spray of hot sparks. Instantly, the old man raced forward. The black power of his wand gathered at its tip for a final assault. Ilien fell forward, back upon the Buried Road. He pulled his foot to safety and his wits returned, but there was no time to react. The old man bore down upon him, his outstretched wand ablaze, black eyes narrowed.

Ilien shielded his eyes from the old man's blinding gaze. "Inhibi inhabi hababi viru!" he cried.

The old man screamed in rage as Ilien disappeared. A bolt of green fire streaked through the air to his left, catching him by surprise. It tore the wand from his grasp and ignited his long, crimson robes. He spun in fury, a pillar of flames, desperate to reach his assailant. No one was there. Another jet of fire struck from behind. Ilien appeared, his hands pouring forth torrents of emerald green magic. The old man crumpled to the ground. A shriek split the air, a wailing cry that shivered Ilien's spine. He extinguished his magic and clutched at his ears.

From the burning remains of the old man's body rose a pale and wavering shadow. It hovered in the roiling fumes of his ruined shell, darkening the rising smoke. It pained Ilien to look at it, as if the shadow leeched away his very sight. But he could not look away. He had seen this shadow before. He knew what he looked upon.

And it knew him.

"Necromancer! You have returned!" it called as it streaked into the air, up into the flat grey sky, and vanished.

Ilien fell to his knees.

Rose rushed to Ilien. "Are you hurt?"

"Kale!" gasped Ilien.

The boy stood a dozen paces away, a slanted smile stretched across his misshapen face. Sweat streaked his swollen features and he held his Breach in both hands.

"They have fled," said Kale. "You defeated the Onegod and they fled."

Ilien looked to Rose, his face hopeful. "It's over? It's done?"

He knew what Rose was about to say, even before he saw the grim look fall across her face. It wasn't done. The Evil was not destroyed—for that's what it was, what it had been, the same Evil he had encountered in the tunnels beneath the Long Dark Road back home on Nadae.

"Don't be foolish," said Rose, releasing his arm. "You defeated the Onegod, but defeated is not destroyed. You defeated only one of its forms. There are many others that still may find us even now." She turned to Kale. "Lead on. Quickly."

"Yes, but you do have the power," gushed Kale as he approached Ilien. "Now you must know that you can destroy the Onegod."

Ilien glanced uneasily at the smoking remains of the old man, then at the flat, grey sky where the shadow had fled. "How many servants of this Onegod are there?"

"They are not servants," answered Rose. "They are him. Often they are old men, but he can possess any form he chooses. Many forms, one god." She strode past Ilien and urged Kale onward. "We should be far from here before he returns. Let's go."

"How do you know he'll return?" asked Ilien.

"Because now he knows where you are."

Kale tucked his Breach beneath his arm and jogged forward. "Come. The next stonehall is still far away."

Chapter IX

Flight to the Stonehall

They traveled quickly through the hard, grey land. Kale led the way with the assurance. Still, Ilien stumbled along behind him in a constant state of fear—fear of being found by the Onegod again, fear of stepping off the Buried Road and being swallowed by the agony of the Desecration. As he followed, intent on placing his feet where Kale's left their mark, a new fear gripped him. He stopped and spun around.

"What are you doing? Keep going!" barked Rose as she nearly collided with him.

Ilien pointed behind them. "Look."

Rose turned and scanned the horizon, her face rigid. "Are we being followed?"

"Not now." Ilien gestured at the clear trail of footprints they were leaving behind them. "But we will be soon."

Kale came up behind them. "Manna break?"

"No, Kale," said Rose. "It's our tracks."

"They'll follow us right to the stonehall," said Ilien.

Again, Rose searched the horizon for signs of pursuit. "It can't be helped," she said. "Our only hope is to stay ahead of them. When we reach the next stonehall, Kale will backtrack and cover our trail. It may stop the Onegod from finding the stonehall."

"And us," added Kale, a wry grin splitting his craggy face.

"Now move, Kale," said Rose. "We need to double our speed."

Kale smiled and reached beneath his tunic. He pulled forth a large hunk of Manna. "Then we'll need some of this."

Ilien grimaced, but accepted his piece as gratefully as he could.

"Not too much at once," warned Kale. "Remember the Consumption, Ilien. Small bites. Small bites as we go."

Several hours later, Ilien found himself nibbling the last bit of his Manna. The small piece Kale had given him had empowered him to run the entire afternoon without tiring. The sky was beginning to darken, signaling that somewhere beyond the perpetual cloud cover the sun was sinking. They had run single file to minimize their tracks, and though Ilien feared veering off the Buried Road, the invigorating power of the Manna pushed that fear to the back of his mind. Now, with any luck, they would make it to the next stonehall well ahead of any pursuit. As Ilien swallowed the last of his Manna, he wondered how far they had left to go.

They ran until darkness fell. It fell quickly, and none-too-soon as far as Ilien was concerned. The effects of the Manna began to wear off not long after he ate his last bite. He was dead tired and hoped the stonehall was near. His fear of falling off the Buried Road returned with a vengeance.

"It'll be night soon, Kale," said Rose. "How much farther to the stonehall?"

Kale slowed, then stopped. Ilien lurched to a halt behind him, doubling over in exhaustion. Rose quickly conjured her magical flame. The invading darkness seemed to overwhelm the tiny flame, and it cast a sickly light upon them all.

"I don't know," said Kale. His facial deformities pooled with shadows. "We should have been there by now. I think we passed it."

"Passed it?" cried Rose, straightening. "How?"

Kale looked desperately around, then hung his head.

"What's the big deal?" said Ilien. "We'll turn around and go back."

Rose took a deep breath to calm herself. "Okay. How far back is it?" she asked, her face strained in the wavering light of her magical flame.

"Too far, I think," said Kale.

Rose clenched her hands into fists, eyes wide.

"What's wrong?" asked Ilien, a growing panic building in his chest. "Can't we camp right here?"

"Night in the Desecration is complete," whispered Kale.

"That's good," said Ilien, looking from Rose to Kale. "It'll cover our tracks. Right?"

Rose's magical light flickered then dimmed. "Night in the Desecration is a death sentence." She placed a trembling hand on Kale's shoulder. "Unlike the Cyclops, the Onegod will not protect us." She lifted Kale's chin and stroked his malformed face, her eyes filled with sudden forgiveness. "It's not your fault. I do not blame you."

The air grew quickly darker, bringing with it a suffocating pressure. Ilien grabbed his chest. He looked around desperately. There was nowhere to escape.

Kale threw his arms around Rose as she gazed into her wavering flame. "No one's ever survived a night in the Desecration, Ilien. No one." The flame flickered, then died.

Darkness rushed in, so complete that it quenched the light from Ilien's mind, snuffed the very images from his thoughts. He gasped, struggling to breathe. Evil pervaded the night—mind-numbing, overwhelming Evil, the same blinding blackness that assailed him in the tunnels below the Long Dark Road, the same absence of everything that he'd driven away once before.

"Kinil ubid illubid kinar!" he cried with the last of his breath. Choking, he drew the Light rune, right hand thrust forward.

Like a white-hot spark born from the clash of swords, Globe jumped to life in his palm. The blackness pressed in, obscuring her shining brilliance. She sputtered and hissed in Ilien's hand like an ember on water, fighting for life. But slowly the void receded as her brilliance returned and drove the darkness from Ilien's thoughts. Unable to breathe, Ilien shouted the spell in his mind. Again and again he drew the rune. Globe began to grow. Her silvery light fell upon his face. He gasped in a full, clean breath of air and shouted the magical words once more. "Kinil ubid illubid kinar!"

Globe burst into a dazzling, burning sun, forcing Ilien to avert his eyes. Her brilliant radiance drove back the blackness, pushed it past Ilien and held it at bay ten feet away. Rose and Kale huddled together by the edge of the light, their eyes wide. They gulped in air then rushed to Ilien. Globe lifted from his palm and floated above them, her shining rays keeping the night from falling in on them.

Ilien dropped to his knees beside Kale. "How far is it to the next stonehall?"

Kale stared up at Globe, his misshapen face bent in awe, his uneven eyes wide.

Ilien grabbed his shoulder. "How far, Kale? We can't stay out here much longer. I don't have the strength to keep Globe going until morning."

Kale ran his hand across the lumps on his forehead. "Too far," he said. "We have to go back, back to the one I missed." He looked desperately at Ilien. "I'm sorry. I shouldn't have missed it."

Rose put her arm around Kale. Her face was ghostly white. "It's okay, Kale. Do you know how to get back to it?"

Kale shook his head. "I think so."

"You *think* so," said Ilien. "Kale, you need to be sure. I don't know how much longer I can keep this up."

Globe suddenly flickered, and Kale's face dropped.

"Don't worry," came a soothing, woman's voice. "I am stronger than you know." Ilien looked up at Globe as she spoke again. "I will light the way for you," she said, pulsating with each word.

"But for how long?" asked Ilien. "How long can you resist this darkness?"

Globe bobbed in the air. "For as long as it takes."

Kale's swollen lips stretched like scars across his face. "I can lead you to the next stonehall. I will not fail you."

"How far is it?" asked Rose. She peered into the impending blackness that threatened them from all sides.

Globe dimmed and the darkness encroached upon them. They huddled closer as her circle of illumination closed in like a noose. Ilien felt trapped in a witch's crystal ball. A growing sense of helplessness filled his heart.

"It's far," said Kale, his voice strained with worry. "But if Ilien can light the way, I'll get us there. I promise."

Ilien rose to his feet. Shrugging off his dread, he offered Rose a hand.

"Are you sure we shouldn't go back and search for the stonehall we missed?" she asked.

"You heard Kale," said Ilien. "He's not sure where it is. We might not find it. Even if we do, we'll be heading in the wrong direction." Ilien shot Kale a worried glance. "You do know where it is?" he asked.

Kale planted his Breach before him. "I will not fail you."

They followed Kale in single-file, pressed together against the impenetrable blackness all about them. Several times, Globe dimmed her light, sending panic through the small company. But each time she quickly brightened again. In this way they traveled in weary silence through the absolute night of the Desecration. They heard no sound save for their own quick breathing and shuffling footfalls. They saw only what lay within Globe's small sphere of light. As they moved, the ground below their feet emerged from the blackness before them—grey, flat, purged of all life. Several steps later it disappeared behind them as the blackness swallowed it again. Twice Kale stopped and pondered the way before moving on again. He plodded in the lead with his head bent, eyes upon the ground.

They stopped only once to rest and nibble some Manna. Even then, the respite was brief. Soon they journeyed on, hopeful of finding the next stonehall, eager to see the day again, even if it held nothing more than dreary, grey dullness. When at last weariness overtook them, and Ilien felt he could not travel on without falling asleep where he stood, the pitchblende of night began to pale. It was subtle at first—a feeling, a lessening of the dread surrounding them. The air grew less oppressive and there was a sense that they neared their destination. Globe seemed to dim again, yet this time she didn't brighten as before. In truth, her light remained constant. The utter blackness was giving way to normal night.

They continued on through the dull, grey dawn at a much faster pace. Kale led they way, head up, sure of his way. Ilien and Rose no longer followed on his heels. Globe still shined above them, but shrank in size as the air brightened around them.

"Come," said Kale, his voice sounding loud in the half-gloom. "It's not far."

The landscape around them had grown hillier overnight. They now marched single-file in a narrow gully with steep dirt slopes on either side. Ilien looked behind them. There was no sign of pursuit. He wondered if the Cyclops had followed them through the night, protected by the Onegod. If so, they might not be far behind.

"Up ahead," said Kale, breaking Ilien out of his thoughts. "There it is." He quickened his pace, his Breach slung over his shoulder.

Up ahead, the sloping ground leveled, revealing a tumble of broken, grey boulders piled in a great, jagged heap. Ilien guessed that the entrance to the stonehall lay beneath, and he hurried to follow Kale. Globe floated along above him while Rose scrambled forward, eager as he was to enter the relative safety of the secreted cave.

Moments later they both joined Kale in climbing from rock to rock as they ascended the pile. Near the top, Kale suddenly disappeared. Ilien rushed forward, thinking he'd fallen. Instead, Kale waved up at him from a tiny, rock-walled chamber below. Ilien quickly determined the way down and soon stood beside him, with Rose at his side. Globe hovered in the rear, casting their shadows thin and wavering before them.

"Follow me," said Kale.

They were beneath the boulder pile now, and Kale led them forward, winding his way along a narrow, sloping corridor. The air grew dark, but Globe joined Kale up front. They descended further beneath the boulders until the corridor opened into a small, stone chamber. Kale smiled at Ilien, his swollen lips stretched in a pink smear across his lumpy face.

"Home, sweet home."

Ilien sent Globe to search the rest of the room. As she flitted from here to there, her light revealed a stack of casks in one corner, a collection of barrels in another, and a small stone table in between. Globe came to rest above the table. The broken remains of two wooden chairs, destroyed by time, were visible opposite each other.

"There should be some water in those casks," said Kale, "and something to eat in those barrels." At that, he turned to make his way back along the narrow, sloping corridor.

"Where are you going?" asked Ilien.

"I'll be back." He disappeared into the darkness.

"He's going back a ways to erase our tracks," said Rose in answer to Ilien's worried gaze. "It may keep the Onegod from discovering the stonehall."

Ilien walked to the stone table and sat heavily upon it. "How much farther until we get out of this place—this Desecration?" He regarded the pile of decaying wood that was once a chair. "Time destroys all things," he said.

"Not the Onegod," said Rose, moving to the pile of casks in the corner. "He's only grown more powerful over time." She rummaged about and came up with a small, stone cup. She tapped one of the casks and was rewarded with a hollow echo. She did the same with the others. They were all empty.

"Looks like there's no water," she lamented.

Ilien looked to the barrels in the other corner. They looked almost as decayed as the chairs. "I'm betting the food in this place isn't much to look at either." He squinted up at Globe. "So how much farther until we escape this Desecration, anyhow?"

Rose moved to inspect the barrels. "I'm not sure," she answered.

"What do you mean, you're not sure?"

"Empty," she whispered, disappointed. She turned to Ilien. "Only Kale knows for sure. Kale's the Watcher. I'm just a tag-along."

"I thought the Watchers worked alone. You never did answer my question when we first met," said Ilien, raising an eyebrow. "Why are you here?"

Rose looked to the corridor where Kale had left. She joined Ilien, sitting next to him on the stone table. "The Watchers do work alone."

"Then how do you fit in?" Ilien studied her in Globe's slanting light. "Why are you here?"

Rose let out a sigh. "It's a long story." When she saw Ilien's expression, she added, "The short tale is that years ago I, too, crossed to this place from somewhere else."

"Years ago? How many years ago?"

Rose frowned, revealing deep lines around her eyes. "About thirty years ago," she said, "when I was about your age."

Ilien tried to picture her as a child. "Where did you come from?"

Rose thought for a moment. "From another place, another world. Like you."

Ilien pondered what she's said, trying to make sense of it. He knew there were many other worlds, all connected by the Crossings. But why come to this one?

Rose answered as if reading his mind. "Like you, I came here seeking help. I came here to find the wizardesses."

Ilien didn't know what to say. Could it be that there were other worlds in the same predicament as his? *Of course*, he thought. The War of the Crossings had trapped Nomadin and NiDemon on many different worlds. But how did Rose know that the Nomadin wizardesses had fled to this world? It didn't make sense.

"The war between the Nomadin and NiDemon rages on many different worlds, and spans many different times," continued Rose. "I crossed seeking aid from the wizardesses who had fled my world, and I was brought here. I was found by a young boy with a face like Kale's, and mistaken for the one they were waiting for. I was mistaken for you. It didn't take long for the mistake to be discovered, though. For one, you are a boy. Secondly, the Desecration did not harm me, as it harms you."

"Of all the places in this crummy world, you arrived in the Desecration?" said Ilien, hardly believing it.

"Yes. Bad luck, wasn't it. But that's all in the past now. The Watcher who found me took care of me, raised me, until the next Watcher took his place. Over time, I learned what they were watching for, *who* they were watching for. I've been with each successive Watcher ever since, helping them however I can."

Ilien felt a sudden kinship with Rose, and a sudden sorrow. Like him, she had crossed to this horrid place to seek help for her people. Like him, she was trapped here, too. "So you've never been outside the Desecration."

"No. I haven't. And I'm just as eager as you to get out of this wretched place." She looked at the decaying barrels in the corner. "If only to get a decent meal."

Globe flickered and dimmed causing their shadows to jump and waver beneath them.

"You must be exhausted," said Ilien, peering up at Globe. "I forgot how long you've been lighting the way."

Globe paled and floated down to rest between Ilien and Rose. Her light waned further until she was little more than a luminescent ghost in the blackness.

"We're safe now," said Ilien. "You brought us to safety. Why don't you fade and get some rest?"

"You talk to your light as if it's alive," said Rose.

"She is alive." Ilien placed a hand beneath Globe, and she slowly shrank in size.

"I'll take it from here," said Rose. With a mumble and a flick of her wrist, she cast a magical flame into the air. Globe went out with a muffled pop, leaving the room lit in ruddy shades.

"How do you do that?" asked Ilien, regarding her magical flame as it warmed the air above them. "What kind of spell is it? Is it a Kindle Candle spell?"

Rose stood and stretched her weary legs. "No," she said as she brushed the dust from her bottom. "Well, partially."

"So which one is it? The Kindle or the Candle?" said Ilien, grinning.

Rose smiled back at him, and Ilien was struck with a sudden image of Windy, smiling at him after he'd made a stupid joke. He missed her. He missed home.

"Very funny," quipped Rose. "I say partially because I don't have to use all the words. I only use one."

Ilien frowned. "But that's impossible. The True Language is very precise. Gallund always told me not to use slang or unnecessary adverbs, and to always watch my tenses. A spell is a magical sentence, not a phrase, and definitely not a single word."

Rose's smile widened. "Oh, really." She pointed to the space above Ilien's head and said, "Illubid."

Ilien ducked as another one of her tiny flames flared to life with a pop and a hiss.

"It won't burn you, Ilien. At least, it won't if you don't stick your hand in it. You see, one word is all it takes."

Ilien's frown deepened. "Gallund never taught me that."

"Gallund? Your teacher?"

"My father," said Ilien. "And my teacher." He looked about in confusion. "I don't get it. Illubid isn't the word for fire. It's the word for light."

"It's both," replied Rose. "And neither."

Ilien gazed at her blankly. Not for the last time, he suddenly wished he'd paid better attention to Gallund's lessons.

"The word illubid is in both the Light spell and the Kindle Candle spell, is it not? The other words, the ones that differ in each spell, affect the meaning of the word illubid and the outcome of the spell."

Ilien's eyes lit up. "But you skip all those other words, don't you? With just the one word you're able to evoke fire when there's nothing to burn. It's pure magic."

In his excitement, Ilien stood and began to pace. "I could conjure all sorts of things if I knew more words. If only I still had my spell book. Fire would just be the beginning. Heck, if I knew the word, I bet I could conjure water."

He stopped and looked at Rose, his face hopeful. "You can teach me."

"No," said Rose. "I can't."

"What do you mean, you can't? What else is there to do while we're holed up in these stonehalls? And it could only help. You saw what I did to that old man. Imagine what I could do if I knew what you knew. I'd be unstoppable. The Onegod wouldn't stand a chance."

"You already know what I know," said Rose

Ilien shrugged off her comment. "If I knew the word for sugar I could actually make Manna edible. If you taught me the word for death, I could destroy the Onegod and go home. You have to teach me!"

"I said you know what I know and that's the truth!" said Rose, her voice rising. "The only word I know is fire."

Ilien froze. In the brief silence that fell, he plainly heard a distant cry for help.

Chapter X

Breach

"It's Kale!" Rose raced back up the narrow rising corridor, her magical lights trailing her, dancing madly as they went. For a heartbeat, Ilien was left alone in the blackness, his mind turning in circles. Kale cried out again and he chased after Rose, his heart pounding wildly.

Ahead, Rose's magical flames pursued her in the darkness. She was moving fast, and Ilien heard Kale's cry again, closer, above him, from outside. The darkness gave way to dim light. He stopped in the small, rocked wall chamber and looked up to see Rose framed against the grey sky as she climbed her way up. Already she was at the top, pulling herself up and out, onto the top of the boulder pile.

Frantically, Ilien began to climb. Near the top he heard Rose call his name. In moments, he stood atop the pile of boulders that hid the stonehall below.

"Get back, Ilien!" cried Rose.

A rock sailed past his Ilien's head and shattered on a nearby boulder. Another hummed only inches over his head as he stumbled back, catching himself from falling down the hole behind him.

Below, Kale stood surrounded by three Cyclops. They navigated around him, keeping out of range of his Breach, each clutching a rock in his massive hand. The one directly in front of Kale lunged forward, feinting to the right, while the Cyclops behind Kale launched a rock at his back.

Ilien gasped. Quick as a cat, Kale blindly swung his Breach behind him, blocking the stone and sending it whirling into the air. The other two Cyclops threw their deadly missiles, intent on catching Kale off guard. In a blur, Kale sent them sailing back. One stone caught its thrower beneath the chin, dropping him to the ground unconscious. The other sent a Cyclops stumbling back out of its path.

Ilien spotted Rose below as she picked up her own stone. She raised the fist-sized rock in her right hand and shouted, "Propel!"

In a blur, the stone streaked from her hand toward the nearest Cyclops. With a sickening thud, it struck the monster in the back of the skull. The Cyclops collapsed to the ground in a cloud of grey dust.

The final Cyclops circled around Kale, its single eye wide with fear. Rose stooped for another stone. It wheeled and ran, its long, bandy arms flying out in all directions as it went.

Rose raised the stone up high. Kale shot her a disapproving look.

"It's fleeing," he said. "Let it go."

Rose smiled grimly. She lifted one eyebrow. "Propel."

The stone launched from her outstretched hand and pursued the escaping Cyclops. A moment later, it found its mark. The Cyclops stumbled to the ground and lay still.

Ilien climbed down from atop the pile of boulders, painfully aware of how useless he'd been during the fight, and hugely impressed with Rose's magical attack.

"You said the only word you knew was fire," he said as he jumped from rock to rock to reach her. Soon he stood panting before her. "How did you do that?"

Kale shook his head, his swollen lips pursed in a perverse, grotesque sneer. "The question is not how, but why. Our enemy was fleeing. He was beaten. Yet you attacked him anyhow."

"Our enemy was not beaten. He was fleeing," said Rose. She gestured to the fallen Cyclops. "Now he's beaten." She turned to Ilien. "And yes, I know the word for Move."

"Which is what I suggest we do before any more enemies find us," said Kale, slinging his Breach across one shoulder.

Ilien couldn't believe his ears. "Move? You mean leave the stonehall now?" He was exhausted after journeying all night through the quenching darkness of the Desecration. He looked at Kale and wondered how the boy could even stand after all he'd been through. "We just got here. We need to rest."

"We're not leaving the stonehall," said Rose. "Ilien's right. We need to rest."

"What we need to do," Kale stated flatly, "is leave here before those Cyclops wake up."

Rose's face flushed a deep shade of scarlet. "We're not leaving. The next stonehall is too far!"

"We can make it there before nightfall," said Kale, turning to leave.

"No, Kale. We can't."

Kale spun and glared at her, his facial features twisted in sudden anger. "Yes, we can!"

Ilien sensed the struggle between the two was about more than just staying or leaving.

Rose took a deep breath and let it out slowly. "Kale. Take Ilien back into the stonehall."

Kale's eyes hardened. Behind him, the Cyclops stirred.

"Go, Kale," said Rose. "Do it now."

The Cyclops raised its head with a moan.

"Maybe Kale's right," said Ilien. "Maybe we should go.

That Cyclops is—" He fell silent as he realized what their argument was really about. "You can't just kill them," he whispered.

"Why not?" Rose turned on him suddenly. "Do you suggest we wait here until they wake up and attack us? Then Kale can use his precious Breaching Arts until they drop unconscious again from exhaustion?" She reached beneath her faded, green cloak and pulled out a knife. The blade was small, the handle worn. "I don't practice the Breaching Arts, Ilien. We're staying here. If you don't approve, you have ten seconds to come up with a better idea. Otherwise, I suggest you get back to the stonehall."

Ilien didn't know what to do. How could Rose just kill the Cyclops without a thought? He'd been in battles before, saw creatures die. He had even killed a Groll. But that had been in self-defense. But this was different. It was knifing someone in their sleep. It was wrong.

"There's no other way," said Rose, as if reading his mind. "We won't make it to the next stonehall before nightfall, and if we stay the Cyclops will only attack us again, or worse, tell the Onegod where we are."

"Wait," said Ilien, frantic to find another solution. "Why not tie them up? If we tie them up so they can't escape, we can rest here until morning, then—"

"There are crueler things than death," said Rose. "Leaving someone tied up to starve is one of them."

"Someone may find them."

"Who do you think will find them but more of the Onegod's servants? And if they do, they'll hunt us down all over again, only this time there'll be more of them."

The Cyclops snorted as its wits began to return.

Rose held her knife out in front of her. "Now get into that stonehall."

Kale grabbed Ilien's arm and pulled him forward. "Come. Let the barbarian do her job. I'll have no part of it." As Ilien followed Kale, his mind churned. Deep down, he knew what Rose was doing was necessary. The Cyclops would attack them again. Even if they fled, the Cyclops would hunt them down. They would never stop. But he also knew that what Rose was doing was wrong. It just felt wrong. But what else could they do? There was no other way. And if there was no other way, was it truly wrong?

"Hurry, Ilien," urged Kale as he began to climb the pile of boulders, hopping from stone to stone.

There has to be something I can do, thought Ilien. *But what?* It would all be over in moments if he didn't do something.

A flash of movement caught Ilien's eye. A small, brown toad hopped back into the depths of the rock pile. It was the first living thing he had seen in the Desecration, and it startled him. *It must live beneath the boulders, perhaps in the stonehall*, thought Ilien. Somehow it survived in this desolate place. Of all creatures—a toad.

That was it! A toad! He knew at once what he could do. He stopped at the top of the pile. Kale had already begun climbing down the hole leading to the stonehall. Rose knelt before the nearest Cyclops. She brought her knife to its neck. Its sharp blade glinted dully.

"Stop!" shouted Ilien.

Rose froze. She turned and looked up at Ilien. The Cyclops came to its senses and lashed out with one giant arm, striking Rose in the back. Rose let out a strangled cry as her body launched into the air. She cleared twenty feet then tumbled to the ground in a motionless heap.

Ilien staggered back in shock and bewilderment. *What have I done?*

"No!" he cried. "Rose! No!"

The Cyclops climbed to its feet. It stood swaying in confusion, trying to clear its head. Behind it, the other two Cyclops began to stir.

Kale came rushing back up, his Breach leading the way. Seeing Rose's crumpled form, he screamed in anguish and leaped from the top of the pile. In two great bounds he reached the ground and sprinted toward Rose.

The Cyclops grabbed a rock at its feet. The two behind it stood and followed suit. In unison, they advanced on Kale, armed with deadly missiles.

Kale reached Rose and dropped to his knees. Casting his Breach aside, he fell upon her and called out her name. The three Cyclops rushed him, intent on attacking while their enemy was unarmed.

"Mitra mitari mitara miru!" shouted Ilien. From his outstretched hand raced shooting stars of green and gold. They volleyed into the charging Cyclops, detonating in a cloud of silver dust.

Kale never noticed. His grief was too deep as he cradled Rose in his arms. But behind him, when the silver dust settled, three single-eyed toads hopped frantically away as fast as they could.

Ilien raced to Kale. "Rose!"

Rose lay on her side. Her face was still, her breathing shallow. A painful, red scrape stretched across her forehead and ended in a purple bruise on her left cheek. Kale lifted her cloak and peered beneath it at her back. He ran a hand over the swollen area where the Cyclops had struck her.

"She's badly hurt," said Kale, his lumpy face stretched tight with worry and streaked with tears. "She's damaged inside."

Ilien put a hand on Kale's shoulder. Kale beseeched him

with his large, crooked eyes, brittle with fear. "Can your magic help her?" he asked.

Ilien looked in horror at the wound on Rose's back. Already it was turning purple and had spread to cover most of her lower back. The blow had broken something inside her—bones, no doubt, but perhaps more. He had healed the Swan in the tunnel of the Long Dark Road, but these injuries were much more severe. He wanted desperately to promise Kale that he could save her, but he couldn't.

"Stand back," he told Kale as he closed his eyes. "And keep quiet. I need to concentrate."

Kale knuckled the tears from his eyes and stepped away from Rose. He stood frozen in silence, biting on his swollen lower lip with his cat-like teeth.

Ilien envisioned the Healing rune in his mind, one dimensional, intricate and complex, like a story held in a single letter. But this time he wasn't daunted by the task of recreating it. He knew its secret and understood what he needed to do. He just hoped he could do it. Instinctively, he turned the rune in his mind's eye. As he did so, it shifted and split into two separate runes, one behind the other. Two runes. Two hands.

Too easy, thought Ilien.

He opened his eyes and carefully traced each rune, one with each hand. His fingers left no shining marks in the air. No glowing runes hung before him as he knew they should. He quickly drew the Runes again, closing his eyes once more, studying the runes carefully to be certain he drew them properly. When he opened his eyes next, he saw only Rose lying still on the ground before him, her back more swollen than before. The bruise on her cheek had spread to her temple.

"The runes hold no power out here!" His hands balled

into fists. "We have to get her into the stonehall."

Even as he spoke the words, he realized how impossible that would prove to be. Rose was a full-grown woman. Though there was two of them, they were kids. Even working together, Ilien doubted they could carry Rose up to the top of the boulder pile, let alone climb down the hole and into the stonehall with her in tow. It was impossible. Yet it was the only way. Without the True Language, Nihilic magic didn't work outside the stonehall. Somehow the one needed the other, and Ilien didn't know the Healing spell.

"I will carry her," said Kale. He held his Breach out to Ilien. "You carry this."

"Hold on," said Ilien, eyeing the Breach with disdain. "First of all, you can't carry Rose all by yourself. Secondly, if anyone was going to carry her it would be me. I'm bigger than you."

"Bigger is not always stronger," stated Kale. He tossed his Breach at Ilien, forcing him to catch it. He stooped, scooped Rose up in his arms, and lifted her easily off the ground. "Come."

Ilien watched in awe as Kale began climbing the pile of boulders with Rose balance precariously in his arms. Though she was nearly twice as large as him, Kale navigated his way upward with little difficulty. Soon he stood atop the pile. He set Rose down at his feet.

"I said come. Unless that Breach is too heavy for you." A grin flashed across Kale's twisted features. Without a word, Ilien followed.

"How do we get her inside?" asked Ilien when he reached the top. Truth be told, he was more than a little embarrassed. He had nearly tripped twice while climbing up with Kale's Breach in his arms.

Kale studied the hole that led down into the rock pile. "If

only I could grow wings," he muttered. He frowned, then added, "I guess I'll just have to carry her down."

"That's a great idea," said Ilien.

Kale cast Ilien a dirty look.

"No. I can fly her down," explained Ilien. "My Nihilic spells don't work without the True Language, but the True Language works just fine without my Nihilic runes."

Kale's dirty look stretched into one of confusion.

"I don't know why," said Ilien, "but it's true. I happen to know the word for Fly in the True Language." He peered down into the hole. "It's wide enough. I should be able to fly down with Rose in my arms."

Ilien tossed Kale's Breach back to him, stooped, put his arms gently beneath Rose, and—

"She's too heavy," he moaned, straining to lift her.

With Kale's help, Ilien soon stood teetering on the brink of the hole with Rose's limp form in his outstretched arms. He didn't know how long he could hold her, so he incanted the spell quickly.

"Lever belie, belever beflie."

The pressure on his arms subsided as the spell began to work, lifting both him and Rose off the ground. Weightless, they floated gently down the hole and into the small chamber below.

Kale climbed down to join them. He took Rose from Ilien's arms. "Come. You have work to do," he said as he led the way into the stonehall.

Ilien followed Kale, hoping beyond hope that his Nihilic magic could heal Rose. He still didn't understand why the runes he drew outside were ineffective, while spoken spells still held magic. He still didn't quite understand how drawing runes produced magic at all. His hunch was that tracing a rune pulled magic from the air, much like picking an apple

93

from a tree. But from where?

There came a clatter from ahead of him in the darkness.

"Light, Ilien. I need light," said Kale.

Ilien conjured Globe. She lit the chamber with her soft, white glow. Ilien drew the Light rune and she brightened in response.

Kale carried Rose to the stone table and set her curled up upon it. He staggered back and dropped to his knees on the floor. "Your turn," he said between long, ragged breaths.

Again Ilien marveled at Kale's surprising strength. The boy's twisted features hunched into a gory grimace of worry and pain.

Ilien leaned Kale's Breach against the wall and moved quickly to Rose. He closed his eyes and drew the Healing rune, his fingers flowing assuredly through the air. In his mind's eye he saw the two runes shining before him, one behind the other.

"It's working," whispered Kale.

Ilien opened his eyes. The two runes hung in the air above Rose, glowing with power. They floated down and melted into her body. Rose moaned and stirred. Her face contorted in pain. Her cheeks flushed crimson.

"I think it's working," repeated Kale.

Ilien wasn't so sure. When he had healed the Swan there had been no moans of pain, no grimaces. He rolled Rose on her side, lifting her cloak to reveal her welted back. He drew the runes once more and guided them to the injured area. They melted into the ugly black and blue bruise that had spread to cover most of her lower back. Again Rose moaned in pain, but the bruise faded away. The swollen lumps receded within moments. Her back looked nearly normal.

He moved to examine the scrape upon her forehead. The magic was working. The skin had already healed, but the deep purple contusion on her temple remained. Once more, Ilien traced the magical runes, guiding them to the injured area. He watched as the wound shrank. He breathed a sigh of relief as the blood beneath her skin vanished and the swelling subsided. The crimson drained from Rose's face as the pain abated. Her breathing steadied.

"Is she healed?" asked Kale, his own knotted features smeared with worry.

Ilien leaned heavily against the stone table. The Healing rune had done all it could. So had he. He was spent. He looked up at Globe, who dimmed in sympathy with his weariness.

"I think she'll be okay now," he said. "We should let her rest a while. Help me move her to the floor."

With Kale's help, Ilien carried Rose to a comfortable looking spot on the floor. He removed his tunic and bunched it up under her head.

"Why doesn't she move?" asked Kale, his face betraying his lingering worry. "Why doesn't she wake up?"

"She just needs more rest," said Ilien, not knowing what else to say. The truth was that he was worried, too. He had healed her visible wounds, but he feared there was deeper damage that the Healing rune could not mend.

"Let her rest," he said as he pulled Kale back to the small, stone table. "She'll be all right," he reassured him.

Kale reluctantly left Rose's side and sat beside Ilien upon the table. Their legs dangled above the floor. Without his Breach, Kale looked like any ordinary boy to Ilien. He had long become accustomed to Kale's deformed face so that by now he saw only the sad child beneath.

"Tell me about the Breaching Arts," said Ilien, attempting to alleviate the somber mood that permeated the stonehall.

"What do you want to know?" Kale sat slumped over, his eyes upon the ground.

Ilien hopped off the table and snatched up Kale's Breach from against the wall. "Well, for one, what's this thing made of? It's extremely light but hard as metal. It feels like some sort of bone." He tapped it on the ground. It rang off the stone like a sword.

Kale gave Ilien a sideways glance. "It is bone," he replied. "Gorgul bone. All Breaches are fashioned of Gorgul bone."

Ilien held the Breach at arm's length. He thought of Pedustil and wondered how Kale, or anyone for that matter, could condone the killing of such a magnificent creature in order to create a weapon.

Kale saw the look in Ilien's eyes. He hopped off the table and approached with a crooked smile. His cat-like teeth gleamed in Globe's luminescent light. "Don't worry. No Gorgul has ever been harmed to make a Breach."

Ilien gave the bone staff an approving look. An inch and a half thick, it fit snugly in his palm. Ilien wondered which one of a Gorgul's bones was so long and slender. "If you don't kill a Gorgul to make a Breach, how do you get the bone?" He lifted an eyebrow. "You don't rob Gorgul graveyards, do you?"

Kale looked crossly at Ilien. "Of course not. That would be very unwise. A Breach is gifted."

"Gifted? From who? A great-uncle or something?"

"What's a great-uncle?" asked Kale, his expression still critical.

Ilien had forgotten that Kale had no parents—never had parents—so of course he wouldn't know what an uncle was.

"Anyhow," continued Kale. "The bone is gifted from a Gorgul."

Ilien fumbled with the Breach in his hands. "The Gorgul gives it to you while it's still alive?"

Kale shook his head. "Not only would that be impossible, it's just plain sick." He hopped back onto the table and situated himself comfortably. "The bone is gifted from a Gorgul, but it doesn't come from a living Gorgul. It's gifted from an ancestor to someone they deem worthy."

"And that would be you?"

Kale frowned. "I have never seen a Gorgul. My Breach is a hand-me-down. It was given to me by the Watcher before me." He brightened suddenly and added, "But they say there are still Gorguls around. It's said that the last wizardess keeps one as a pet."

Ilien thought of Pedustil, his green luminescent eyes, his leaky gill vents, how he looked like a fat snake when he tucked his wings away.

"Where I come from, there are definitely still Gorguls around. There's one in particular I'd give anything to see right now."

"You've actually seen a Gorgul?" marveled Kale.

"I've ridden one," said Ilien, smiling.

Kale's twisted face filled with awe. In Globe's pale light he looked suddenly so normal that Ilien stood and stared at him.

"What was it like?" asked Kale. "Do they fly fast? How high did you go?"

A low moan from Rose interrupted Ilien's answer. Kale hopped off the table and ran to her side. "She's waking up!"

Ilien wasn't so sure. Rose lay on her back just as they had left. The crimson flush had returned to her cheeks. Another low moan escaped her lips, but her eyes remained closed.

"Rose," whispered Kale. "Rose, wake up."

"She needs more rest," said Ilien, trying to pull Kale away.

Kale shrugged him off and knelt beside Rose. He felt her forehead. "She's burning with fever." He turned to Ilien. "Use your healing spell again."

"Come away from there," said Ilien, grabbing Kale's shoulder. "She needs more rest, not you poking and prodding her."

"Just use your healing spell again. She needs more healing."

Rose lay still and quiet. Her breathing sounded weak and shallow.

"Kale," said Ilien.

"Just do it!" shouted Kale, whirling to face him. "Why won't you just do it and heal her?" Anger and worry worked Kale's face into a gruesome sight. Tears added a fearsome glow beneath his crooked eyes. His cat-like teeth shined in Globe's dim light. "Why won't you use your healing spell one more time?"

Ilien met Kale's pointed gaze. "I've done all I can," he said. "My magic isn't powerful enough to heal what ails her."

Kale stood and wiped away his tears. "Then we must leave here immediately."

"What are you talking about? We can't just leave her here!"

"We're not leaving her," stated Kale. "We're coming back." He started toward the exit. "Let's go."

Ilien refused to follow. "Go where, Kale?"

But Kale had already disappeared up the winding passage that led outside.

"Kale!" called Ilien, chasing after him.

He caught up to Kale in the small stone-walled chamber. He seized him by the shoulder. "Where are we going?"

Kale began his ascent, easily pulling away from Ilien's grasp. "To the next stonehall."

Ilien stood dumbfounded. Kale called down to him from the top of the boulder pile above. "Now come!"

Ilien followed. The harsh, grey landscape pained his eyes after having spent so long in the dark confines of the stonehall. He rubbed at his eyes. Kale already stood below him at the base of the boulder pile.

"Come!" yelled Kale. "We don't have much time."

"I'm not climbing down until you tell me what's going on!" replied Ilien. "Why are we going to the next stonehall?"

Kale peered up at the perpetually clouded sky. "It's already late morning! Now let's go!"

Ilien stood defiantly upon the rock pile, his hands at his hips. He grimaced as he realized how ridiculous he must look—like a petulant child disobeying his mother.

"There is something at the next stonehall that will help you," said Kale. "It will help you heal Rose."

Something that can help me, thought Ilien. "What is it?" Kale walked away without a word. "What will help me heal Rose?"

"I don't know what it is," replied Kale, rounding on him. "But I know it's there and I'm going to get it."

"How do you know that it will help me do anything, let alone heal Rose? We can't just leave her here alone on a hunch, Kale. What if more Cyclops come? What if the Onegod finds Rose alone and helpless?"

"The Onegod will not come. The Cyclops will not come. They are after you. I will hide any tracks that lead to the stonehall. Anyone who comes will follow us away from here, if they follow us at all. Rose will be safe until we return."

Ilien shook his head. "You haven't answered my question, Kale. How do you know that what ever is there will help me? How do you even know it's there at all?"

Kale's crooked eyes hardened. He pursed his swollen lips. "Every Watcher knows it's there, and none know what it is. It was placed in the stonehall and locked away almost two thousand years ago, after you left us. It awaits your return. It will help you in a great many ways. It will help you destroy the Onegod. Right now we have to get it and bring it back here and heal Rose." Kale pinned Ilien with a withering look. "Is that too much to ask?"

Ilien nodded mutely. *You'd better be right*, he thought.

Chapter XI

End of the Road

Kale quickly and thoroughly hid any sign that they had ever set foot near the boulder pile and the stonehall below it. He then returned to Ilien, who waited uneasily for him upon the Buried Road.

"Promise me you won't lead me off the Road by accident," said Ilien.

"Just follow in my footsteps and you'll be fine," replied Kale. He fumbled out two pieces of Manna from beneath his ragged shirt. "Eat the whole thing," he said, handing one to Ilien. "We need to get there fast."

But what about the Consumption?" asked Ilien, taking the damp and smelly bread.

"You can sleep when we get back," said Kale.

Ilien felt the Manna's energizing effects as soon as he struggled down the last bite. "How far to the next stonehall?"

Kale smacked his lips. "You mean the last stonehall." He pointed to the distant horizon. It was then that Ilien saw the grey peaks of low mountains in the distance, blending in with the grey of both ground and sky. "We'll be there by nightfall," said Kale. He took off running.

Kale set a grinding pace. Were it not for the Manna, Ilien would have never kept up. Even so, it was obvious that Kale was the more fit. His muscle-hardened body barely seemed to touch the ground, while Ilien began to mentally count each footfall with growing weariness.

The landscape changed little save for an occasional dip or rise. Lifeless, barren, bleak, the grey peaks in the distance loomed closer with every step they took. Ilien's mood lifted. Beyond those mountains lay the world outside the Desecration. Beyond that lay his only chance of getting back home. There was only the matter of returning to heal Rose, then they'd all make it out of the Desecration together.

After that, of course, they still had to seek out the last wizardess who had concealed herself from the world to who-knew-where.

And then there was still the Onegod to deal with.

This adventure stuff is a real drag, thought Ilien, his mood falling fast. How he wished he could be laying out in his backyard by the small, meandering stream, hoping not to catch a fish. Those days seemed ages past, and yet it wasn't so long ago that he'd first set off that early spring morning with Thessien and Gallund, headed for Evernden.

Ahead, Kale ran with mounting intensity. Ilien quickened his pace, painfully aware that the boy was driven by his concern for Rose. Though Kale had been raised by his people to have no attachments, his love for Rose was evident.

Ilien grit his teeth against his growing weariness. He would not let Kale down. He would do whatever he could to save Rose. He owed the boy that much. He lowered his head and concentrated on shoving one foot in front of the other. They needed to reach the last stonehall before nightfall.

As the day progressed, the low peaks before them grew taller on the horizon. The usually flat land began to slope noticeably upward and the ground became rockier. Oftentimes the Buried Road was nothing more than naturally exposed ledge—the far-flung bones of the approaching mountains.

Above the rounded peaks, Ilien thought he saw pale, blue

streaks in the distance. *Could it actually be blue sky?* he wondered. *Is it true? Are we really approaching the end of the Desecration?* The thought of seeing green plants, hearing song birds chirping and smelling the sweet scent of flowers drove an energy into Ilien's stride that superceded the waning power of the Manna bread. Ahead of him, Kale, too, had quickened his pace. Ilien wondered how long it had been since the boy last saw blue sky himself, or smelled the intoxicating perfume of roses.

Ilien's eyes drifted from the deepening grey of the looming peaks to the tiny patch of blue above them. That's when he noticed the thin column of smoke rising up from the base of the mountains. Kale noticed it as well and stopped. As Ilien caught up to him, he saw the disbelief on Kale's sweat-streaked face, the fear in his eyes.

"It's the Onegod."

"The Onegod?" said Ilien. "Then they've discovered the last stonehall."

Kale shook his head. "No. They know nothing of the stonehalls, I assure you."

"Then why are they blocking the way?"

Kale surveyed the horizon, his crooked eyes scanning the mountains from left to right. "There," he said, pointing.

Ilien glimpsed another column of smoke in the distance.

"This is the border," said Kale, "the edge of the Desecration. The Onegod has many such camps on the border. They guard the way out."

Ilien trained his eyes in the opposite direction and saw yet another encampment far to the right of the first.

Kale sat down. He pulled out another hunk of Manna. "They are only a few miles apart, with watchtowers and scouts all looking for you." He broke the Manna in two and handed a piece to Ilien.

103

"How are we going to get past them?" asked Ilien. He eyed the magical bread uneasily.

"We wait until nightfall and sneak past." Kale chewed thoughtfully. He saw Ilien's eyes go wide. "Don't worry. Your globe of light can guide our way."

"But won't they see us?"

"Remember, Ilien, night in the Desecration is absolute. We won't be seen." He nodded. "Now eat your Manna before the Consumption takes you."

Ilien snatched the bread from Kale's outstretched hand. "This stuff is worse than Awefull, you know."

"It's not that bad."

They didn't have to wait long before the grey overcast sky began to quickly darken. Kale was right. Night in the Desecration was complete. If not for Globe, the all-pervasive blackness would have overwhelmed them.

"I hope you know the way," said Ilien.

Kale nodded. "Follow me and keep close."

They plodded through the inky blackness, their eyes trained on the rocky ground at their feet as it emerged from the nothing in front of them. Several steps later it vanished back into the nothing behind them. With every footfall, Ilien hoped desperately that Kale knew exactly where he was going. Stepping off the Buried Road now could prove fatal. What if he toppled into the blackness before Kale noticed? He'd suffocate in the impenetrable night as the earth wracked his body with waves of agony.

Ilien quickened his step to stay that much closer to Kale.

The low mountains were only a few miles away, but it took hours to finally reach them. The ground grew steep, making travel difficult. They scrabbled their way forward, their feet slipping on loose stones. The clatter of their passage sounded unusually loud in their small bubble of light, but Kale assured Ilien that the Void was impenetrable. No one would hear the sound of their passage.

"The Road is ended," said Kale. He stopped and planted his feet firmly on the hard stone beneath them. "You are safe from the curse of the Desecration. The ground can no longer hurt you."

Ilien felt the muscles of his legs relax. He hadn't realized how tense he'd been. Now that he could step wherever he chose without fear, his legs felt a bit wobbly and loose.

Kale smiled and showed his jagged, cat's teeth. "It's not far now. Soon we'll be in the last stonehall." He turned to lead the way. "We'll find what awaits you. Then you'll be able to heal Rose."

They traveled faster through the night, half-running, half-walking. Ilien's heart beat wildly in his chest as he struggled to keep up with Kale. The boy led the way with marked assurance, head up, eyes trained on the blackness before him. It was then that Ilien noticed that the absolute night around them was brightening.

How can that be? he thought. *Morning is still hours away.*

Before he could think any more about it, Kale stopped so fast that Ilien crashed into him from behind. They stumbled forward into a solid wall of stone.

"Watch where you're going!"

"Sorry," said Ilien, stepping back and collecting his wits.

Before them, rising up until it disappeared into the gloom beyond Globe's circle of light, a grey, stone cliff blocked their way.

Kale pointed upward. "Up we go."

Ilien trained his eyes upward. He thought he could see a few feet into the blackness. Yes. The absolute night was definitely not so absolute.

105

"We are at the base of the mountain," continued Kale before Ilien could mention what he'd noticed. "There is a hidden stair nearby. At the top of the stair is a hidden door. Through that door lies the last stonehall."

"Wait—"

Kale raised a hand. His smile drained away as he regarded the night around them. His eyes grew wide with sudden fear. "Come!" he whispered fiercely. "Come quick!"

He ran to the left, keeping one hand against the cliff side as he went. Ilien chased after him, his heart in his throat. He could clearly see the landscape outside Globe's bright circle.

"What's happening?"

Kale stopped and spun around. He clamped a hand over Ilien's mouth. "Extinguish your light," he said urgently. Globe disappeared, leaving them trapped in darkness—ordinary darkness. Ilien could see the savage look on Kale's misshapen face through the gloom.

"This is the edge of the Desecration," whispered Kale. "Night here is not absolute. We can be seen and heard. Let's pray we haven't yet been spotted." He shook his head in self-reproach. "I should have realized."

Kale removed his hand from Ilien's mouth. "We must find the stair."

Ilien stumbled through the shadows after Kale. In his fear, the clatter of rocks beneath his feet sounded like boulders crashing around them. His breathing rasped loudly in his ears. Surely they would be heard, if not seen.

A shriek split the night, a wailing cry that rose like a siren in the distance. Ilien had heard that scream before. It was the howl the old man released when Ilien destroyed his body. They'd been discovered!

Kale stopped before the cliff side and searched it with his eyes. He fumbled his hands across its uneven surface, groping at the rock with his fingers.

"It's here!" he cried as he found two shallow depressions in the cliff. "The hidden stair!"

Ilien thought he could see it. There were small indentations pressed into the rock. Toe and finger-holds. They were spaced a few feet apart. They ran straight up the cliff in a meandering line.

"You've got to be kidding," he mumbled under his breath. "That's not a stair. That's a deathtrap."

The wailing shriek of the Onegod shatter the air around them. There was no time to complain. Kale reached up and dug his fingers into the nearest depression. With a heave, he pulled himself up. He kicked his foot into a toehold below.

"Come on!" His twisted face showed the strain of trying to climb the impossible stair. "There's no other way!"

The Onegod screamed again and emerged from the gloom behind them. Clad in black robes, the old man stood before Ilien, his silver wand raised. A deep hood hid his face, but the shadows beneath were pierced by two black eyes filled with blinding darkness. A gnarled, bony hand leveled the silver wand at Ilien.

It was a wand Ilien had seen before.

"Lever belie, belever beflie!" cried Ilien. He sprang into the air, grabbed Kale by the tunic, and sailed up the cliff side, gritting his teeth against stress of Kale's added weight. "How far up?" he shouted.

Kale looked down at the receding Onegod. "Fly faster!" Below, the old man had raised his silver wand.

Ilien cried out and tightened his grip on Kale. "How far?"

Kale trained his eyes upward. "There! That small ledge. That's it!"

Ilien saw it—a narrow shelf of rock not twenty feet

away. He sailed up to it, crashed into the cliff side, and landed on top of Kale in heap. Together they scrambled to their feet, their backs against the cold stone.

"The Onegod will follow us," said Kale, breathing hard. He spun and faced the cliff. A circular hole had been cut into the rock at chest level. Kale pushed a finger into the hole. "This is it!" In a flash, he held his Breach in his hands. "The key." He inserted the tip of his Breach into the hole. The Onegod screeched in fury down below. "Hurry!" urged Ilien.

Kale pushed his Breach further into the hole. Ilien expected the Breach to stop at some point, but it kept on going. Half its length had disappeared into the cliff side, and still Kale kept feeding it forward. Soon, only a few inches of the Gorgul bone staff protruded from the rock before them.

"Stop!" yelled Ilien. "It's not working! It's taking your Breach!"

Kale shrugged him aside. He pushed the last of his Breach into the hole. It disappeared without a sound.

A vicious blast of wind struck Ilien from behind and swept him off his feet. Kale reached for him but his fingers closed on empty air. Ilien was blown from the small, stone landing.

"Lever belie, belever beflie!" Ilien hovered in the air, arms and legs stretched out like a frog's. He glanced wide-eyed at Kale. "That was close."

Kale pressed his back against the cliff. His swollen face twisted with sudden fear. He instinctively reached for his Breach, but it was gone.

Ilien righted himself in mid air. The old man hovered before him. His black robes flowed in the gusty air around his haggard frame. His hood blew back to reveal his bony face.

"No!" screamed Ilien. He hovered back in fear. "It can't be!"

The face was Gallund's.

Ilien refused to believe it. But it was undeniable. Though gaunt and sunken, with hollow eyes and ashen skin, the face was Gallund's.

"Ilien!" cried Kale from the landing behind him.

In his fright and bewilderment, Ilien hovered senseless before the Onegod, not daring to move. The Onegod leveled his silver wand at Ilien's chest, power emanating from its tip like spewing black smoke. For the briefest of moments, the darkness in the Onegod's eyes faded, leaving an empty expression across Gallund's face.

"Ilien!"

Ilien spun. Kale stood framed by an open doorway, his Breach held out to Ilien. In a flash, Ilien seized hold of it. Kale yanked him back to the small stone landing.

"Keep flying and hold on!" commanded Kale. He turned and ran through the entryway, pulling Ilien behind him.

The Onegod gained the landing. He aimed his silver wand at his fleeing prey, thought better of it, and gave chase.

"Run faster!" shouted Ilien. "Much faster!"

Kale's labored breath rasped loudly in the small tunnel. His footfalls pounded out a steady beat on the stone floor.

"Light, Ilien!"

Globe sprang to life and raced ahead to light the way. The tunnel stretched into the distance with no end in sight. It ran straight, with smooth walls and a flat, even floor. Unlike the other stonehalls, someone had taken considerable time and effort to construct this one.

Ilien glanced over his shoulder. The Onegod had closed the distance between them. Without warning, Kale stopped. He flung Ilien further up the tunnel. Ilien sailed off like a shot, with Globe still leading the way.

"Kale!" he cried as he watched the boy disappear in the darkness.

Ilien crashed to the floor and tumbled to a stop. Globe hovered above him. He would not let Kale face the Onegod alone. He struggled to his feet, shouted his battle cry and ran back down the tunnel.

A booming crash shook the air and Kale came sprinting back toward them. A roiling cloud of dust and debris chased after him. The Onegod was nowhere in sight.

"Go! Go!" shouted Kale, waving them back the other way.

Ilien skidded to a halt, but Globe sailed forward before he could stop her. She flew past Kale, into the cloud of dust, and disappeared.

The tunnel was thrust into darkness. Ilien turned and stumbled blindly up the corridor but Kale slammed into him. The blow pounded the air from his lungs, knocking him senseless to the ground. His head struck the tunnel floor. He heard the rush of wind in his ears, tasted dirt, and knew no more.

Chapter XII

An Old Friend

"**A**wake, Ilien."

It was a command, not a request. There was no concern in the voice that gave it, but there was no malice, either. It was simply a command, and Ilien obeyed.

He opened his eyes to the clear, blue sky stretching overhead. Tall grass waved in a warm breeze all around him. He lifted his head and took stock of his surroundings.

He lay on a large, flat stone beside a small pool of water. A stream emptied from the far end of the pool and meandered away toward a distant grove of pines bordering a grassy field spotted with yellow blossoms. A small, white farmhouse huddled beside a towering, grey barn in the distance. It was Farmer Parson's house, but this wasn't Southford. Ilien knew where he was immediately, though he'd been there only twice before. He rubbed his head where it had struck the tunnel floor, and found he was unhurt.

"Good. You're awake."

He turned to see Gallund standing before him, his silver wand clutched in one hand. The wizard's face wasn't sunken and grey, but he wore a long, black robe. Ilien leaped to his feet, his hand instinctively reaching for his back pocket.

"Looking for this?" asked Gallund, holding Ilien's pencil by its tip, eliminating any reply the pencil might give.

Ilien gasped and stepped back. *The Onegod here? But how?*

Gallund advanced on him, stashing the pencil beneath his robes and raising his silver wand. "How many times have I told you?" he said, wagging his wand at Ilien like a scolding finger. "Your pencil is for spellwork, not schoolwork. I warned you, Ilien. Now you've lost it."

"Stay back!" shouted Ilien, his back to the pool.

Gallund's ruddy cheeks flushed a deeper shade of red, but he suddenly stopped. "Ilien. Calm down. What's come over you?"

Ilien locked eyes with the wizard. Deep within, past the outward twinkle normally present, Ilien saw what he searched for.

"You are not my father," he said. "Stay back or I'll destroy this body as I did your last one."

Gallund's eyes dimmed, their sparkle disappearing as they filled with night. His black robes fluttered in the breeze, which had suddenly turned cold. "Destroy this body if you can. Kill as many as you'd like, but you cannot destroy me," said the Onegod.

Ilien shielded his eyes from the Onegod's blinding gaze. "You are not my father. I will destroy you. You cannot trick me." Words to an unsummoned spell echoed in his mind.

"Ilien, my boy." It was Gallund's voice again, gentle yet commanding. The shadows had fled from his eyes and his face softened with concern. "Don't be so angry. You'll get your pencil back. It's for spellwork, after all, and you'll have studying to do soon. Yes, you'll have work to do."

Ilien's sight returned and he jumped back, unsure what Gallund would do next. The wizard's face froze and the color drained from his cheeks as a battle waged within him. He stood motionless like a black pillar in the green grass, his wand at his side. A moment later, he opened his coal-black eyes.

"You have no power, Necromancer!" shouted the Onegod. "Kill this body if you can!" He swept his silver wand through the air. Ilien dodged, his spell forgotten.

No magic came.

"It is you who has no power," said Ilien, standing tall.

The Onegod laughed, a high-pitched peal that sent the grass shivering around them. "You wish to see my power? See what I have made!"

Ilien heard the distant crack of boughs and thunder of falling earth. He turned and gasped. The pines in the distance moved. One by one they kicked themselves free of the ground in an explosion of dirt and rocks, their roots mimicking a multitude of powerful legs.

"I am the Creator!" screeched the Onegod. "You are nothing!"

"Mitra mitari mitara miru!" Ilien shouted forth his spell over the Onegod's laughter, strengthening it with Nihilic runes. Green flames leaped from his fingers. The sickly fire arched over the stream and rained down upon the pines as they struggled to free the last of their roots from the earth.

Needles and boughs burst into flames, fed by the sap of their unnatural blood. Frenzied, the trees fled in all directions, shedding sparks and smoke wherever they went. They didn't go far. Soon, five small bonfires crackled and hissed beside the stream.

Ilien turned back to face the Onegod, straining against his blinding gaze. "I will find you in your castle of stone," he said. "And I'll destroy you. I will end all the suffering you have caused."

Ilien's sight returned and Gallund stood before him again, trembling, his grey eyes locked onto his. "You will get your pencil back, Ilien. And when you do, you will have to kill me."

Ilien cried out and sat up in the darkness. A stab of pain brought him to his senses. A full moon hung in the air before him, a ghostly face visible in its pale light.

"Kale?"

The boy sat opposite him in the gloom, Globe resting in his lap and his Breach at his side. His oversized eyes glowed softly with Globe's light.

"Are you hurt?"asked Kale.

"A little," replied Ilien, reaching up to rub the lump on his head and peering into the shadows. "Are you? What happened? How long have I been out?"

Globe lifted from Kale's lap and floated lazily over to Ilien.

"A couple hours," answered Kale. "The tunnel entrance collapsed and you hit your head pretty hard." He pulled his Breach closer. "We're safe from the Onegod, for now."

Ilien squinted painfully and waved Globe away.

"How?" He eyed Kale's Breach in disbelief.

"No," said Kale. "I didn't do it. The Onegod did."

Kale continued before Ilien could inquire further. "There is a hidden door that falls from above, a secret gate to seal us in if ever the stonehall is discovered. All Watchers are told of it. I ran back to close the gate before the Onegod could catch us. I was too late. The Onegod had already reached it. I thought he would kill me, but instead he tried to close the gate himself. When he couldn't, he smote the ceiling, collapsing it between him and me."

Ilien sat in silence as he digested Kale's words. "Why would he do that?"

"That's a good question. But an even better one is, how did he know the gate was there to begin with?"

Ilien's eyes went wide. "You don't think he knew about this stonehall from the beginning, do you? That he purposefully sealed us in?"

Kale struck a fighting pose with his Breach. "I don't think so. But we'll have to be on our guard."

"On our guard?" said Ilien. "Didn't you just hear what I said? If the Onegod sealed us in for a reason, then he's been here before, and if he's been here before then this place is a death trap."

Kale struck the stone floor with his Breach. The sound reverberated in the dark tunnel. "Then I suggest we be extra careful."

Ilien locked eyes with the boy. The resolve in Kale's gaze could not be argued with.

"There's no going back," said Kale. "We can only go forward. If the Onegod has something in store for us, then so be it. It changes nothing. We must find what we came for. We must get back to Rose."

Ilien blinked and looked away. He peered into the blackness where the entrance lay collapsed. "Did you see that old man?" he said. "The Onegod—he looked like my father." Ilien turned back to Kale. "You say the Onegod takes many forms. Can he make you see what he wants you to see?"

"I suppose so," replied Kale. "But do not be mistaken. The old men are real. They are the Onegod's favorite form for it's said that they were once his greatest enemies."

Ilien sucked in a sharp breath. Those old men were once the Nomadin wizards who had inhabited this world! It made sense. The robes. The wands. The Onegod had somehow overpowered them and now they were his servants. Ilien remembered his dream and shivered. That last one had looked so much like Gallund.

Ilien climbed to his feet. He dimmed Globe until her light was little more than a glimmer in the gloom. "We can't be too careful," he whispered. "Let's get going."

Kale led the way along the smooth, stone tunnel, his Breach held ready in one hand. Globe hovered above him, shedding a wavering light all around. Despite their fear that something unknown and dangerous lay waiting for them, they walked quickly. They both knew they were nearing the one thing that could help Ilien save Rose. It was also the one thing that could keep them safe from whatever the Onegod had in store for them. Though neither of them knew exactly what it was, they drew a measure of urgency from the knowledge that it was there.

They also knew that if the Onegod had indeed known about the stonehall from the start, it was there that the danger would be the greatest.

Ilien drew near Kale and whispered, "How much farther?"

"Not far," answered Kale, his voice hoarse in the dark. "This tunnel will branch up ahead. We must take the left passage. There is a chamber at the end of that passage."

They trod in silence for a moment.

"It's in that chamber?" asked Ilien. "What we came for is in that chamber?"

Kale nodded. "There are three gated alcoves," he said. "The key is in one. The talisman is in the other."

Ilien breathed heavy as he walked. "What's in the third alcove?"

"A book, I think," said Kale. "Now keep quiet. The passage splits up ahead."

A book? thought Ilien. *A spell book?*

They strode a while longer in the dark before Kale raised his hand and stopped at a fork in the tunnel. The echo of their footsteps traveled ahead into the blackness.

"Where does the right passage lead?" asked Ilien, peering into its endless depth.

Kale slung his Breach over his shoulder and turned to take the other passage. "That's the way to the world outside." Ilien stepped forward. "The world outside?" Kale grabbed his arm and pulled him back. "First the talisman, Ilien."

A sudden thought brought Ilien up short. "Kale, if the tunnel behind us is collapsed, then how do we go back for Rose?"

Kale smiled broadly, his swollen lips threatening to split apart. "We'll fly there."

Ilien stared at the boy in disbelief. "That's impossible. It doesn't work like that. I can't fly over a mountain."

Kale's smile remained. "You will," he assured him, "Once we retrieve the talisman, we'll fly back to rescue Rose."

Ilien rubbed at his temples. "This is insane. You don't even know what it is, or if it's still there. And I can't fly over a mountain!"

Kale's face grew still. His smile slipped away and his eyes filled with a vulnerability Ilien hadn't seen before. It was then that Ilien understood. Kale believed because he had to. Kale believed because if he didn't, Rose was as good as dead.

"Alright," said Ilien, placing a hand on Kale's shoulder. "Don't worry. We'll fly there." Even as Ilien said it, he knew it was a lie.

They proceeded with more caution down the lefthand passage. They both understood that if the Onegod had anything in store for them, this is where they would find it. Suddenly it dawned on Ilien that if the Onegod had known about the stonehall from the beginning, then he undoubtably knew about the item they sought—the item that could help Ilien destroy him. A chill moved along Ilien's spine. He searched the tunnel floor but saw no tracks, no sign that anyone or anything had been that way before them. "This is it," whispered Kale, turning to face Ilien. Globe floated before a rusted portcullis that blocked the way, an aged metal grate that hung from the ceiling to prevent their passage forward. Her dusky light threw a lattice of shadows beyond it.

"Why didn't they just give the key to the Watchers?" asked Ilien. "It doesn't make sense. Why keep it where anyone can find it?"

"What if the Watchers lost it?" asked Kale, his crooked face filled with shadows. "Besides, anyone can find the key, but only you can retrieve it."

Ilien peered past the portcullis into the darkened chamber. "Only I can retrieve it? That doesn't sound safe." He turned to Kale, his face white in Globe's light. "What do you mean by 'retrieve?'"

"Only the One who left us, the One who is prophesied to return and destroy the Onegod, can retrieve the key," said Kale. His putty-like lips smeared across his face in a gruesome smile. "It's a test."

"A test?" said Ilien with a sideways glance. "What if I don't pass this test?" He thought of all the test he'd taken at school, and swallowed hard.

Kale prodded the bars of the portcullis with his Breach. "Don't worry. You will."

"And if I can't," pressed Ilien. "Will you believe I'm not who you think I am, that I've never been here before?"

Kale grinned, his twisted face hunching into a knot. "I will never believe that you're not who I think you are."

Ilien had to smile despite himself. "That's a mouthful. Let's hope you're right."

With that, they each grabbed hold of the portcullis and

lifted it from the floor. The aged, rusted gate groaned as it slid up and into the ceiling. Dirt and debris fell from above, cascading into their hair and littering the ground about their feet. They stepped quickly back as the portcullis disappeared into the stone with a loud clang.

"Brighten your light," said Kale, dusting himself off. "There's no point in being too cautious after all that racket." Ilien drew the Light rune and the room beyond jumped with bright light. Kale and Ilien ducked behind the edge of the entryway, but their fears were unfounded. The room before them lay empty, cavernously empty.

The chamber was vast. Roughly the size of the great, gem-encrusted main-room of Ledge Hall, its size was secondary only to its emptiness. No furniture. No casks or barrels. Only dusty stone from top to bottom. Here the walls were made from blocks of stone. At the far end of the chamber, just visible in the dim recesses of the room, three arched exits stood guard-like in the gloom, armored with heavy bars.

They made their way toward the far end of the chamber. Ilien kept watch on the shadow filled corners but saw no evidence that the Onegod or his servants had ever been there. The dust lay undisturbed. But he couldn't shake a growing dread that he was missing something. The Onegod—the old man who had looked like Gallund—had shut them in here for a reason. He just couldn't fathom what that reason might be.

"Look!" whispered Kale as they approached the barred archways. "There's writing above each of them."

An unlit torch was mounted on each side of the center arch, and without thinking Ilien whispered, "Illubid." The brands guttered to life, casting bright firelight on the stone-block walls. Words had indeed been carved into the rock above each arch, but Ilien's attention was drawn to what lay beyond the center arch, past the heavy bars and the deeply etched message. In the crisscross of dark shadows cast by the iron gate stood a tall, stone pedestal, the top of which shimmered with a pale, red light. Ilien drew closer, pressing his face between the rusted bars, straining to discern what lay glowing upon the pedestal.

"The key!" cried Kale. "The key is here!"

Ilien jerked away from the iron gate. Kale stood before the lefthand arch, his hands grasping the bars. His Breach leaned against the dusty wall and his misshapen face was stretched with awe.

"It's the key. Look how it floats in the air."

Suspended as if it hung on invisible string, a large, silver key revolved slowly in the air. Ilien leaned in for a closer look. Something in the recesses of his memory pulled him up short. He had seen that key before.

"Look here!" said Kale. He had moved back to the center arch. "This is the only gate that has a lock."

Ilien inspected the other two archways. Kale was right. The bars were mortared into the stone. There was no way in. Only the center arch was accessible with a key.

"But how do I retrieve it?" mumbled Ilien.

Kale moved next to the right-hand arch. "There's something back there," he said, peering into the gloom filled space beyond the bars. "It looks like a chest."

Ilien stood in thought before the left-hand arch and watched the key as it revolved in the air. He'd seen that key before, he was sure of it, but he couldn't remember where.

"I have an idea," he said. "Give me your Breach."

Kale snatched up his Breach and held it close. "What for?"

"Maybe we can reach the key with it," said Ilien. "Don't worry. I'll give it back."

No matter how he tried, Ilien couldn't reach the key. Every time the tip of the Breach neared it, the key would float out of reach. He finally gave up in frustration. There was no way in, no way past the bars, and the key was out of reach. He wished Anselm was there. The Giant could have pulled the bars wide enough apart for him to slip through. Ilien took a deep breath and went through a mental checklist of the spells he knew, but he couldn't see how any of them could help.

"Ilustus bregun, Ilustus bregar," he said. The bars remained. "Well, they're not illusions," he surmised.

"I was keeper of the key. Speak my name and enter."

Ilien snapped out of his thoughts. "What did you say?"

Kale stood behind him, staring overhead. "The writing above the arch. It reads, 'I was keeper of the key. Speak my name and enter.'"

Ilien stepped back and viewed the carved words for himself. "I was keeper of the key," he read. He regarded the revolving silver key once more. "Keeper of the key," he muttered as he approached the bars and leaned in to get a better look.

"And this one says, 'I stole the wand that wasn't,'" said Kale from below the right-hand arch, the one with the chest behind it. He looked over at Ilien, his lumpy brow bent with confusion. "The wand that wasn't?"

Ilien's mind was still wrapped around the riddle of the key. "I know I've seen that key before."

"What's the wand that wasn't?" asked Kale.

"That's easy. My pencil," answered Ilien without thinking.

Kale's swollen face pinched to a point, if that was possible. "What's a pencil?"

Ilien was still searching his memory, when Kale said,

"And who stole it?"

Ilien realized the answer, and found himself standing before the right-hand arch, peering at the small chest that sat ten feet beyond.

"Peaty," he said. "Peter Wilson. He stole my pencil. But how in the world—?"

Before he could finish, the metal bars blinked twice, and disappeared.

"It worked!" cried Kale. "Now open the chest!"

Ilien stood dumbfounded. Disappearing bars he could handle. He'd seen such magic before. What he couldn't yet understand was why the writing above the arch referred to Peaty back home, and his penchant for stealing his talking pencil.

"Open the chest!" urged Kale. "The talisman must be inside!"

"The talisman," muttered Ilien, his confusion deepening.

"The item that will help you heal Rose," answered Kale, shoving him forward. "Now open the chest."

In a daze, Ilien stumbled toward the chest, reached down, and lifted the lid. For a long moment he didn't move. He just stood there with Kale prodding him from behind.

"Well what is it?" Kale asked. "What's inside?"

Ilien's heart jumped. His hand shot out and clutched the item he saw. Straightening, he staggered back. "How is this possible? I left you with Gallund back on Nadae."

He opened his hand and blinked. His pencil lay silent in his outstretched palm.

Chapter XIII

Riddles Revealed

"What is it?" asked Kale. He regarded the pencil as if was a strange animal he'd never seen before. When the pencil wriggled in Ilien's hand, he raised his Breach defensively.

"How are you here?" said Ilien. "It's impossible. Gallund had you last. He took you from me before I crossed."

"The key," said his pencil. "Retrieve the key and open the lock. All of your questions will be answered."

Ilien walked numbly to the left hand arch where the silver key revolved silently in the air. His head spun so furiously with each revolution that he closed his eyes against the vertigo, but the key remained transfixed in his mind. He'd seen that key before, but where? It came to him suddenly. The silver key. The magical silver key that Windy kept. Yes! That was it! The one that opened the polished silver lock on her chest of talismans. He had seen that key before and like his pencil, it was somehow there.

"Answer the question," said his pencil. "Solve the riddle. The keeper of the key, you know who it is."

Ilien read the riddle aloud as he tried to understand what was happening. "I was keeper of the key. Speak my name and enter." He couldn't understand how it could possibly be, but he said the answer out loud.

"Windy. It's Windy."

The metal bars blinked, then vanished. The key fell to

the floor with a dull metallic clink, kicking up a small cloud of dust. Ilien stared at it, still dumbfounded. It seemed impossible that both his pencil and Windy's could key be there in the stonehall. And the riddles—how could anyone in this godforsaken world have known about Windy or Peaty?

"Take it," said his pencil. "Take the key."

Kale stood behind Ilien, his misshapen face stretched with awe, but he held his Breach in white-knuckled hands. Ilien approached the key cautiously, remembering its penchant for flying about the room and spearing him in the backside. But the key lay motionless on the floor, and for a moment Ilien thought it might not be the key Windy kept after all. Then it lifted from the floor and streaked to his hand, poking him savagely in the thumb.

"Ouch!" cried Ilien, clenching his fist around the mischievous attacker to ward off further attacks. He held his pencil and the key side by side. "This is unbelievable."

But it wasn't. They were in his hand, the two magical talismans he'd left back on Nadae, the two magical talismans that someone had placed in the stonehall nearly two thousand years ago after he'd left. His head began to spin again as he realized what it meant.

He walked to the center archway. Inscribed above it was a single, unintelligible word: *Eligo*. Ilien inserted the silver key into the lock. It fit perfectly and the lock sprang open with a click. He half-expected the metal bars to disappear, but the door swung inward instead. Beyond, still glowing faintly with a pale, red light, the stone pedestal remained. Ilien now saw what lay upon it.

"It's a book," said Kale behind him. "I told you so."

The book lay open. At first, Ilien thought it might somehow be his old spell book, but the writing within was unfamiliar, and Ilien moved closer to get a better look. It wasn't until he stood directly before the stone pedestal that he discovered he wasn't looking at the book, but at a handwritten letter placed upon it. Both shimmered with red magic.

Ilien lifted the glowing letter and read it out loud. "Ilien Woodhill, if you are reading this, you have returned. How much time has passed between your departure and the present can only be guessed. I am sure that much you have known has changed. This book records many events that have transpired in the years after you left, but we cannot foresee the future. There may be upheavals that yet alter the world, rendering it is unrecognizable to you."

A chill climbed up Ilien's back. He glanced down at the open book, glowing with red magic. With a trembling hand he closed it and read on the cover, "The Fall of Nadae."

Ilien staggered back and almost dropped the letter. "It can't be."

"Keep reading," urged his pencil. "You need to know the truth."

Ilien reluctantly read on, a growing panic filling him. "If you have not guessed already, you never left Nadae. You crossed, but through time only, to a future the horrors of which I can only guess. I am writing this letter some fifty years after you left. Much of the East has already succumbed to the Onegod, for that is what he names himself. Whatever the name, he has overcome even the Nomadin. Only a few of us have not yet fallen prey to his influence. Our time is short, for his power grows daily, and I fear that by the time you read this letter, I, too, will be under his control. It will be up to you to reverse all that has been undone, to destroy this Onegod. But you will not be alone. You will have your wand, which you have found already. If you are reading this, you have allies. Trust in them. They will prove invaluable.

"Lastly, I must warn you. There is something you must never do. It may be that you would not have thought to do this but for my admonishment. Nevertheless, I must warn you. Under no circumstances should you return to this time. These are cold words to read so far from home, but your very life depends upon this. There is nothing you can do to change the past. Only the future matters. This book is the record of our demise. We hope that the spell we placed upon it has kept it preserved from the ravages of time. Perhaps hindsight will help you do what we could not. There may yet be something between these pages that will help you set things right.

"I will close this letter with my warning repeated. Never return to this time. If you do, you will die. Do not ponder how I know that. Just know it is true. Always remember who you are. With fondness for you both, Gallund."

Kale placed a hand on Ilien's shoulder. "Now do you believe me? You have been here before."

Ilien's head began to spin. This was Nadae. This was the world two thousand years later. Everything he had ever known, all his friends, his hometown, his mother, they were all gone. The immensity of it crushed the air from his body. He dropped Gallund's letter to the ground and fell to his knees. Gone. All of it gone.

"Why did he let me cross?" he whispered. "Why didn't he stop me?"

"He couldn't have stopped you," said Kale. "You are destined to destroy the Onegod. It has been foretold."

Ilien glared down at Gallund's letter. He was sick and tired of hearing about everything he was destined to do. All he ever wanted to be was a normal boy from a small town. He never wanted any of this. He suddenly wished beyond all wishes that Gallund had never agreed to take him along on his ridiculous adventure. If he had just stayed home that early spring morning instead of being allowed to tag along to Evernden his life would have been commonplace.

Ilien sucked in a sharp breath. He stared wide-eyed at the letter before him and read the final words again. *With fondness for you both, Gallund.*

"Windy!" cried Ilien.

Gallund had written the letter to two people. That could only mean one thing. Windy had crossed with him after all!

"She's here!" exclaimed Ilien, flying to his feet. "Windy's here!" He turned to Kale, who suddenly looked away. "But you knew that already, didn't you?" said Ilien. "You've known she was here from the start."

Kale clutched his Breach. "I did not," he said defiantly.

"Then Rose knew that Windy had crossed. I should have seen it. The way she reacted when I mentioned Windy's name. But why didn't she tell me?"

Kale glanced across the room, his face attentive, his crooked eyes wide.

"That means she's out there somewhere!" shouted Ilien. "She's been out there all this time! Alone!"

Ilien stormed over to Kale and knocked the Breach from his grasp. It clattered to the stone floor. "Did you hear what I said?"

In a flash, Kale snatched the Breach from the ground and ran to the chamber entrance. He stood with his back to the wall, listening. Then Ilien heard it, too. Boots on stone, distant but growing closer.

"The Onegod is coming," said Kale. "We must get back to the exit-tunnel before it's too late."

"The Onegod? But how?" The old man had collapsed the tunnel behind them. The old man! Ilien realized the awful truth. *I fear that by the time you read this letter, I, too, will be under his control.* That old man had been Gallund after all. The Onegod had possessed his body and now he returned with a company of Cyclops.

"Come on!" cried Kale, his Breach held out before him.

Ilien scooped the glowing book into his arms and sprinted after Kale. They raced from the chamber, Globe dancing madly above their heads. But Kale proved too fast, and Ilien quickly fell behind. It was all he could do to shove one foot in front of the other while keeping a firm grip on the book and his pencil without tripping in the dark. Then suddenly, Globe disappeared up ahead. Kale had reached the exit-tunnel, which doubled-back the other way.

Ilien gasped and put on a burst of speed. Farther ahead, he saw the glimmer of torches. The Onegod and his Cyclops soldiers surged forward out of the darkness, closing the gap between them. It was a race to reach the exit-tunnel, and Ilien was slowed by the heavy book he carried. With rising panic, he realized that he wasn't going to make it. In desperation, he raised his hand, leveling his pencil at the approaching torches.

But Globe reappeared, dazzlingly bright, and darted toward the charging Cyclops. In her light, Ilien saw Kale take up position ten feet from the exit-tunnel. He held his Breach out before him, prepared to make a stand against the onslaught. He glanced back at Ilien, eyes beseeching him to run faster.

"Kinil ubid illubid kinar!" shouted Ilien.

The Cyclops' torches flared violently. The startled Cyclops fell back and dropped their guttering brands. The Onegod screeched in rage as the torches spun and danced like wild snakes on the tunnel floor, blocking their passage.

"Run!" cried Ilien as he reached Kale. Together they fled down the exit-tunnel, Globe once again leading the way.

Behind them, the torches continued their fireworks display, filling the tunnel with smoke and clatter.

"That little stick is handy!" shouted Kale. "Almost as useful as my big one!" Kale grinned at Ilien as they ran.

"Little?" protested the pencil. "Who are you calling little?"

Ilien stashed the pencil in his pocket. His eyes burned ahead into the darkness. "How much farther until we're out?" When Kale failed to answer him, he added, "Because those torches won't last much longer."

"It's far, I think," said Kale. "But we'll be safe once we reach the outside world. The Cyclops hate the sun. It burns their eye."

"What about the Onegod?" asked Ilien.

Kale fished beneath his shirt and pulled out a piece of Manna. "This is the last of it," he warned. "Try to eat it slowly. It should sustain us until we reach the exit."

Ilien snatched the Manna from Kale's outstretched hand, and nearly dropped the book. "The Onegod, Kale! What about the Onegod?"

Kale chewed on his Manna, his swollen cheeks balling into two lumpy knots. "The old man, we'll have to fight."

Ilien took a bite of his Manna, grimacing at more than just the sour taste. Fighting the old man who followed them meant fighting his father.

The Manna bread once again gave them the energy they needed to put distance between them and their enemies. They ran like madmen through the straight and narrow corridor. Globe's light was like a beacon of freedom before them, leading them onward toward the outside world, the world beyond the Desecration. They jogged for hours, and Ilien guessed they had trekked more than ten miles, when they suddenly stumbled into a wide cavern. Here the smooth, cut stone gave way to natural rock. The walls glistened with moisture and the dirt floor was strewn with rocks and debris that caused their footfalls to echo loudly about them. They stopped and looked around, panting in the dark. Ilien doubled over in exhaustion, clutching the heavy book in his arms. He noticed that it still glowed faintly red from the remnants of the Preservation spell Gallund had cast upon it.

"This must be it," said Kale. "This is the end of the stonehall. The exit is near."

Ilien peered into the darkness behind them. There was no sign of pursuit, but the Onegod and his Cyclops soldiers were back there, gaining on them at that very moment.

"Quick!" he urged. "We have to find the way out!"

They scanned the cavern but saw no exit, no open archway, no door left ajar. They searched the perimeter of the cave, scrambling over rocks and boulders as Globe's light glistened off the damp cavern walls. Kale tapped the stone with his Breach, searching for the exit concealed beneath the grime and dirt.

"It's here," he said. "It has to be."

Ilien froze as he heard the distant drum of feet. "They're coming."

Kale grew frantic. He began digging in the dirt as if he could tunnel his way out.

"Didn't they teach you how to get out of this place?" cried Ilien. "They told you where every stonehall was, how to find each one, but they didn't give you a clue how to get out of the most important stonehall of all?"

Kale shoved one end of his Breach into a promising looking crack in the wall. "All they said was that I would have no trouble finding it."

Ilien stood in thought. *No trouble finding it.* That meant it had to be right in front of them. But where? Somehow they were overlooking the obvious. He glanced over at Kale, who pried violently at the rock with his Breach, sweat beading on his lumpy forehead.

"Wait!" said Ilien. "We're looking in the wrong spot."

Kale knocked loose a section of dirt from the wall. "What do you mean, we're looking in the wrong spot? This is the only cavern here."

Ilien directed Globe away from the wall.

"Hey!" shouted Kale, as he was left in the dark. "Bring back that light!"

Globe moved toward the center of the cavern.

"What's the most obvious place in any room?" Ilien asked as Kale scrambled to join him. Globe illuminated the center of the cave. Below her, plain for all to see, yawned a hold in the ground. "Its middle," said Ilien. "There it is! Come on!"

They stumbled over the dusty rocks that covered the cavern floor. When they reached the hole, they stopped and peered inside. Shadows shifted and jumped in Globe's wavering light.

"I suppose we'll have to climb down," said Ilien nervously.

Kale tilted his head. "What's that sound?"

Ilien heard it too. A faint whirring. Ilien knelt and listened closer. The whirring grew louder.

"It sounds like wind," he said. "This *has* to be the way out."

Kale retrieved a stone at his feet. With a grimace, he dropped it into the hole and watched it disappear into the blackness. They listened, but never heard it hit bottom.

Globe descended into the hole. "Look," said Ilien. "There are stairs to the right side, ten feet down." Directly below, the earth opened into a gaping black pit, but stairs encircled the open hole, spiraling down into the darkness.

The drum of marching boots echoed loudly into the cavern. Ilien jumped to his feet, clutching his book in both hands. "They're here!"

Kale jumped feet first into the gaping hole. Ilien gasped, but the boy landed firmly on the stairs ten feet below. "Jump!" he shouted. "I'll catch you!"

Ilien leaped as the first Cyclops stormed blindly into the cavern. "Lever belie, belever beflie!" he shouted, and sailed down beside Kale on the winding stairs. The whirring they heard earlier grew to a dull roar.

They took the stairs two at a time as Globe danced before them. One misstep and they would fall into the open, bottomless pit. The stairs grew increasingly slick, and Ilien knew the source of the roaring sound below them. The thunderous shaking of the air, the damp spray upon the rocks—an underground river surged beneath them.

"Kale! Stop!" Ilien called, but the boy was already too far ahead to hear him over the roar of the rushing water.

Ilien jumped from the stairs. "Lever belie, belever beflie!" He sailed downward at an alarming pace, but with a thought he slowed himself and landed back on the stairs ahead of Kale, blocking the boy's way. "Stop!"

Suddenly, past Kale, Ilien saw dark shapes moving on the stairs above. He snatched up a loose stone from the stair and shouted, "Propel!"

The stone flew from his palm and sailed into the darkness. He heard a muffled cry. A moment later, a Cyclops came crashing down from above. The screaming beast bounced off the stairs and tumbled past them, arms and legs flailing wildly. It disappeared into the darkness below with a faint splash.

More Cyclops descended upon them, and Ilien looked for

another rock. "Keep going!" he shouted to Kale. Kale continued on, surefooted. Encumbered by the book, Ilien slipped on the wet stairs. The Cyclops were gaining on them.

"Propel!" shouted Ilien as he grabbed another stone from the stair. A second Cyclops fell headlong into the river with a thunderclap of water.

"There it is!" Kale stopped a step away and pointed.

Globe hovered in the open air, shining her light on the roiling river below. Quick, black water raced by, heaving its way through a narrow stone channel. A frigid mist shimmered in Globe's radiance as Ilien and Kale shuffled to the foot of the stairs. Below them, an inlet had been excavated from the stone, creating a pool of calmer water where a moored rowboat bobbed up and down. It shimmered with a pale, red light and was chained to a narrow shelf of rock that acted as a dock.

Kale leaped from the stair onto the stone landing below. "They're coming! Jump now!"

Ilien glanced over his shoulder. The Cyclops stumbled frantically down the spiral stairs. Not far behind, the Onegod raised his silver wand—Gallund's silver wand.

Ilien sprang to the landing beside Kale. A black bolt of power crashed anvil-like upon the stairs behind him. It shattered the rock and sent sparks leaping into the water. The book nearly slipped from Ilien's grasp. He tripped, and pitched toward the river. Kale grabbed him by the shirt and hauled him upright, pushing him toward the boat.

"Get in!" he said as he struck at the chain with his Breach. The Gorgul bone staff rang off the rusted, metal links. Kale grimaced in pain and the chain snapped in two. Ilien jumped in as Kale thrust the boat from the inlet and leaped into the bow. He held tight to his book as the river swept them madly away.

Chapter XIV

The World Outside

"Keep your head down!" Kale shouted over the din of the river.

Ilien hunkered down as far as he could. Globe hovered in the bow beside Kale, illuminating the boy's fear-stretched features. The boat around them radiated a faint red light, the same red light that imbued the book, and Ilien hoped that Gallund's spell would protect it as the river crashed over them. Battered and bruised, he sheltered the book under his arms and closed his eyes, hoping the wild ride would end soon. Spell or no spell, the boat couldn't take much more damage.

The river thundered through the darkness, heaving through the mountain's veins as it coursed between its rock-lined channels. The boat plummeted downward, careening off the rocks. Kale cried out in fear. Then suddenly the roar of the river quieted. The water calmed and the boat sailed smoothly along as they floated out into a wide pool surrounded by rough-hewn walls of stone. At the far end, daylight streamed in through a wide opening where the river exited, sluggish and lazy. A high stone ceiling stretched overhead.

"We made it," said Ilien. "Kale. We made it."

Kale sat up and stared at the mouth of the cave and the golden beams of sunlight pouring in. He knuckled the water from his eyes. "It's beautiful."

Ilien stared, too. It seemed an eternity since he had last seen the sun, or blue sky. Its crystal glass rays filled him with sudden, overwhelming happiness. But the feeling fled as quickly as it came. Windy was somewhere back in the Desecration. Rose, too. They would never get back to them now because there was no returning the way they had come. Rose lay wounded in the stonehall, slowly dying. Windy was lost and alone, or worse. A growing sense of sadness grew in Ilien, and he hung his head.

The book still glowed faintly red, even in the sunlit cave. No harm had come to it, but not so the boat. Despite the magical spell that protected it, water seeped in through a long crack in the bottom and sloshed about their feet. Kale pushed them toward shore using his Breach as a pole.

Up ahead, the river issued from the cave and meandered between banks of tall grass. They caught a glimpse of bright blue sky, and the green, growing scent of trees. Kale looked at Ilien with a gleam in his crooked eyes. His swollen lips parted in a fleshy smile, revealing his cat-like teeth as he leaned on the Breach, pushing the boat faster.

A warm breeze gusted into the cave, blowing back Ilien's long, unkempt hair. A tingle ran up his spine as he breathed deep the clean, living air. It spread to his arms and prickled his scalp, relieving the growing dread in his chest. The quiet of the cave receded, replaced by the hiss of the wind through tall grass. The sound tickled his ears, and he smiled until his cheeks hurt. The buzz of insects, a noise he had often taken for granted, sounded musical. A bird blew a long, clean note from near the water's edge and it felt to Ilien as if the very world was singing. He had never known how beautiful the average world was until now, after he had experienced the utter, grey lifelessness of the Desecration.

They burst from the gloom of the cave into the sunshine,

dancing like madmen in the sinking boat, shielding their tear-filled eyes from the dazzling light. Kale lifted his Breach above his head and howled at the crystalline blue sky. Ilien pulled his pencil from his pocket and cast green and silver stars into the air. They whooped and hollered, skipped and jigged until the boat took on more water than it could handle. It sank around them, but they didn't care. The water was shallow, and they splashed their way laughing onto shore, carrying their few possessions above their heads. They fell into the mud along the banks of the river and lay back in the tall marsh grass, glad to be alive.

Their enthusiasm for mud and water soon wore off, though the sheer joy of seeing the sun and hearing the birds and smelling the good land remained, and they trudged their way to higher ground. Not far from the muddy riverbank, the ground grew level and sandy. Beyond, they saw a line of green trees in the distance—the beginnings of a sparse forest of oaks. They sat in the sand, feeling the sun on their skin, but beneath their joy lurked a sinking feeling.

"We have to go back," said Kale. His smile slipped away, replaced by grim determination that turned the mud on his face into something sinister. "We cannot wait any longer."

Ilien looked away toward the trees on the horizon. He knew they had to go back, but he didn't know how to tell the boy that he couldn't simply fly them there at will. He had his pencil back, and he was no longer under the smothering cloud of the Desecration, but he still couldn't pull that one off. He peered up at the snow-capped mountains they had journeyed beneath. Perhaps somewhere in that tangled mess of rock was a passage back to the other side, but it would take them weeks to get there. Rose would be dead by then. Windy most likely, too.

"Kale," he said. "There's something I have to tell you."

Kale stood and brushed himself off. "We're going," he said.

"You don't understand," said Ilien. "I can't just fly us there. I don't have that kind of magic."

Kale closed his eyes and lifted his face to the sky. Ilien felt his heart break, not only for Rose and Windy, but for Kale as well. Rose was the only mother Kale ever knew. Now he was telling Kale that he couldn't save her, that she would die in the Desecration, alone in the stonehall.

Ilien couldn't bear it. There had to be a way back. Maybe Kale was right. Perhaps he *could* fly them over the mountains. He was supposed to be the Creator, after all, or Necromancer, if you chose to believe the Onegod's lies. If anyone could fly over mountains, it was the Creator.

He would attempt it! Kale deserved that much. Rose and Windy did, too. He would try, even if it drained him completely, even if it killed him.

"Okay." His voice betrayed his doubt. "I'll try it."

Kale opened his eyes and looked to the sky. "It's easy," he said. "Just hold on tight."

"Hold on tight?" He followed Kale's gaze. The sky stretched overhead, a crystal blue dome above the flat, moving river. A single white cloud hovered high in the heavens. Small at first, it grew larger as if by magic. Then Ilien saw that it wasn't actually growing larger, it was growing nearer, and it wasn't a cloud. Within it, Ilien could just make out the form of a massive, winged creature.

"A Gorgul!" he cried. "But how?"

Kale stared up at the approaching Gorgul, a wide smile stretching his swollen lips tight. "I told you we would fly back after we found your talisman. I didn't say *you* would fly us back."

Ilien shielded his eyes. "How did it find us?"

"When you retrieved the key and unlocked the gate," said Kale. "They know you are here now. Only you could have done so. Only you knew the answers to the riddles. Now they know."

"They?"

"The Gorguls, the last wizardess. It is she who sent the Gorgul to find us."

Ilien peered up at the roiling white cloud with the large winged beast in its middle. It was still far away and grew more immense by the minute. "How did it know where to find us?"

Kale smiled. "This Gorgul is somehow bound to you, or so I've been taught."

Ilien squinted into the bright sky. His eyes flew wide. "Pedustil?"

The sky exploded in a roiling cloud of steam and scalding vapor as the Gorgul closed in for a landing. The sound of a steam engine crashing off its tracks split the air, and Ilien and Kale ran for cover. They crouched in the tall grass by the river and watched as the massive Gorgul passed above them. It spread its wide, leathery wings and quickly descended, clawing its way to a stop along the riverbank, kicking up mud and rocks in all directions. It stretched out its long reptilian neck, vapor and silver-hot fumes spraying from its gill-vents. Then the Gorgul dipped its snout into the water and drew a great draft of the cool, clear liquid into its body. Blasts of hot steam belched into the air, obscuring the Gorgul from sight.

"You rode that?" asked Kale, swallowing hard.

Ilien swallowed, too. If the Gorgul was Pedustil, he was far larger than he remembered. "Yes. I did. Now you'll ride him, too."

Ilien emerged from the grass and approached the great cloud of swirling vapor. He prayed the Gorgul was Pedustil, but he had his doubts. He'd been gone for two thousand years. He didn't know how long Gorguls lived, but he doubted they lived that long. A sudden gust of wind sent eddies of steam into the air, revealing a scaly green tail as thick as a tree trunk. The tail lifted up like a wary cobra, then plopped back down with a heavy thump. Ilien stopped. He thought it wise to wait for the rest of the Gorgul to appear before rushing headlong to hug it.

"Be careful!" called Kale. "It's been a long time. He might not recognize you!"

The wind cleared away the steam from the Gorgul's flanks. Ilien wasn't sure it was possible for the Gorgul to be Pedustil. He'd never seen a creature so large, and the thought of startling it sent the blood racing from his head. Pedustil's fangs had been the size of giant icicles. He felt his legs go wobbly as he imagined the size of the fangs of the behemoth before him.

"Perhaps you'd better wait back here with me!" shouted Kale.

Perhaps you're right, thought Ilien. He turned to make a hasty retreat when Kale's misshapen features blanched white. A moist breeze tickled the back of Ilien's neck. The ground groaned behind him and a deep growl froze him in his tracks. Kale grimaced and hunkered lower in the grass. Ilien slowly turned around.

"Boo!"

A blast of thick, white vapor blew Ilien off his feet. He landed on his back, dripping wet but undamaged, and glared at Pedustil as the Gorgul fell into a fit of thunderous laughter. Torrents of mud flew into the air and jets of steam lashed the sky. It was as if a dozen furnaces had blown all

139

their gaskets at once. When Pedustil was done and the air had cleared, he sat before Ilien, smiling a caveful of stalactites.

"Did I scare you?" he asked.

Ilien stared in awe at the tremendous Gorgul. Pedustil's wings now spanned a small apple orchard and his back could accommodate a company of soldiers, but his face remained the same—a long, scaled snout above a wide, smiling mouth, thoughtful green, luminescent eyes amidst an expression-filled face. It was Pedustil—times four.

Ilien jumped to his feet and flung his arms around the Gorgul's massive snout. "It is you! I don't know how, but it's you!"

The Gorgul laughed, sending Ilien tumbling to the ground. "I'm glad you are safe," he said, his voice like the deep rumble of a falling water. "I have waited a very long time to see you again, my friend."

"You found me," said Ilien.

"Yes," said Pedustil, swinging his giant head down closer to Ilien's. "I told you my fate was bound to yours. It still is."

There was movement in the tall grass by the river, and Kale stepped out from his hiding place, his Breach grasped firmly in one hand.

"Ah!" said Pedustil, lifting his long neck into the air to get a better look at Kale. "The Watcher that brought you through the peril. Well done, Watcher."

Kale laid his Breach at Pedustil's feet and bowed. "My Breach is yours to command."

Pedustil lowered his massive head and eyed the Gorgul bone staff, his gill vents trailing wisps of vapor. "You must be especially skilled to wield a Breach so long."

Kale smiled his jagged, little teeth. "Yes, I am."

Pedustil let out a steamy laugh. "No doubt you are, but retrieve your Breach, young Kale. The Lady is waiting for you both. I am to fly you there at once."

Pedustil shifted his weight and lowered the great bulk of his body. He laid his tail down so that it ended before Ilien and Kale, forming a ramp that led around to his back.

Kale looked purposefully at Ilien, and Ilien spoke up. "The wizardess will have to wait a little while longer. Our friends—we have to go back for them."

Pedustil frowned. "I was told to bring you back to the Lady, Ilien. Your safety is all that matters now. I cannot take you back into the Desecration."

"The Princess," said Ilien, "she's back there. And Rose, the woman who helped us escape the Onegod. We have to help them."

"The Princess?" Pedustil bared his fangs, revealing molars the size of tree stumps. "Climb on my back and hold tight. Things could get a little bumpy."

Chapter XV

The Fall of Nadae

Ilien sat back comfortably and watched the white peaks of the mountains loom closer. Flying on a massive Gorgul was far better than flying on a small one. To begin with, the sheer size of Pedustil negated any turbulence. He remembered how the old, smaller Pedustil had bounced about when he flew. This newer model seemed to float effortlessly along. Then there was the seating. The small impression in front of Pedustils wings was now a row of deep, cushy seats. Ilien sat in one, Kale in another, with the book between them. The small spike Ilien had once used to steady himself now grew as tall as a light post.

"Kale?" Ilien examined the eight foot spike. "This is where your Breach comes from, isn't it?"

Kale simply nodded, his face blending perfectly with the steam trailing from Pedustil's gill vents.

"Don't worry," said Ilien. "You'll get use to it. My first time up was on the back of a giant bird."

"Where exactly is the Princess?" asked Pedustil as they climbed steadily upward on the wind. "Is she far?"

Ilien chewed on his thoughts and watched the approaching mountains. Windy was alone in the Desecration. It had been days since they had crossed, and though she had food and water in her pack, it would be running low by now. He had no idea where she was, but he had a hunch Rose did.

Pedustil blew a jet of steam out his gills. "Ilien?"

"We left Rose in a stonehall," said Ilien. "It's not far. Once we cross the mountains, fly low."

They ascended higher, and the air grew frigid. Ilien sat beside Kale and whispered, "Temper clement." The air around them warmed, and Kale nodded in appreciation. He seemed to have settled in, for his face was no longer pale, and he smiled weakly. Still, Ilien could tell Kale longed for the ground beneath his feet by the way he clutched his Breach.

"We'll be there soon, Kale," said Ilien. "We'll heal Rose and she'll be just fine."

Kale nodded again, and Ilien pulled his pencil from his pocket and sat back comfortably. "Now, about this healing matter," he said to his pencil, "you do know a Healing spell, right?"

His pencil lay stiff in his palm. "I told you before that all I can do is help you remember. I can't cast spells myself. I have no magic of my own."

"Then let's start helping," said Ilien. "What does it start with?"

"You know it doesn't work like that."

"Just a hint?" Ilien smiled expectantly.

"I don't have any hints!"

Ilien closed his eyes and tried to open his mind to his pencil's most inner thoughts.

"You said you would never leave me again," said his pencil. "Remember? When you left me with Peaty?"

Ilien started to object, but cradled the pencil in his palm instead. "I'm sorry. I didn't mean to."

Only the rush of wind could be heard as they flew higher above the white-capped peaks below. "I know," said his pencil. "It's alright."

They both fell silent again, and Ilien looked out across

the open expanse of sky to the west.

"Restori somana restori siruz."

Ilien sat up. "What did you say?" He held the pencil at arm's length. "That wasn't a spell, was it? Because that sounded like a spell."

The pencil sat in tacit silence.

"You've been holding out on me," said Ilien, his eyes narrowing. "You've known spells all along, and yet you refused to tell me them. I can't believe it!"

Ilien's hand flew to his mouth. "That time in the Giant's tent when I needed to disappear, you held out on me even then! How could you?"

"It's not like that," said the pencil. "I didn't know spells back then, and I don't really know them now. But I haven't just been lying around for the past two thousand years. One does overhear a few spells in all that time. I'm not completely brainless, you know."

Ilien's face creased in disbelief. "Are you telling me that you never knew that Invisibility spell? It just popped into my head exactly when I needed it?"

The pencil fell silent again.

"I knew it! Now you tell me you just happened to overhear a Healing spell, and you just happened to remember it after all these years?"

"I *did* overhear that Healing spell," said the pencil.

"When? Did someone get annoyed with you and break your tip off again?"

"I heard Gallund cast it on King Thessien when the Onegod slew him."

Ilien blinked and sat back. "Thessien Atenmian. King of Asheverry. Dead?"

"Of course he's dead, Ilien. Everyone you've ever known—"

The pencil sighed. "I'm sorry. I forget that all this is new to you. But you must understand, this is Nadae two thousand years after you left it. Almost everything you've ever known is gone. Every living person who walked upon the earth when you were last here is but dust of the dust now. And yes, I do know that spell. I remember it because I was there the day Thessien died."

Ilien already knew everything the pencil was saying. He knew that Thessien was dead. His mother back in Southford, too. Southford was gone as well, no doubt.

"It's still difficult to accept sometimes, that's all," he mumbled.

"Read the book," said the pencil. "Read it as Gallund suggested. Everything's in there. You may not find it comforting, but it may help you in other ways."

Ilien eyed the book warily. *The Fall of Nadae.* The title left little to the imagination. Still, he did have some time before they reached the Desecration. Gallund had said he might find something between its pages that would help him set everything right again.

Ilien scooped it up and opened it to page one. A faint magical aura still imbued the paper, protecting it from damage. The book was worn and tattered, nonetheless. The pages were yellowed with time, the binding stiff and cracking, but it was still in readable condition and the writing plainly was Gallund's. The contents page indicated the book was divided into twelve smaller books, each recording a span of one hundred years. The first entry in Book One was labeled: Year One. Third Month.

Third month? thought Ilien. *What happened to the first two?*

He placed his pencil between the pages, and began reading.

Year One
Third Month

Thessien Atenmian, King of Asheverry, has spoken openly of his fear that the Nomadin are mustering forces at Kingsend Castle. Though it has only been three months since the Witch Queen and her sisters were defeated, and nearly as long since the ambush at the Crossing, it is believed the Nomadin have not been idle.

This starts three months after I left, thought Ilien. *Ambush at the Crossing? What ambush?* Ilien read on.

Wierwulf scouts have been caught near Beckett and Weifleet, further adding to the King's suspicions that all is not well in the Southland. Several of his own scouting parties have not returned from forays near Kingsend. Thessien has called for all able-bodied men from both the West and the East to join the King's Army. Still no word from Anselm. What's more, the search for Ilien's mother has proved futile—a blessing, perhaps, considering all that has happened.

A blessing? What was he talking about? Ilien skimmed the rest of the passage but could find nothing else concerning his mother. He skimmed the next page as well. Nothing. He'd just have to keep reading. *And what was that about Anselm?* The last Ilien remembered, Anselm was returning home to face his son and enlist the Giants in helping to defeat the Nomadin. Three months with no word didn't bode well. There was no further mention of any ambush at a Crossing. He flipped ahead to another page. The book was filled with such passages, each marked with a date. Ilien returned to where he left off and continued reading.

Year One
Fourth Month

A scouting party has returned from the South to report that Thessien's suspicions are correct. The Nomadin have gathered an army of Southlanders who believe the East has joined with the Giants and are intent on invading the South. Adding to this army are many wierwulf men and women who have infiltrated their ranks. A Groll is said to command their army. Thessien is preparing for an inevitable attack that he is sure will come before the winter sets in. His own army swells with fresh recruits. No word from Anselm yet, but Thessien believes he will succeed in bringing the Giants in league with the East.

Year One
Fifth Month

The attack came from the South as expected, but the stroke fell to the west of the Midland Mountains. The Nomadin's first blow was more symbolic than strategic. They burned Dell, Spence and Southford before laying siege to Evernden. There, King Allen has proved a worth ally. Evernden may yet fall, but until then, many wierwulvs will meet their end. Thessien has reinforced Evendolen and Berkhelven to the north, and sends his army south to the Quinnebog to meet the Southlanders there. The battle for Nadae has begun.

A chill moved through Ilien. *Southford—burned to the ground. Why would the Nomadin do such a thing?* His hometown   destroyed. His school, his house, all gone. Everyone he knew, Peaty and Stanley, his neighbors and teachers, all probably killed. Why? How could the Nomadin be so cruel? He thought he suddenly knew the answer, and it sickened him. *The Nomadin's first blow was more symbolic than strategic.* They did it because of him. He read the next few passages, anger driving him on.

Year One
Sixth Month

Evernden has fallen. Battle has come to the Near Plains before the snowfall as Thessien predicted. Still no word from Anselm. Scouts have not returned from the Westland where the Giants abide. We fear Anselm may have failed. The Giants are sequestered in the far West, but they cannot stay out of the battle forever. Thessien has sent an open emissary to beseech the Giants for aid. We can only wait and see which side their might comes down upon. The battle goes well for now. If we can but hold the Southland army until winter, they will be forced to retreat.

Year One
Seventh Month

Berkhelven burns. Thessien and his army were pressed back from the Quinnebog by an overwhelming force of men and wierwulvs. The Near Plains ran red with their blood, yet still they came. We have been forced to abandon Berkhelven in favor of a retreat to Evendolen, as Thessien now fears that the Nomadin and their army will make a push for the Eastland through the pass to the north. There has been no word from our emissary to the Giants, and we fear now that there never will be. We must hold the enemy at Evendolen.

Year One
Month Eight

Food grows short, but we still hold the northern pass.

Ilien noticed that the writing here was in a different hand, and wondered where Gallund had gone. He continued on, riveted by the course of events.

We have an ally in the cold. Winter beats down all in her path, but we have Evendolen to protect us. The Nomadin and their army have retreated to Berkhelven, lest they freeze in their boots. Supplies are on their way from the East out of Brookfield, and should be here in a few weeks. Things look up. We will hold the line here.

Year One
Month Nine

Supplies never came. Men are starving. A sickness has taken hold of many. We eat snow to keep our bellies full, but some say the Nomadin have cursed the snow to make us sick. We long for a turn in the weather, but fear it will only bring the Nomadin and their army to our doorstep. We have not the strength to fight. King

Thessien speaks of aid still to come from the Giants. We shall see.

The next passage was written once again in Gallund's hand.

Year One
Tenth Month

Anew terror raises its head in the East, one the Nomadin did not foresee, one Thessien could never have guessed. I, myself, first felt it awaken some months back, but I was not sure, so I set out alone to search for myself. I found him at Ledge Hall. He names himself the Onegod, and claims rulership of all Nadae. Though he would not come out to meet me, I knew what he was. An Evil of Old, one whose desire it is to destroy all Creation. No doubt the NiDemon, Bulcrist, has a hand in this Evil.

The Evil of Old. Ilien had fought that black void beneath the Long Dark Road. He had destroyed its serpent, but not the Evil itself. And Bulcrist. Somehow Ilien had known he would come to no good. The two of them together would be a formidable enemy. He resumed reading, his heart racing.

Perhaps by some sorcery Bulcrist has released the Evil upon us to avenge his defeat at Asheverry. But he has bitten off more than he can swallow. This Evil is stronger than he realizes. I sense it. If not defeated soon, its power will grow. Even now, its power surpasses mine. I must parley with the Nomadin. Surely, they will see the danger before us all. Only together can we hope to

destroy this Evil before it spreads unchecked. If only my son were here.

Ilien smiled grimly at mention of himself. It was the first time Gallund had written directly about him, and it made him suddenly wonder why. As of this entry, Ilien would have been gone for some ten months now. Ten months since he had disappeared through the Crossing, and yet there was only one mention of him, and none of Windy. Gallund must have been wondering why he hadn't yet returned with the wizardesses. In fact, there had been no mention of the wizardesses, either. Why was that? It was as if Gallund didn't expect him to return. It bothered Ilien so much that he skipped ahead, skimming the passages until he came to one that mentioned him again.

Year One
Twelfth Month

The Giants have come from the West. Led by Anselm and his son, they have routed the Nomadin's army at Berkhelven and are marching toward Asheverry, driving the Southlanders and their wierwulf cohorts before them. The Nomadin, for their part, have finally seen the wisdom of my warnings, but I fear it is too late. The Onegod's power has surpassed that of our own. Still, he sits upon a throne of his own making at Ledge Hall. I fear he waits until we spill the last drops of our blood on the battlefield against each other. Then like a vile carrion eater he will devour us. I can only pray that the Giants are mightier than even the legends say.

I miss my son. It's a year today. It is impossible to put words to my sorrow. So much lost. There never was

any report on the fate of his mother. Perhaps they are finally together. I long to visit his grave in Asheverry Castle, but I fear I may never do so again.

The passage continued, but Ilien could read no further. If he read it right, he was dead!

Chapter XVI

A Glittering Sign

Ilien jumped when Kale shook his shoulder.
"Good read?" asked Kale, his swollen features more grotesque than ever with weariness. "I think we're almost there."

Ilien blinked and put down the book. He'd been so engrossed he'd almost forgotten he was riding ten thousand feet in the air on the back of a ten ton Gorgul. He stared down in wonder at the text he'd just finished reading. How could he be dead? He pinched himself. Ouch! He definitely wasn't dead. But there it was, in black and white. His grave was in Asheverry Castle!

Ilien snatched the book back up and flipped back to the very first passage. He read:

Though it has only been three months since the Witch Queen and her sisters were defeated, and nearly as long since the ambush at the Crossing . . .

Ambush at the Crossing! They were ambushed? He was killed there? It didn't make sense. He would have remembered being ambushed. Certainly, he'd remember being killed. Then he remembered the voice that had shouted, "No! Stop!" It had sounded like his voice, his very own voice.

Ilien dropped the book to his lap as he remembered

Gallund's warning. *There is something you must never do. It may be that you would not have thought to do this but for my admonishment. Nevertheless, I must warn you. Under no circumstances should you return to this time. These are cold words to read so far from home, but your very life depends upon this. There is nothing you can do to change the past.*

"I must have gone back," said Ilien aloud. "Somehow there's a way to get back home to the very time Windy and I crossed. And when I went back, I was ambushed and killed at the Crossing. But by whom?" Ilien's mind raced. "And why would I go back?"

Of course! It was obvious! Gallund warned him that there was nothing he could do to change the past.

"I must have gone back to try and stop us from crossing!"

It was brilliant! If he could return before he left, he could prevent any of this from happening in the first place.

"Wait! According to Gallund, I did go back and I was killed. That's why he warned me not to go back."

His head began to spin. Kale looked at him as if he'd gone mad.

It hardly made any sense, but there it was in black and white. He somehow had returned to try to stop himself from crossing in the first place and was ambushed and killed at the Crossing. If Gallund wanted him to stay where he was, it sounded like sound advice.

Kale looked him up and down. "It must be the thin air."

Ilien shrugged him off. "Are we almost there?"

Dour, grey clouds blanketed the land of the Desecration below. It wasn't yet midday, and the sun shone brightly above, a dazzling ball that reflected off the snow of the glittering white peaks in a blinding cascade of prismatic colors. But the beaming sunlight never made it past the shroud that cloaked the dying land before them, stretching as far as the eye could see. Ilien tried to recollect what the land looked like before he had Crossed to this time, before the Onegod and Bulcrist had blighted it and cursed the very ground to kill him. There had been a vast forest covering the land. The Damp Oaks, with its myriad trees and brush and squirrels and birds. There had been streams and frogs and insects. Life. Precious life. Now all that was gone. And it was all Bulcrist's fault.

He sits upon a throne of his own making at Ledge Hall.

Ilien knew exactly where he would go if he made it back to his own time.

"Hang on!" shouted Pedustil. "We're going in!"

They dove into an ocean of soot and smoke. The rancid air howled in their ears as they coughed and gagged, their throats on fire and eyes streaming hot, muddy tears. Ilien held tight to the book, afraid it would blow off Pedustil's back. Kale labored to breath beside him. All Ilien could do was squeeze shut his burning eyes and wait for it to be over.

They burst from the reeking pall of dust and fumes like a meteor from the heavens, trailing smoke and ash behind them. Ilien gulped in a fresh breath of air, if it could be called that, and clawed the smudge from his eyes. Kale sat beside him, coughing, clutching his Breach in both hands.

The world below was as flat and indistinguishable as a desert. Mottled grey and brown, the landscape stretched out into the distance in an unbroken collage of desolation. Ilien's heart sank as he realized he couldn't differentiate one section of land from another. How would they ever find the stonehall where Rose lay wounded?

"We'll have to land and retrace our steps," said Kale, as he, too, thought the same thing. "Fly to the right," he called to Pedustil. "Over there toward that brown area."

A patch of dark earth in the distance contrasted sharply with the pale landscape around it. As far as Ilien could discern, it seemed to be in the direction they had traveled. The he saw something that made his heart race. Faintly, almost imperceptibly, the earth was marked with crisscrossing spidery lines. The lines weren't lighter or darker than the surrounding terrain. They were like ripples on water. They formed a loosely woven web, and Ilien thought he knew what they were.

"It's the Buried Road. You can just make it out from up here."

"I see it!" cried Kale. "There's where it leads to the last stonehall!"

The intersecting pathways came from far and wide, crossing each other on their way to all the various stonehalls that peppered the Desecration, but one path broke from the main collection and ran straight toward the mountains. It was the part of the Buried Road that led to the last stonehall.

"Can you see it, Pedustil?" shouted Ilien, remembering the Gorgul's poor eyesight. "Can you see the intersecting lines below us?"

"Of course, I can see them," answered Pedustil. "I'm near sighted, not blind!" The Gorgul snorted in indignation and banked sharply to the right. Ilien felt his stomach rush to his chest.

"Look," said Kale, tugging at Ilien's shirt.

Ilien squinted. In the distance, along the base of the mountains, he saw the rising columns of smoke from the many encampments the Onegod had built to keep watch for him. "Do you think they saw us when we flew over?"

Kale grimaced and shrugged. "We had better find Rose, and quick."

Ilien searched the gloomy sky for any sign of winged

pursuit. He was certain the Onegod couldn't fly this high himself, but who knew what sort of flying creatures served him. He breathed a sigh of relief when he saw only grey gloom above. For the moment, they were safe.

It took Kale a few minutes to get his bearings, but once he did he had no trouble guiding Pedustil down to the stonehall where Rose lay wounded. As they neared the ground, Ilien saw the worry on Kale's face. It was a worry he felt himself. They'd been gone a day and a half, and though Ilien had healed Rose's outward wounds, he'd been unable to heal what ailed her inside. What if they were too late? It would be a devastating blow for Kale to lose Rose. She was like a mother to him, and he a son to her. But another worry ate at Ilien, one that twinged his conscience for even thinking it. If Rose was dead, so were his chances of ever finding Windy.

Pedustil spread his massive, leathery wings and they glided to a perfect landing amidst the swirling dust. Kale didn't wait for the Gorgul to arrange his tail so they could disembark. He grabbed his Breach, walked to Pedustil's flank and slid down to the ground.

"Come on!" he cried. "Let's make this quick!"

Ilien scrambled along Pedustil's tail and ran to the pile of boulders. Kale was already half way up. By the time Ilien reached the top, sweating, with a bruised ankle where he had smashed his leg on a rock, Kale was racing along the darkened tunnel below. Ilien incanted Globe and sent him chasing after the boy, then began his arduous climb down. Near the bottom he heard Kale cry out.

We're too late! thought Ilien. He jumped the rest of the way down and raced along the sloping tunnel, crashing into the walls in the darkness. He saw globe ahead, throbbing with light. Kale knelt on the floor where they had left Rose, his head in his hands, shoulders hunched in sorrow.

"We're too late!" sobbed Kale. "She's gone!"

Ilien's throat tightened and tears sprang to his eyes. He staggered toward Kale, his heart broken for the inconsolable boy, his mind numb with the knowledge that Windy was gone forever too. He looked down where Rose lay.

Rose was gone.

Kale flew to his feet. His tears shined fiercely beneath his crooked eyes. "The Onegod has her! No one else would have taken her!"

"You don't know that," said Ilien, stepping forward. "Maybe she left on her own. She might be out looking for us." Even as he said it, he knew it wasn't true.

Kale grabbed his Breach where he'd propped it against the wall. "The Onegod took her. I know it."

"But how could he have found her. He doesn't know about this place."

"I don't know how he found her, but he did."

Ilien searched the room. It was exactly as they had left it. "Why? Why would he take her?" he said. "Why not just kill her as he tried to in the first place?"

Kale seized Ilien by the arm. "Because the Onegod is hoping we'll come after her, that's why. What he wants is you. Now let's go."

Ilien pulled away. "Go where? Where would he take her?" But he knew the answer even before he completed the question: Ledge Hall.

"To his castle in the mountain," said Kale. "That's where we must go."

Ilien felt sudden panic. Things were moving way too fast. "We can't just fly there and expect him to hand Rose over," he said. "Don't you think we need help?"

"Who, Ilien? Who will help us?"

"The last wizardess," said Ilien. "We'll get her to help."

Kale threw his hands up in exasperation. "There is no time! Rose is wounded and can't last much longer. We must go now!"

Ilien winced. The boy was right. The Onegod may have taken her as bait, but he surely didn't care wether the bait lived or died.

Kale strode from the stonehall and Ilien followed after him, but Globe remained behind, hovering over the table.

"Let's go!" barked Ilien. "What's the matter with you?" He marched back to get her, then stopped. In Globe's slanting light, something shined in the corner. Globe flitted over to it and brightened. The gleaming object burst into life, showering the walls with dancing red lights. Ilien watched from across the room, mesmerized.

His heart leaped in his chest. "It can't be!" he cried. He raced to Globe and scooped the glittering red gem off the floor. It was the crystal he'd given to Windy before they had crossed, the one he had miraculously made with his magic. Windy had been in the stonehall with Rose! She must have left the gem for Ilien to find as a sign that she was alive and well. But that meant the Onegod had both of them now. Ilien stashed the crystal in his pocket.

"Hey!" came the muffled cry from his pencil. "It's crowded enough in here already!"

Globe bobbed in the air, then flew from the room. Ilien chased after her, his hope renewed. Windy was alive! If the Onegod wanted Ilien, he'd get him. But he'd get more than he bargained for, Ilien would see to that.

Outside, Kale was already astride Pedustil. He stood pointing and shouting. From atop the pile of boulders, Ilien saw a cloud of rising dust in the distance. In its midst, a hundred or more Cyclops charged their way.

159

"Run!" shouted Kale, waving him forward. "Run!"

Ilien descended in leaps and bounds, jumping from rock to rock. A chorus of guttural shouts shook the air as the Cyclops spotted him. Sudden panic stole Ilien's breath. The Buried Road! Where was the Buried Road? Kale must have seen his error for he cried, "Left! Left!" Ilien leaped from the last rock, praying Kale was right, that the Buried Road would be beneath him. He tensed as his foot hit the ground, but found himself running safely across the ground.

"Climb on!" bellowed Pedustil.

Ilien was half way up the Gorgul's tail when they started moving. Kale thrust out his Breach and Ilien reached for it frantically. As he grabbed hold of its tip, the book behind Kale slid from its resting place.

"No!" cried Ilien, leaping forward. It was too late. Pedustil heaved his vast, leathery wings and surged into the sky. The book fell to the ground in front of a hundred screaming Cyclops.

"We're not out of this yet!" warned Pedustil as he banked sharply.

From down below, great fist-size rocks sailed up at them. Some struck the Gorgul's hard, scaled underbody and bounced off harmlessly, but many more rained down upon Ilien and Kale as they clung to Pedustil's back. Amidst the deadly hail, Ilien knew it would be only moments before they were pelted unconscious. His pencil wriggled in his pocket. He tore it out and circled it above him. "Propel ador!" he shouted.

The barrage of rocks above them wheeled and launched back toward the ground. The was an explosion of cries from below. Ilien held his pencil ready, prepared to counterstrike again, but no more rocks came their way. Pedustil climbed steadily upwards as the moans from below faded away.

"That was impressive!" said Pedustil. "You've learned much since we last met!"

Ilien lay back in the soft indentation on Pedustil's back and breathed a sigh of relief. It had been impressive considering he didn't know what the word *ador* meant.

"The book!" he cried, rising up. Kale pulled him back down.

"It's gone, Ilien. There's nothing we can do."

Ilien hung his head, closing his eyes against his bitter disappointment. Gallund had said there might be something in the book that could help him set everything right. Now he would never know.

Pedustil banked sharply. "Prepare yourselves! We're flying out of this godforsaken place, and that means back into that cursed dust cloud."

They rose toward the threatening pall, and Ilien gave one last look at the Desecration below. The flat, grey world looked like a filthy, unhealed wound. The crisscrossing patterns of the secreted Buried Road spread through the land like cracks in a vast scab. Ilien marveled at the suffering that generations of people had endured for his sake, and a deep gratitude sprang within him. He vowed then and there not to let them down.

He called out to Pedustil. "Fly us to Ledge Hall! There's an ungod to deal with."

Pedustil shook his great, scaly head, and they swayed back and forth through the air as he did so. "No. We're going to see the Lady. You need her help."

Kale looked wide-eyed at Ilien. Ilien spoke up angrily. "Windy and Rose are in grave danger! Now fly us to Ledge Hall!"

Pedustil ignored his outburst and climbed higher into the sky. The dirty ceiling of dust and smoke loomed closer.

161

"Please!" said Kale. "We can't leave Rose! She's hurt! She may die! Please, she needs our help."

Pedustil flew as if alone.

"Then set us back down!" shouted Ilien. "We'll get there ourselves!" He tried to stand up but a gust of wind knocked him clumsily off his feet. He landed on top of Kale, who shouted and tried to push him off.

"I was told to bring you back to the Lady, and that's what I'm going to do," stated Pedustil.

Ilien climbed unsteadily to his feet. "Put us back on the ground. We're going to Ledge Hall. You can go see the Lady alone, and when you do you can tell her that, unlike you, we would not abandon our friends."

Pedustil roared in sudden anger, tucked away his wings and dove toward the earth, angling back to where they'd been. Ilien fell into the soft indentation on Pedustil's back and held onto Kale. Kale clutched his Breach, white knuckled, his misshapen features twisted by fear.

"Slow down!" shouted Ilien. "You'll kill us all!"

Pedustil heaved out his wings and swung back into the air. Up they rose, over the boulder pile that hid the stonehall. Pedustil roared again and banked sharply toward the rocks. A hundred yards away, a company of Cyclops, still nursing their wounds, turned angrily as their foes landed before them.

"You think you can handle the Onegod?" asked Pedustil, steam escaping his mouth with a sharp hiss. "Have at it then."

He shrugged his wide shoulders and jettisoned his passengers off his back. They landed in a heap at the base of the boulders. He flapped his wings twice, lifted from the ground, and disappeared into the flat, grey sky.

"Where's he going?" screamed Kale, jumping to his feet. "He can't just leave us here!"

162

Ilien scanned the ground, his breath caught in his throat. Luckily, he'd landed on the Buried Road. He looked up to see a hundred rage-filled Cyclops charging toward them. His luck had run out.

Kale leaped in front of Ilien, his Breach unmoving in rock-steady hands. "To the stonehall! The Cyclops are too big to enter!"

Ilien yanked his pencil from his pocket and searched the sky for Pedustil. "We get the point!" he shouted. But the Gorgul was nowhere to be seen. Ilien grabbed Kale's arm. "No, Kale. Not here. We'll fight them from atop the rocks."

They raced up the mound, bounding from stone to stone, Ilien leading the way. The Cyclops poured in, surrounding the small heap of rocks that kept them temporarily out of the fray. They jeered and shouted and many stooped for rocks at their feet. Kale steadied his Breach, awaiting the deadly missiles he knew must come. Ilien raised his pencil, intent on burning the first attackers to ash.

An explosion shook the ground, rattling the boulders and knocking Kale and Ilien off their feet. Pedustil crashed upon the Cyclops like a mountain let loose from the sky, crushing a dozen where they stood. Like a landslide, his tail plowed a dozen more to their death, their broken bodies smashing into their brethren, who stumbled to the ground, crumpled and maimed. A storm of scalding vapor came next, boiling all in its path, scattering a slew of survivors, leaving their rough skin blistered and peeled. Several Cyclops attacked the Gorgul from behind, but Pedustil wheeled and cut them down with a snap of his steaming jaws. He flung their mangled bodies amidst the fleeing remnant, then heaved himself into the air with a push of his powerful wings and gave chase.

Ilien watched in disbelief as Pedustil slew the rest, swooping and diving, pouring forth his burning brew of deadly steam upon the screaming horde. The last Cyclops fell headless to the hard-packed earth, and Pedustil wheeled about with a sudden roar. He bore down upon the two horror-stricken boys and landed beside the boulders, laying the head of his foe before them. Its single eye stared blankly up at them.

Ilien pushed to his feet and staggered back. "Why did you do that!" he screamed. "You killed them! You killed them all!"

The Gorgul thrust his massive snout into Ilien's chest, knocking him back to the ground. "These are only one-eyed animals the Onegod kills for sport. You wouldn't last five minutes before him. You need help and you are a fool to reject it!"

Kale rose and surveyed the carnage. The brutish bodies of Cyclops littered the ground in all directions. He closed his eyes, repulsed by what he saw. When he opened them, he turned to Pedustil and said, "It is you who kill for sport."

Pedustil bared his sword-like fangs. "Do not be naive. I kill Cyclops whenever I can. They would kill you and Ilien without a thought. Especially Ilien, who they call Necromancer. They are an evil, warped race. They would kill themselves if they knew what they once were, what they have become."

Kale looked away. He held onto his Breach as if it kept him from falling.

Ilien stared at the bloody head that lay on its side. "What were they?" he asked.

Pedustil lowered his head and sighed. His eyes softened. "It's best we leave. The Lady is waiting for you and we are already late."

"Rose will die," said Kale, turning on him, "but you don't care about that, do you?"

Pedustil breathed out a stream of moist air. "She will not die," he said.

"You don't know that for sure," said Ilien. "She's badly injured."

"She is a Nomadin," said the Gorgul. "Nomadin do not die so easily."

Ilien pinned Kale with a stare. "Then she *is* a wizardess."

"No," replied the Gorgul. "She is not."

"How do you know all this?" asked Ilien. "You've never even met her."

Pedustil laid the tip of his tail before them. "I have met her, though I doubt she would know it now. But it is the Lady who knows all this, and more. She sees much. She has been watching her for a long time." He gestured to the proffered tail. "Now climb aboard. We have far to travel."

Kale reluctantly followed Ilien to their place on Pedustil's back. When they were seated, he said, "He'd better be right, because if Rose dies I'll make these Cyclops look like child's play."

Ilien looked around them and winced. "In case you didn't notice, they were child's play."

Chapter XVII

Wiped from the World

They fought their way through the dust and smoke and soon reemerged into the bright sunlight. Kale and Ilien sat wearily and closed their eyes against the dazzling brightness of the cloudless sky. The clean, crisp air cleansed them of the clinging stench of the Desecration, and it wasn't long before the tug of exhaustion pulled them into a fitful sleep.

Ilien awoke shivering in the dark. Beside him, Kale lay asleep, curled in a tight ball with his arms wrapped around his legs in a subconscious attempt to ward off the cold. Ilien invoked a Warmth spell. He sat up and rubbed his hands together as the frigid air fled before his magic.

Pedustil's wings beat a slow, steady cadence amidst the moan of the wind as he winged his way through the inky blackness. The sky was riven with stars, crystal-white against the depthless void. Ilien looked down. It felt as if they hung above a vast, empty chasm.

"Where are we?" wondered Ilien. His voice sounded unusually loud.

"We are somewhere over what used to be the city of Brookfield," answered Pedustil, "if I recall the name properly. We're headed for a little known pass through the Midland Mountains, where the river that you once called the Quinnebog flows into what used to be plains on the other side."

"Why do you keep talking like none of those things exist anymore?"

Pedustil's wings fell silent as he glided on a sudden current. "Because they don't. Much can change in two thousand years, the least of which are names. Brookfield is entombed beneath the Black Woods. The Quinnebog has been named the Fen River for as long as anyone can remember."

"And the plains on the other side? What happened to those?"

Pedustil beat his wings twice, then glided once more. "They are swampland now."

"Swampland? That must be one big swamp."

Pedustil resumed his toil through the night. "There is something you should know, Ilien. Everything south of the Fen River is swampland now. The once fortressed city of Evernden, even your hometown of Southford, they rot amidst foul waters and have long since perished."

Ilien felt a shadow darken his heart. He pictured his small, two story farmhouse drowning in mud, Farmer Parson's neatly plowed fields stewing in muck, Parson's Hill rising like a gravestone from the murky water.

"How is that possible? The Far Plains were enormous. The land all about was hilly and dry."

"The Onegod has desecrated much. The land you once called your own has been hardest hit. He dammed the Quinnebog long ago and flooded everything south to the Three Lakes."

"But why destroy so much?"

"The Onegod only knows destruction. Look what he did to the Damp Oaks after you Crossed. The Desecration, like the swampland, is his attempt to wipe you, and the memory of you, from the world."

167

Ilien peered up at the star-filled night. "Why is he so bent on wiping me from the world? I've been gone for two thousand years. You'd think he'd have forgotten about me by now."

"He remembers because he fears you. He remembers who you are. That is why he names you Necromancer. His reign over this world for the past two millennium has been solely about making the world forget who you truly are."

Ilien shivered despite the warm air he'd conjured. "Once we pass through the mountains, what then? Where is this last wizardess, anyhow?"

"She is with the Lady in the only place still unreachable by the Onegod."

Ilien thought for a moment. "I thought the Lady *was* the last wizardess."

Pedustil's back shook as he laughed, and Ilien bounced up and down. "No. The Lady is no wizardess. I am surprised that you have forgotten her so quickly. She is the Lady of the Wood, Ilien, though you know her by another name."

"The Swan!" said Ilien. "We're going to the Drowsy Wood?"

"Yes," answered the Gorgul."

Kale let out a loud snort and rolled over in his sleep.

"The only way in is through an exit-grove," said Ilien, remembering how he had to weave through the trees just so. "The last known exit-grove was outside Evernden."

Pedustil banked to the left and a gust of wind buffeted Ilien's Warmth spell, sending eddies of cooler air spiraling around him. "Yes again," replied the Gorgul.

"But that grove can't possibly still be there. Even if it was, it would be under water."

"The pine grove has long since drowned in the rancid waters of the Far Swamp," said Pedustil. "That's one reason the Onegod hasn't yet found his way in. But the entrance is still there, if you know how to find it."

Ilien forced a smile. "And you know how to find it?"

"No. But you do."

Ilien wrung his hands together. "I thought you were going to say that. The last wizardess? Is she there too?"

"Of course," said Pedustil. "And others who will help you defeat the Onegod, but first you must get in, so sit back and get some rest. We've a ways to fly."

It was the Gorgul's way of saying the conversation was at an end. Ilien took the hint, but he wasn't in a sleeping mood. There was too much he didn't know, too many variables to work out, not the least of which was how to enter the Drowsy Wood. He had always thought the pine grove was the key. Visitors had to enter the trees in a certain place, then weave through the forest in a very particular way. It was always, "enter the forest five trees from the left, go three trees in, left two and right three more." Now there was no pine grove. There was nothing to weave through. Yet Pedustil had said that the entrance was still there, if you knew how to find it. Ilien sensed it was some sort of riddle, and he really hated riddles.

Ilien reclined on the Gorgul's back as they winged their way through the night and pondered every possible solution he could think of. An hour later, he fell asleep, no closer to an answer than before. He dreamed he was back home on Parson's Hill, trying to pick apples from a giant apple tree. The tree was bursting with juicy, red apples, but it was so tall he couldn't reach them. Now and then a breeze would blow and knock an apple free, but when he stooped to pick it up, it would promptly disappear before he could take a bite. He shouted at the tree to throw down its fruit, but to no avail. He tried to climb it, but every time he did so the trunk grew taller and taller until he slid back to the ground in exhaustion. All he could do was glare at the apples and wish he had longer arms.

Ilien woke, his mouth dry, his stomach hungry. The sky shimmered in deep shades of pink and blue with the first light of dawn. Kale still slept soundly, stretched out now in the warm shelter of Ilien's magic, the trace of a smile upon his swollen lips. Ilien studied the boy, and wondered how he was able to still smile after all he'd been through in his life. Horribly deformed, raised with no parents to care for him, and cast all alone into a lifeless world of danger and destruction, the boy had not only survived but had thrived. Despite his face, Kale was a model specimen of fitness and health. No more than ten years old, by the look of him, he could defeat several Cyclops at once using only an eight foot staff.

As Ilien gazed upon him, he saw a dark purple bruise just below his collar bone. Most of it was covered by Kale's shirt, so he hadn't noticed it before. He must have been struck by a rock and never said anything. He hoped nothing was broken. Ilien slowly pulled back Kale's shirt to get a better look at the wound.

Kale awoke with a start and shot up violently, slapping Ilien's hand away. "Leave me alone!"

"Kale!" exclaimed Ilien, startled by the boy's reaction. "I'm sorry, but you're hurt. That bruise looks terrible."

Kale pulled his shirt tighter around his lean frame. "I'm fine. It's just a bruise. It's not as bad as it looks."

Ilien let out a deep breath. "You scared me. I thought you were sleeping. I nearly jumped off Pedustil's back!"

"I *was* sleeping," said Kale. "You shouldn't go poking people in their sleep."

"Sorry," said Ilien.

Kale suddenly grinned, showing his sharp, little cat-like teeth. "Nearly jumped off Pedustil's back, huh? I would have liked to seen that one."

Ilien shook his head and stretched. The sun cast its first golden rays over the white peaks of the mountains, but he felt its warm fingers only briefly before Pedustil descended and they flew back into cold shadows below. Ilien realized then that they had crossed the Midland Mountains. The world below still slept in darkness. The sun wouldn't rise for an hour, but as Ilien looked to the horizon, he realized there was no one there anymore to see it. Dark water and tufted, brown hummocks stretched as far as he could see.

"That was once the Far Plains," said Pedustil, swinging his giant head around to greet his two riders. "The Drowsy Wood lies to the southwest. We'll be arriving shortly, Ilien."

The implication was not lost on Ilien. That meant he needed to figure out a way into the Drowsy Wood without using trees. He rubbed at his temples. Hunger had given him a headache. He remembered his dream and longed desperately for an apple or anything that might give him the energy to think more clearly. They were about to arrive at their long awaited destination, and he would be the spoiler.

Why can't the Swan just come out and get us? She's supposed to be a seer, isn't she? Shouldn't she realize it's us and just open the door?

That would be too easy. Instead, they had to trace some stupid pattern through trees that weren't even there anymore. Even when the trees had been there, Ilien never understood why they had to weave in and out of them just so. One misstep and you had to start all over again. How could they possibly weave that same pattern when the trees had been gone for nearly two thousand years? It was ridiculous!

"Hey!" cried Kale, excited. "Look at this!"

Ilien drew the Light rune in the air to see what Kale was talking about—and froze.

Kale held out a small piece of Manna, fished from the deepest recesses of his shirt. "Look what I found. One last piece."

"That's it!" exclaimed Ilien.

"Calm down," said Kale. "I'm gonna split it with you."

"Not that," replied Ilien. "The way in! It's a rune!"

It made perfect sense! The way you wove between the trees made a pattern on the forest floor, just as a rune made a pattern in the air. Enter the forest five trees from the left, go three trees in, left two and right three more.

Ilien traced out the pattern on Pedustil's back. Whereas the Light rune looked like an E with a tail, this rune looked like an angular S with an elongated bottom and no top at all. He could easily draw the Light rune. In fact, he remembered the first time he'd drawn it in the sand basin back at Ledge Hall. He had placed three fingers in the sand, pulled his hand sideways then down, creating the rune in one deft motion. That had been the key. Fluidity and ease of movement were crucial.

He studied the S shaped rune in his mind. He wished he had that basin of sand now. It was much easier to practice tracing runes when he had something visual in front of him. The S-shaped rune wasn't as complex as the Healing rune, but it wasn't as simple as the Light rune, either.

Kale watched Ilien as he used various fingers and combinations of fingers to try and trace the pattern upon Pedustil's back. "It looks like the Breaching Arts in miniature," he commented.

"How's that?" asked Ilien, without looking up. He thought he almost had it.

"It looks like you're tracing Breach patterns," said Kale.

"Breach patterns," muttered Ilien, focused on his fingers like some mad mathematician.

"Yeah. Breach Patterns. When you're trained in the Breaching Arts, you learn ways to move your Breach that strengthen your abilities, patterns that draw energy from the air around you. What you're doing is similar."

Ilien glanced up then. "Patterns that draw energy from the air?"

Kale took a bite of his Manna. "Yeah," he said, chewing.

Ilien had often wondered how tracing a rune in the air brought forth magic. What Kale said made sense, sort of.

"I think I've figured out how to trace it," said Ilien. "We'll see when we get there." He looked down at the vast swamp below, an ocean of green, slimy water studded with brown lumps. "If we get there," he said. "How is he ever going to find the exact place where the exit-grove used to be?"

"You just worry about getting inside," said Pedustil, overhearing his concern. "I know where I'm going. We're almost there."

Ilien sat back and practiced drawing the rune in one fluid motion. His thoughts kept returning to what Kale had said. If runes drew magic from the air, then that meant there was magic all around them, just waiting for someone to gather and use it. But then how did the True Language work? How did words do the same thing?

"Hold on!" called Pedustil. "There's a small hill that rises from the swamp up ahead. We'll land there."

Ilien tried to remember what the land had looked like two thousand years ago. It wasn't hard. As far as he was concerned, it had only been a month since he last fled into hiding in the Drowsy Wood with a Groll hot on his trail. He remembered the land well. The small grove of pine trees that he and Windy had zigzagged through had been surrounded by a wide, open field. There had been a hill nearby, the hill where he'd seen the Groll silhouetted against the moonlit sky. It was that hill they were headed for now.

"There it is," whispered Ilien, as if he looked upon some ruined civilization from some ancient time. Rising from the murky water, the once lush, green hill now hunched brown and lifeless in the distance. Beyond it, Ilien could see the other hills and small rises that marked the outskirts of the Kingdom of Evernden and the end of the Far Plains. He tried not to think of the parapets and towers of Evernden Castle lying in ruin, the vast gardens moldering, the outlying forests nothing more than swollen stumps as far as one could see. Somewhere beyond that lay his hometown of Southford, wiped clean from Nadae.

Pedustil landed heavily upon the hilltop, his feet digging up great tracks of spongy, wet earth. "Hang on!" he cried.

The sour odor of rot and decay filled the air as he slid to a halt amidst the decomposing muck. The murky swamp stretched to the horizon, and Ilien pictured the exit-grove as it used to be, growing in perfect rows not far from what was now a muddy shoreline.

One by one, Pedustil pulled his feet from the mud with giant sucking sounds. "Let's get inside before I start sinking."

"Don't you think we should get closer?" asked Ilien. "The pine grove was somewhere out there," he said, gesturing toward the festering swamp.

"I'm sure it was," said Pedustil. "But the Drowsy Wood is somewhere all around us, so it doesn't matter that we're not in the exact same spot as the pine grove."

"Draw the rune," urged Kale, holding his nose against the penetrating smell of the swamp.

Ilien closed his eyes as he always did when he drew a new rune. It helped him concentrate. He pictured in his mind the angular S with its elongated bottom and missing top. Then, as he had practiced, he traced it in the air in one deft stroke.

Chapter XVIII

Jallara

"It's amazing!" exclaimed Kale.

Surprisingly, they still stood on Pedustil's back. The Gorgul, though, stood flat-footed in a wide glade hemmed by towering pine trees. The evergreens grew so tall and massive that even Pedustil looked up at them. Their sap-streaked trunks rose like pillars around the clearing, filling the air with the smell of pungent spice.

"You did it," said Pedustil as steam leaked from his gill vents.

Ilien gazed at the flat, grey-paper sky. It was just as he remembered it. What he didn't remember was finding himself in a wide glade when he last entered the Drowsy Wood. The entrance, or mud room as Anselm had called it, had been a young pine forest with pressing rows of straight-trunked conifers and narrow lanes carpeted with fallen brown needles. This looked more like the Drowsy Wood itself, where the trees grew so large that entire houses could be carved within their golden marrow.

"So much has changed," he said sadly. "The centuries have taken their toll even here."

"Yes," said Pedustil, stretching out his leathery wings. "But time moves slower here, and thankfully so for the forest would have died from age long ago. Then the Lady would have had us planting seedlings night and day."

Ilien recalled how Anselm had caught him in his trap,

and he wondered if the Giant's cabin was still there. Surely, Anselm's wife had long since passed away, but the cabin might still be standing. He longed suddenly to see it, if only to see something familiar again.

Kale stood gaping at the trees in the distance. "They're so big."

Ilien smiled. "You ain't seen nothing yet," he said. "Wait till you see Hemlock."

Ilien remembered how Anselm had magically transported them to his cabin by weaving through the trees in a particular way. He now knew that the Giant had been following a rune pattern, and he tried to recall exactly how Anselm had moved. *Was it "in three trees, right two more" or "in two trees, left three?"* he wondered.

"This is as far as you go!" cried a familiar voice behind him.

"Penelope!" he cried, spinning about and calling the Swan by her true name.

The Swan sat on the needle-covered ground, her large webbed feet hidden beneath the bulk of her feathered body. The plumage on her head was a bit thinner, more wispy down than quilled feathers, but all in all she looked the same as the last time Ilien had seen her.

"Not so fast!" said the Swan, her voice devoid of friendly favor. "No one gets into the Drowsy Wood without first passing by me!" Her brow furrowed in sudden annoyance as she looked upon Kale. "Who is this lump of a boy? You were to bring me Ilien, nothing more."

Ilien felt a chill run down his arms. This was not the Swan he knew. He had expected her to be happy to see him. On the contrary, she was cold. Her voice cracked with bitterness and her once caring, black eyes now scrutinized Ilien suspiciously.

"He's with me," said Ilien. "He saved my life."

The giant bird nodded begrudgingly.

"You!" she said, peering at Ilien and shaking her tail feathers. Several flew into the air and fluttered to the ground behind her. "Yes, you! You may think you left me only days ago, but I have waited here two thousand years to see you again." She struggled to her feet and waddled fiercely toward Ilien. "Now give me a hug before I die of old age!"

Ilien staggered uncertainly into her feathery embrace. The Swan had become like Gallund, crotchety and impatient. *Was this what old age did to everyone?* he wondered.

"It is so very great to see you again! How I've missed you!" She held Ilien at wing's length. "You've left us a real mess here, you know," she said. "That Onegod, he's out to kill you! Don't listen to those fools, Ilien. He'll do just that if you face him! He'll kill you for certain!"

Ilien forced a smile. "It's great to see you, too. Things have . . . changed just a little."

Ilien shot Pedustil a questioning glance. The Gorgul spiraled the tip of his tail in the air where the Swan couldn't see it. Kale frowned in confusion.

"Come now!" shouted Pedustil, lowering his head so the Swan could read his lips. "Don't you worry about him! He'll be just fine. It's time to see the wizardess."

The Swan pinned Kale with a rheumy stare. "Who is he?"

Ilien spoke up. "His name is—"

"The wizardess, Penelope!" barked the Gorgul. "Take us to see the wizardess!"

The Swan perked up at the mention of the wizardess. "Yes! The wizardess! I should take you to see the wizardess!" She forgot about Kale and waddled off toward the edge of the clearing. "Come! We're late. I think."

As they followed after her, Ilien slowed, motioning for Pedustil to do the same. "What's the matter with her? Has she lost her mind?"

"Time moves half as fast in the Drowsy Wood," replied Pedustil. He nodded at the Swan. "But a thousand years, even for a magical bird, is a long, long time. She's mostly deaf, if you didn't notice. She's a bit forgetful, too. And mistrustful."

"Let's not forget cynical," added Ilien. "What was all that about the Onegod killing me? I thought I came here for help, not discouragement."

The Swan turned and made her way back to them. "You came here for help, not disillusionment," she said, fixing Ilien with a biting stare. "I hear more than you think!" She spun and continued on her waddling way, leading them toward the edge of the glade once more.

"We'll take the shortcut," she said. "Follow me and stay close."

As they neared the forest, Ilien wondered how Pedustil would be able to follow. The trees grew a dozen yards apart, but even so the Gorgul would have a hard time squeezing through the wide lanes with his vast wingspan. Ilien remembered Pedustil's penchant for tucking his wings away, and turned to see the Gorgul, looking like a enormous fat snake with feet, bringing up the rear.

They entered the towering trees and passed into a wide, open lane quilted with fallen needles. Several yards in, the Swan turned sharply to the left and vanished. Kale's eyes flew wide, but Ilien assured him everything would be okay, and with a quick pat on the back and a small shove from the rear, they soon found themselves in the center of a vast, grassy field. A mountainous line of trees commandeered the horizon, stretching as far as the eye could see, towering over the grassland like cliffs above the ocean.

Ilien knew precisely where they were. Behind them, like a great, fallen mirror, slept the glassy lake where he'd first met the Swan. The sun hung poised above it, unmoving, a giant, red ball locked in perpetual morning.

"Some things don't change," whispered Ilien.

"Don't lollygag about!" shouted the Swan, already far ahead of them as she shuffled toward the forest. "We're to meet the wizardess at Hemlock!"

Hemlock! Ilien's heart raced at the mention of the giant, secreted tree house with its hidden front door and wide, shuttered windows that glowed in the gloom of the forest like enchanted eyes. He ran to catch up with the Swan, eager to see the cozy sanctuary once more. Carved from the very heart of the ancient tree, with amber walls and honey-domed ceiling, Hemlock was like a golden fortress behind impenetrable forest walls. Nothing could harm him there. Not the Onegod. Not the Evil. Nothing.

As they neared the looming forest, Ilien imagined that the trees weren't trees at all, but towering pillars that held the sky from falling. They rose from the earth, mountainous and imposing, unearthly in their mass. Far above, they stretched out trunk-like boughs into a mighty thatched roof that caught the sun and blocked all light so that beneath lay eternal twilight, and in their heart blind darkness.

The Swan stopped outside the trees. A gloomy forest lane stretched into the distance like a mine shaft. The massive trunks on either side grew so far apart that Pedustil could have stretched his wings and not have touched wood. Ilien wondered how much larger Hemlock had grown in his absence.

"Pedustil dear," said the Swan, turning back to the Gorgul. "Would you mind leading the way? We could use a little light."

"Of course," said Pedustil, giving Ilien a look that said the Swan had forgotten the way. "Light we shall have."

Pedustil's eyes flickered with bright, blue light. The forest lit up like an underwater landscape, bathed in a watery glow as steam simmered from Pedustil's gills.

"Much better," said the Swan as she followed the Gorgul. "My eyes aren't what they use to be."

The small company marched through the heavy shadows, their feet whispering on the needled forest floor. Ilien incanted Globe but kept her small and dim. He looked back the way they had come. The brightness of the forgotten field lay shimmering in the distance. The Drowsy Wood had aged considerably, even if time did move only half as fast here. He brightened Globe, anticipating their arrival at Hemlock.

Pedustil stopped and swung about, his lantern-like eyes temporarily blinding everyone behind him.

"Turn those things down!" demanded the Swan. "I'll be seeing spots for days!"

Pedustil grinned, and his eyes dimmed until they were willow-wisps beneath the trees. "It's just up ahead," he announced. "Penelope, it's probably best if you go first."

The Swan ruffled her tail feathers, then groomed her wings with her beak. "Of course," she said finally.

As the Gorgul stepped aside to let her pass, Ilien's heart nearly skipped a beat. Globe pranced in the air with excitement. Ahead, two bright windows streamed golden light into the gloom. Though the beaming windows were exactly as he remembered, Ilien saw that Hemlock had indeed grown larger. Its trunk now stretched twenty feet on each side of the cunning front door. The overhanging moss that once grew thick and green had been stripped away, revealing two more windows carved into the tree, shuttered with bark and concealed in darkness. Above those, a row of five round portholes peeked out into the night. Ilien urged Kale forward, eager to get inside.

The Swan stopped before the root-laden doorstep. "Listen to me, Ilien. The wizardess means well, but she is misguided, as misguided as your father always was, rest his soul. When you have heard all she has to say, seek me out at the water's edge. There is something I must give you."

At that, she motioned to Pedustil. "Come on. Let's go."

"Go where?" asked the Gorgul, his eyes dimming in confusion, hot vapor leaking from his gill flaps. "Shouldn't we hold counsel with the wizardess?"

"First of all, I have held counsel far too often with that woman. What she has to say is well known to me. Secondly, in case you did not notice, the wizardess is in a tree-house. Retractable wings or not, you'd be lucky to get your head through the door. Now come with me before I forget where we're going. Farewell, Ilien." She looked Kale up and down, shook her head disdainfully, then hobbled away.

Ilien dispelled Globe and climbed the front steps, which had grown taller since he'd been gone. As he reached for the nob, the Swan called back to him.

"Remember, Ilien. Meet me by the water's edge." Her voice sounded frail in the darkness. "I have something to give you."

Ilien breathed deep the heavy scent of sap and spice that greeted him as he entered Hemlock. The gleaming, circular room had been carved from the very heart of the ancient tree and shined like hand-rubbed amber in the light of the hanging oil lamps. Ilien marveled at the vaulted ceiling, high enough even for a Giant to stand beneath. The wondrous cabinets that lined the walls, the wood burning stove and its stack of golden logs, all seemed unchanged. The bed that once rested in the corner had been replaced with a long wooden bench fashioned from Hemlock's golden marrow. The small table and chair where he'd once eaten dinner were gone as well. In their place sat three chairs around a larger dining table.

"Welcome, Ilien Woodhill," came a soft, woman's voice. Ilien spun about, half-expecting to see Globe hovering beside him.

"Up here," said the voice. "Look up."

Ilien gazed at the high vaulted ceiling. It was then that he noticed a balcony now encircled it. A single door opened onto the balcony, and framed within it stood a woman garbed in long, green robes. On her head rested a circlet of woven silver that shimmered in her brown hair. Her face was beautiful, with high cheekbones and gentle eyes. She reminded Ilien suddenly of Rose, without the wrinkles and dirty clothes. She held a silver wand in her right hand.

"Welcome to Hemlock, Ilien. Please, make yourself at home. I will be down shortly."

The woman disappeared through the doorway, and the door closed behind her.

"Was that the wizardess?" Ilien asked Kale.

Kale merely shrugged. "I would guess so," he said, looking around the room as if deciding where exactly to make himself at home. Home for Kale had been one cave or another for as long as he could remember. He was at a loss.

"Let's see if there's anything to eat," said Ilien, moving to the cupboards. "The last time I was here they had this delicious bread with honey."

Ilien rummaged about in the cupboard, but the best he could come up with was—

"No!" he cried, drawing back in horror. "This stuff follows me everywhere!"

An entire loaf of Awefull squatted before him. Grey, glistening damply and smelling like sour mushrooms, the sight of the magical bread sent Ilien stumbling across the room holding his stomach. Kale, on the other hand, sniffed the air and smiled, his swollen lips parting to reveal his jagged little teeth.

"Is that what I think it is?" asked Kale, licking his lips, his face hunching into an excited knot. He quickly leaned his Breach against the wall.

"It's not Manna, if that's what you're thinking," said Ilien, throwing himself into a chair. "It's Awefull."

"It can't be that bad," said Kale, closing in on the loaf like a badger hunting its prey.

Ilien jumped as the woman entered the room through a door that blended so perfectly with the wall that Ilien hadn't seen it. Her emerald green robe was clasped at her neck with a gleaming, silver pin. She spread her arms in greeting, her silver wand absent.

"You have traveled far," she said. "Of course, you must be famished." She drew a series of runes before Ilien. When she was through, she said, "Check the second cupboard to the left. You'll find plenty to eat. But first"—she grabbed Ilien by the arm as he moved toward the proffered food—"we must speak together."

She held up her hand, whispered a word, and an apple appeared. "To keep your wits sharp," she said, handing it to him. "A glutton is never attentive, but neither is a starving beggar." She motioned to the table. Kale and Ilien reluctantly sat down opposite her, where Kale could keep one eye on the loaf of Awefull.

"Do you know who I am?" asked the woman. She folded her long fingers together on the table in front of her.

"You're the wizardess," said Ilien. There was something

oddly familiar about her. Then it came to him, as if he'd known all along. "You're Windy's mother."

"You are very observant," said the wizardess. "There is a certain likeness. But I thought you would have guessed I was your own mother first."

"No," said Ilien quickly, staring at the apple in his hands. "My mother is dead."

Even as he said it, the truthfulness of the statement startled Ilien. His mother in Southford had perished centuries ago. Now that he found himself sitting before the last wizardess, he knew for certain that Gilindilin was gone, too. A pang stabbed his heart.

"Yes, I know," said the wizardess. "I am Jallara, and I am the last of my kind on this world. I have been waiting for you, as have many others." She studied Kale, whose crooked eyes were still riveted on the loaf of Awefull. When she turned back to Ilien, she said, "Where is my daughter?"

"She is in grave danger," said Ilien, gripping the apple tightly. "The Onegod has her."

"Then it's as I feared," said Jallara, her face expressionless. "Penelope foresaw it. She has much vision still, even for one so old."

"Then you'll help us?" said Kale, the Awefull forgotten. "You'll help us rescue our friends?"

"Wait," said Ilien. "You knew it was going to happen, yet you did nothing to prevent it?"

Jallara's face creased with concern. "I could not have stopped it from happening."

"How do you know that?" asked Ilien.

"Because Penelope foresaw that, too."

Kale looked expectantly at Ilien, waiting for his reply.

"I am the last living wizardess on Nadae," said Jallara. "I do not have the power to face the Onegod alone. Only together can we hope to defeat him and save the ones we love."

"Why did they die?" asked Ilien.

Jallara stared at him blankly.

"Gilindilin, the others, why did they die?"

Jallara carefully unfolded her hands. "Did you not read *The Fall of Nadae*?"

"I know that the Onegod killed them. But why? Why didn't he enslave them as he enslaved the wizards?"

Jallara's face hardened at the mention of the wizards. "The wizards were fooled by the Onegod before they knew their own danger. Once they fell under his dominion, there was no need for the Onegod to destroy them. They became his loyal servants, as no doubt you have seen."

"The wizardesses were immune to the Onegod's trickery?"

Jallara smiled. "Perhaps we were," she said. "But that is not why we were killed. You must remember that not long after you were born, we crossed through the same Crossing you did. Like you, we had been gone for two thousand years. When we returned, the Onegod had already come into his full power, and the wizards were already enslaved. The Onegod had his servants. He didn't need any more."

Ilien studied the apple in his hand. The Crossing had transported the wizardesses to the future, but why? Why would they have use that Crossing in the first place? And why did Gallund choose to send *him* through it?

"The Crossing that brought us both to this very time and place should never have been opened," said Jallara, reading Ilien's thoughts. "But the Map of the Crossings had been lost to us for many years. We guessed that the Crossing led to Loehs Sedah. We guessed wrong."

"Loehs Sedah?" said Ilien, shuddering as he recalled

Bulcrist's tale concerning the Land of the Dead, or the Land of the NiDemon as it became known. "Why would you want to go there?"

The wizardess leaned across the table. "We left the Nomadin wizards to prevent the prophesy from coming true. There could be no prophesied child without us."

"But you must have known that Loehs Sedah was the Land of the NiDemon. They were all banished there long ago."

Jallara refolded her hands. "Yes, Ilien," she replied, leaning back in her chair. "But Reknamarken's prophesy said—"

"Believe me, I know all about the prophesy," said Ilien. "The Necromancer foretold that a Nomadin Child would set him free, so the Nomadin forbade themselves from ever having children." He raised his eyebrows. "And here I am!"

"Yes, more than a few of us strayed from that oath," said Jallara, raising her own eyebrows. "You miss my point. You said it yourself, just now. The prophesy concerned the Nomadin, not the NiDemon. It said a Nomadin child would set the Necromancer free. We thought that living among the NiDemon would prevent you from fulfilling the prophesy."

"But the Nomadin and the NiDemon are the same," said Ilien. "It shouldn't matter."

"Yes," said the wizardess. "They differ only in what they believe, nothing more. But it is only our beliefs that truly separate us from one another and make us different, and that is enough when it comes to prophesies." Jallara sighed. "In the end, it did not matter. We left through the wrong Crossing and ended up here where the Onegod tried to kill us all. And here *I* am!"

Ilien stared at the apple he held, then placed it on the table. "Now you want me to destroy the Onegod for you?"

Kale stiffened at Ilien's question.

"Yes," said Jallara.

Ilien blinked. He hadn't expected such a pointed answer. "Do you think I can do it?"

Jallara reached out and grabbed the abandoned apple. "Not by yourself. With help you can do it."

"Help from whom? I see only you," said Ilien. "No offense, but the odds are stacked against us, wouldn't you say?"

"Do you forget Kale?" said Jallara, flashing the boy a smile. "Has he not led you this far?"

"Yes, of course," stammered Ilien. "That's not what I meant."

"Did you not see a mighty Gorgul willing to lay down his very life for you?"

Ilien began to protest, but Kale interrupted him. "We should leave as soon as possible. Time is short."

"Kale is more correct than he knows," said Jallara, rising. "There are preparations to be made and things you need to know. Also there is someone you will meet. But time in the Drowsy Wood is a curious thing. There is more of it here than anywhere else on Nadae. So first you must rest. Then we will talk again."

Jallara straightened her robes. "Eat. When you are through, I will show you to your rooms upstairs." She turned and left through the hidden door before Ilien or Kale could ask any more of her.

Chapter XIX

Undrei

Jallara was right. There was plenty to eat. How the wizardess conjured up the food was a mystery, but it tasted like the real thing. Ilien wasn't sure if the flavor was magically enhanced or that he'd eaten Manna for so long now that his tongue was overreacting. Sweet, red tomatoes burst in his mouth. There were carrots as orange as a summer sunset, aged cheese that crumbled on his tongue. And bread! Golden baked, melt in your mouth, sweet and buttery bread! Every morsel seemed to fill him with a renewed energy beyond what Manna had ever imparted.

Kale, on the other hand, was lost in an Awefull-induced eating frenzy of his own. He'd consumed nearly half the loaf before looking up to see Ilien staring at him. With a sheepish grin, Kale wiped his mouth and sat back contentedly.

"It's just as I remembered it," said Ilien, "but better." He peered up at the encircling balcony, eager to explore the new addition.

"Who is this person we must meet?" asked Kale, following Ilien's gaze.

The door to the room swung suddenly open. Kale and Ilien both nearly fell back out of their chairs in surprise.

"Some would say he is not a person at all," came a rumbling voice from outside. "Some would call him a monster."

Ilien approached the door cautiously. There was no

189

danger to fear in the Drowsy Wood, but he didn't recognize the voice and couldn't help feeling uneasy just the same.

"Who's there?" he asked, peering into the gloom outside. "Show yourself."

A cold breeze blew into the room. The oil lamps flickered. But no reply came. Ilien was about to conjure Globe and send her scouting outside, when a large, hairy hand gripped the edge of the doorframe. An oversized head covered in tufts of black hair stooped through the entrance and a single, watery eye narrowed upon Ilien.

Kale's chair clattered to the floor as he leaped for his Breach. Ilien fell back, his wits gone. How could it be?

The Cyclops pulled himself into the room, his head nearly brushing the high-arched ceiling. "Stop!" he bellowed, raising a meaty hand. "Do not be afraid!" His single eye blinked with a sticky, wet slap. "I am not a monster."

Ilien pulled out his pencil. "Listen to him," it said. "He is not here to harm you. He's here to help."

Kale jumped onto the table, Breach in hand. In a single bound he landed squarely in front of Ilien. Like a whip, his Breach cut through the air. Its tip stopped inches from the Cyclops' lipless mouth.

The room filled with the sound of heavy breathing as everyone froze. Ilien blinked. A Cyclops! Here in the Drowsy Wood! Impossible! But the face of the creature was unmistakable. One off-center eye, two gaping, hairy holes where a nose should have been, skin pulled and smeared like batter in a bowl. The creature's single watery eye blinked again, but there was no malice in its gaze.

"He is a friend," said his pencil as Ilien leveled it at the Cyclops. "I will not cast a spell upon him."

Ilien lowered his wand, but Kale was not convinced. He stood rigid, expectant, his lumpy face expressionless.

"Put down your Breach, Kale," said Ilien. "If he was truly a Cyclops, he would have attacked first and spoken later."

"But it is a Cyclops," said Kale. "It cannot be trusted."

The creature smiled, revealing sporadic, jagged teeth. "I am Undrei," he said. He bowed, and Kale withdrew his Breach to prevent the Cyclops from impaling his eye upon it. "Your pencil is correct. I am a friend."

Ilien eyed the Cyclops suspiciously. "You know what a pencil is?"

"Of course," replied Undrei, standing tall once again. "A pencil is for writing. I know how to do that as well. But your pencil is not only a pencil, is it?"

"What's going on?" asked Kale. He stepped back and repositioned his Breach.

"You don't speak like a Cyclops," said Ilien.

Undrei winked his eye. "So I've been told. On that I'll have to take you word."

Kale fell back into his chair, his Breach forgotten. "An intelligent Cyclops. I've seen it all."

"Do not be so surprised, young Kale," said the wizardess, standing in the hidden doorway. The silver circlet in her hair flashed with topaz light. "Undrei has never seen another of his kind. He was born in the Drowsy Wood. His parents came here after the Deformation, and returned to the outside world shortly after his birth." She turned to the Cyclops. "You're early."

Ilien gripped his pencil tightly, still unnerved standing so close to the same sort of creature that for the last several days had been trying its best to rip him limb from limb. "The Desecration?" he said. "That was two thousand years ago."

"The Deformation," corrected Undrei. He turned his face to show off its scarred surface.

191

"The Deformation began only a thousand years ago," said Jallara. "Since that time, all of Undrei's race has been born deformed."

Kale nodded slowly where he sat. "It's true," he said. "All Watchers are taught so. The Cyclops were not always Cyclops."

"Let me guess," said Ilien, placing his pencil back in his pocket. "The Onegod did this to them."

"Yes," said Undrei. "The Onegod cursed them for not joining his war against men. Born deformed from that moment on, they became outcasts in the world. They were so hideous to look upon that even their own people began to shun them." Undrei glanced meaningfully at Kale. Kale looked away. "Cyclops, they were named, after the one-eyed monsters of tales long since lost. In that way, the Onegod was victorious. When those born before the Deformation had died, all were called Cyclops. With nowhere else to turn, they joined with the Onegod."

"Still," said Ilien, "that was nearly a thousand years ago." He regarded Undrei in disbelief. "That would make you"— Ilien swallowed hard at Undrei's warning gaze—"far older than you look," he stammered.

"Time moves slowly in the Drowsy Wood," replied Jallara, walking into the room to stand beside Undrei. "And Giants live a long time to begin with." She saw Ilien's eyes go wide. "Yes. The Cyclops were once Giants. It is their punishment for siding with men against the Onegod. Now the world only sees them as the Onegod names them. Cyclops. All they truly were has been erased, renamed."

"I know the feeling," said Ilien.

Ilien thought of Anselm and a terrible sadness overwhelmed him. The last passage Ilien had read from *The Fall of Nadae* had told of the Giants marching to Thessien's aid. Ilien had assumed Anselm's and Thessien's fates had been the same. To die in battle, fighting for the freedom of their people, befitted the kings they both were. Now, to find out that Anselm's entire people had been deformed, twisted, enslaved by the Onegod, made Ilien sick. Apart from their similar size, there was nothing in Undrei that resembled his old friend. The Onegod had done his job horribly well.

"So this is who you wanted us to meet?" asked Ilien.

Jallara nodded, her eyes bright. "With Undrei's help you will enter the Onegod's castle and destroy him."

"When you say the Onegod's castle, you mean Ledge Hall," said Ilien.

"Yes," said Jallara.

Ilien eyed the Cyclops doubtfully. "He is only one Cyclops. There will be hundreds, if not thousands, protecting the Onegod. How can he possibly help?"

"The Onegod allows only a single servant to be near him. One servant each day is let into Ledge Hall and brought before him. One Cyclops, and one alone, and that Cyclops is summarily killed the next morning to be replace by another. Such is the twisted way of the Onegod." Jallara placed a hand on Undrei's thick arm. "Undrei will enter the Onegod's castle before nightfall and take that servant's place. So you see, there will be only one Cyclops to worry about, and he will be a friend."

Ilien frowned. "How will he enter Ledge Hall without being seen?"

"There is a secret entrance to the Onegod's castle. You know of it."

"Yes," said Ilien, understanding more of what had to be done now. "The Long Dark Road."

Kale sat quietly in his chair, staring in disbelief at the Cyclops who was offering to help kill the Onegod, perhaps at the expense of his own life.

"Assuming you can still find the hidden tunnel," said Ilien.

"Do not worry about that. Pedustil knows its location."

"Fine, we find the tunnel entrance," said Ilien. "Undrei sneaks in and takes the place of the Onegod's daily servant. So what? He can't possibly kill the Onegod himself. Only I can do that, or so I've been told. Unless I'm with him, and I won't be, what good will it do?"

Jallara patted Undrei's arm and smiled sadly. "The Onegod kills his servant at exactly the same time and in exactly the same way every morning, precisely at sunrise on the altar in the great, gem-encrusted Hall of the castle, the altar made from the bones of the Giant King and his son."

"Anselm?" cried Ilien, his hands clenching into fists. "The Onegod made an altar from his bones?"

"Yes," replied Jallara. "The Giant King and his son paid dearly for their resistance. They fell before the Onegod in battle before the gates of Ledge Hall. Their bodies were taken and never recovered. But they are there, desecrated, used for the Onegod's sacrifices."

Ilien's mind reeled with revulsion. He felt the desire for vengeance rise up in him like vomit, ready to spill out uncontrollably. But he fought back his rage as Jallara continued.

"So you see, we know precisely where the Onegod will be, and precisely when he will be there."

"All I have to do is sneak into the Main Hall just before sunrise and slay the Onegod before he kills Undrei." Ilien shook his head. "It makes no sense. If you know that the Onegod kills his servant every morning in the Main Hall, then why involve Undrei at all? I can just as easily sneak in and slay the Onegod while he's sacrificing his real servant."

Jallara stepped forward. "The Onegod cannot be fully killed unless he is fully present."

"I get it," said Kale, sitting up. "One god, many forms. The Onegod is in many places at the same time."

"Yes," said Jallara. "To truly kill the Onegod, he must be present in his entirety. He must gather himself into one form. If you destroy that form, you will destroy him."

"What makes you think he'll gather himself that way just because Undrei is there?" asked Ilien.

The Cyclops bared his jagged teeth in a grim smile. "Because I know the spell that will force him to do so."

"At the moment he is to be killed," said Jallara, "Undrei will cast the Summon spell he has learned and the Onegod will have no choice but to gather himself into one form. It is at that moment you must strike."

Ilien looked at Undrei incredulously. "Why him? Why not just teach me the Summon spell?"

"Because there is a counter spell," answered the wizardess, "a counter spell the Onegod is sure to know. Surprise is our only hope. If you face him alone, he will expect such an attack."

Silence fell in the room. Ilien couldn't believe that after all he'd been through to get here, this is what they had in mind. A suicide mission with little hope of succeeding. If he was forced to go along with their ridiculous plan, he felt he should know the Summon spell in case something went wrong. He attempted to read it from Undrei's mind.

Ilien clutched his head. He had no problem reading the Summon spell from Undrei's mind. It was a single word, and the Cyclops was repeating it over and over like a kid who had failed to study and was about to take the test of his life. Ilien now knew the Spell, but a headache spread like glue through his mind.

"When do we leave?" asked Kale, stroking his Breach.

Jallara laid a hand on Kale's. "You have done all that was asked of you, young Watcher. Your quest is ended."

Kale's swollen featured jumped into several knots at once and he pulled rudely away. "I am not staying here, if that's what you're saying! I'm going with Ilien!" He tried to rise. "Ilien. We must save Rose! Don't let them keep me here!"

"Kale's right," said Ilien, his head beginning to clear a little. "Our friends are held at Ledge Hall. We won't just forget them."

"No one is asking you to forget them," said Jallara. "The only way to rescue them is to do as we planned. They can only be saved if the Onegod is destroyed."

Kale shot to his feet. "I'm not staying here!"

Undrei lumbered forward to stand beside Kale. "Let him go. He has come this far. He has the right to see this through." He gave Kale a gruesome smile. "One so tiny should have no trouble keeping himself hidden."

Kale glared back. "I have defeated many of your kind with only a stick," he said, brandishing his Breach.

"Calm down," said Ilien. "You're coming, but only to the end of the Long Dark Road. Once we get to Ledge Hall, you will hide until it's done. Jallara's right. If I slay the Onegod, everyone will be saved."

Kale sat down, unsatisfied. "I knew we should never have come here."

Ilien turned to Jallara. "What if I can't kill the Onegod? What if everyone's wrong about me?"

"Then we never had a chance anyhow," she answered. "It's the only way, Ilien. Do not forget who you are. According to legend, the Onegod cannot stand against you."

"How do you know all this?" asked Kale. "How do you

know anything at all about the Onegod if once a day he kills the only one who's ever allowed near him?"

Ilien nodded in agreement. "Kale's right. What if you're wrong about all this?"

There came a clatter at the front door, and the sound of honking from without. The door flew open, letting clear golden light out into the gloom. Frowning there, a bit unsteady on her feet, stood the Swan.

"She isn't wrong," exclaimed the great bird. "She's misguided." Her feathery bulk prevented her from squeezing through the door, but she managed to thrust her long neck into the room. "If you don't mind, Jallara, I'd like a word with the two children."

Jallara smiled. "Of course, Penelope. Undrei, you may sleep here tonight. Ilien, Kale, you will sleep upstairs." She strode to the hidden back door. "We leave early tomorrow, Penelope, so please don't keep the kids up late."

Chapter XX

At the Water's Edge

The shadows beneath the towering fir trees of the Drowsy Wood held a damp chill as Kale and Ilien followed the Swan back toward the distant water. Ilien couldn't help noticing how much the giant bird had changed. She looked old, of course, but it was more than that. She mumbled to herself constantly as they walked. Her gate was slow and unsteady. Her beak rattled constantly, like shutters in the wind. Time had taken its toll on the Swan, and Ilien wondered what she was going to tell them.

They emerged from the forest into the slanting sunlight of the field. The glassy water of the lake reflected the reds and oranges of the perpetual sunrise. The Swan stopped and motioned for them to sit beside her on the ground. Grasshoppers jumped in all directions, but she made no attempt to catch any as she had in the past.

They sat in silence, soaking up the warmth of the sun while the Swan peered across the field toward the lake.

"This is how it should be," she whispered finally. She turned to Ilien. "This is how you meant it to be, when you made it. You don't remember, but you told me that once. You said, 'Penelope, don't let me forget—'" She stopped and looked downcast. "Now I've forgotten what it is I was to remind you about. But you told me once, before you became a man."

"But he's not a man," said Kale. He held his Breach

SHAWN P. CORMIER

upon his lap and squinted up at the Swan. "He's still a boy." Ilien knew what the Swan meant, yet he didn't. She talked as if they'd spoken together in another life. The Swan was always like that. If there was ever anyone who believed he was more than he appeared, it was her.

"Help me to the lake," said the Swan as she struggled to stand. "I want to cool my feet."

They made their way across the field, Ilien and Kale on each side of the giant bird. Now and then she stopped and sat quietly for a moment, catching her breath. Ilien stood beside her, heartbroken at how frail she had become. It seemed only a few days ago that she stood with him before the Crossing, impatient and full of life. Now he could hardly bear to witness what time had done to her.

"A little farther," she said as she waddled unsteadily to her feet. "I want to feel the water once more before I leave."

"Leave?" asked Ilien, gently guiding her by the wing. "Where are you going?"

The Swan eyed him as they drew near the lake. "You know where I'm going. You've been there. A paradise of your making, with lush green fields and a singing stream beside a tall, grey barn. A paradise as beautiful as all this where time stands still. You fashioned it yourself."

Kale frowned, but Ilien knew what she meant. He had been there. Twice. It was indeed a paradise. Farmer Parson lived there. He could see Kink, the giant dog who gave his own life for his, running madly through the grass like some crazed windup toy. And Windy, she had been there, too, until he came and took her away, back to the land of the living.

"That's it," sighed the Swan as she paddled forward in the shallow water. "That feels so nice. Thank you, Ilien. Thank you, Kale."

Ilien watched as the Swan drifted away from shore, and

he was reminded of the first time he met her, there, in that very same spot.

"Ilien," she called, her voice like the gentle rustle of reeds. The weakness in it startled Ilien, and he wished she would swim closer to shore. "Ilien. This is the end," she said.

"What are you talking about? Come back to shore" said Ilien, forcing a smile and wading into the water up to his ankles. "This isn't the end. You heard Jallara. She has a plan. The Evil will be destroyed forever. The Onegod will be no more. Now come back to shore where we can talk."

The Swan shook her tail feathers with great effort. "It's too late for plans," she said as she paddled slowly closer. "The Evil that possessed Bulcrist will possess even you. The balance will be destroyed. All Creation will perish."

As Kale listened, he shrank beside Ilien.

The Swan took a sudden breath and closed her eyes. "You cannot kill Evil, Ilien. Doing so only creates more."

Ilien had to admit that what she said made sense, but this was the real world. In the real world, Evil had to be destroyed. Didn't it?

"Come back to shore," he urged.

She floated aimlessly now. "If you insist on facing the Onegod," she continued, "he will overpower you. The Evil has grown in your absence. Even if Jallara's plan succeeds, you cannot win. I have foreseen it."

"Then it was you," said Ilien. "You're the one who told Jallara about the Onegod. That's how she knows about his servant. Come back and tell me more. I need to know more."

The Swan smiled weakly as she floated farther from Ilien. "I have foreseen much in my lifetime. This I know for certain. If you face this Evil, you will lose."

Ilien watched helplessly as the Swan rested her head upon her chest and strove to catch her breath. "There is something I want you to have," she said. "There, on the shore behind you."

Ilien saw a small, leather pouch laying in the sand. He recognized it immediately. It was Gallund's leather pouch. "Take it," she said. "Take it with you."

Ilien retrieved the pouch. Inside was a frayed piece of cloth embroidered with thick yellow thread. "The Map!" he marveled. "The Map of the Crossings!"

"Take it to Ledge Hall," said the Swan, closing her eyes. "Find the Crossing."

"Ledge Hall? But you said—"

The Swan drifted farther from shore.

Ilien waded out after her. "Penelope!"

"I remember now what you once told me," she said, barely audible now. "Paradise is nothing without freedom. Choice is all we have."

The Swan grew still and several feathers from her wings fluttered to the water. Her voice, thin and frail, came like the cry of a distant gull. "This is the end, Ilien. Go back to the beginning."

Ilien watched helplessly as the Swan floated away from shore. Her head rested on her downy breast as if she slept, but Ilien knew better. His eyes welled with sudden tears. His breath trembled in his chest. He reached out his hand, wishing he could touch the soft, white plumage of his friend and mentor once more. But she was gone. He did not cry out her name. He did not swim madly out to reach her. There was no reason to add such turmoil to a peaceful passing. Her bright, yellow beak seemed to be smiling in the sunlight. Her long, graceful neck curved upward like a chalice handle, and as Ilien looked upon her, it seemed to him that the feathers of her magnificent tail fanned out like an open hand raised in greeting to an unseen friend.

Kale laid a hand on Ilien's shoulder. Together they watched the Swan disappear across the water. When they could see her no more, Ilien looked down at the Map in his hands, still disguised as the witch's scroll. The Swan's last words echoed in his mind.

This is the end. Find the Crossing. Go back to the beginning.

Chapter XXI

Mapping a Plan

That night Ilien couldn't sleep. He tossed and turned beneath his soft, golden covers. Kale, on the other hand, snored softly in the next room. Jallara's response to the news of the Swan's passing left Ilien angry. The wizardess merely shook her head in silence. It was as if she already knew what had happened. She went as far as to say, "Penelope lived a very long and happy life. She was so weak and sickly for so long now that it's a blessing she went peacefully." Then she asked Ilien if she had said any final words to him. Ilien tucked Gallund's pouch deeper beneath his shirt and said nothing. He rudely excused himself, and without waiting to be shown his room, left and found it himself. Now as he lay in bed, still fully dressed, the Map pressed beneath his shirt, the sadness returned and he wished that his mother was there to tuck him in and make everything okay.

"What are you going to do?" asked his pencil from the night stand where he'd left it. "She's right, you know."

Ilien rolled to face his wand and wiped away his tears. "Who's right? Jallara?"

"Not Jallara. The Swan. You have to go back to the beginning."

"You saw what Gallund wrote. If I go back to try to stop myself from crossing, I'll be ambushed and killed. That doesn't sound *right* to me."

The pencil rolled forward in the darkness, stopping at the night stand's edge. "She didn't say to go back to the Crossing. She said go back to the beginning."

"The beginning of what?" asked Ilien, sitting up in frustration. "This whole thing began when I stepped into that Crossing."

"Did it?"

They both fell silent as the question hung in the air. *Of course it all started when I stepped into that Crossing,* thought Ilien. *Everyone I've ever met in this cursed place knows that. They've all told me that the Onegod rose to power because I left.*

"If you go back in time and *don't* stop yourself from crossing, where will you be?" asked his pencil, reading his thoughts.

"I'll be—" Ilien stopped to think about that. *If I go back and don't stop myself from crossing, then I'll be—*

"I'll be back! Of course! I'll be back at the beginning! It will be as if I never left in the first place. They'll see me leave through the Crossing, but I'll actually be back."

Ilien threw off his covers and sat on the edge of the bed. "Gallund wrote that I was ambushed at the Crossing. So if I don't go near the Crossing, I can't be ambushed."

He stood and paced as he worked through his thoughts. "The Onegod's castle is Ledge Hall and the Onegod is Bulcrist, so if I go back and get to Bulcrist before the Evil possesses him, the Onegod will never rise to power and none of this will have ever happened!"

He turned to the night stand. "That's the answer. The Swan was right. I have to go back to the beginning." He reached beneath his shirt and pulled out the Map of the Crossings.

"Kinil ubid illubid kinar," he mumbled, and Globe

sprang to life. "Now let's see what this shows us." He laid the frayed piece of cloth on the bed. "Ilustus bregun, ilustus bregar," he whispered.

In Globe's pale light, the morphing of the scroll into the Map looked strange and eerie, as if it were writhing in pain. But soon the folded Map lay before him and he quickly laid it open.

If Ilien thought Anselm's magical map had been confusing with all its exquisite detail and unintelligible markings, then the Map of the Crossings was like two magical maps written in three different languages. The Map was four times larger than Anselm's, and there were moving circles and colored dots all over it. Some were expanding, some were shrinking, but most were vanishing and reappearing. Even the writing moved from place to place.

"Well, it *is* supposed to show every Crossing throughout the entire Ether," said the pencil.

Hoping his pencil was right, Ilien said, "Show me the Crossing at Ledge Hall."

The images on the map came rushing at him as if they were leaping off the page, or he and everything in the room were leaping through it. The myriad circles and dots all expanded until they burst off the edge of the Map. For several minutes the Map revealed the moving images, but soon they began to slow. One circle then dominated the parchment, growing larger until its circumference surpassed the map's edges. The unmistakable picture of a vast forest as viewed from high above the ground came into focus. Then, as if Ilien was falling from the sky, the forest rushed at him, the landscape grew more detailed. Hills could be seen. Rocky ground. A river. Ilien began to feel dizzy.

"Ledge Hall!" he cried, as the enormous hill with its tall stone cliffs grew larger on the parchment.

The scene on the Map surged forward and Ilien cried out as he passed right through the hillside. The Map went black and the room fell dark. Ilien reached out to touch it, thinking something had gone wrong. As he did, a blurred image began to take shape in the very center of the Map. Pale at first, it slowly brightened and came into focus. The walls of Ilien's room filled with glittering shades of red and blue as the enormous, gem-encrusted Great Hall of the Giant's fortress came into view. Its towering walls of fiery carnelian and high-arched ceiling of blue and white jasper took Ilien's breath away. He reached out his hand, remembering when he and Windy first entered Ledge Hall and marveled at its beauty. The image froze, and Ilien drew back his hand.

"The Crossing is here," he said as he stared at the image on the Map.

"That's just great," said his pencil. "Isn't that where the Onegod sacrifices his servants?"

Ilien eyed the Map warily. "There's one more thing you won't like. If I'm going back, I'm taking Windy with me."

"But you don't even know where she is."

"No," said Ilien, "but perhaps the Map does." He crossed his fingers and said aloud, "Show me where the Princess of Evernden is being held."

The image of the Great Hall slid sideways as the Map moved through Ledge Hall. Ilien thought he knew where it was going. To his relief, he recognized the room where it stopped. It had been Windy's room when they stayed there.

"Now show me Rose?"

The picture of Windy's old room remained. "They're together," murmured Ilien.

"How do you know this thing is telling us the truth?" said his pencil, skeptically. "It seems a bit too easy, if you ask me. Nothing good comes that easy."

"Let me worry about finding Windy," said Ilien. "You just be ready to help me remember some useful spells. Especially that Healing spell."

Ilien regarded the Map, his thoughts churning. "Hey, I wonder if this thing can show me the location of the entrance to the Long Dark Road." Jallara had said Pedustil knew where it was, but it wouldn't hurt to know himself. "Show me the entrance to the Long Dark Road."

The image of Windy's old room disappeared and the room fell dark again. Suddenly, the Map flashed back to life and vertigo nearly overwhelmed him as the image pulled back rapidly to reveal Ledge Hall from the air. The landscape of shining streams and rocky outcrops raced across the parchment, adding to Ilien's dizziness as the room jumped and shimmered with flashing light. The image slowed and Ilien saw a pile of boulders amidst a small clearing.

"Where is that?" he wondered aloud. The image on the Map grew smaller until Ilien saw the outskirts of Asheverry. It was the same pile of boulders where Bulcrist had attempted to kill him, the same pile of boulders that hid the entrance to the Long Dark Road outside the city. If only he had destroyed Bulcrist then, he thought, instead of sending him back to Ledge Hall to live out his days alone.

"Isn't there an entrance closer to Ledge Hall?" he asked.

Ilien closed his eyes as the image on the Map began to move. A moment later, Ilien found himself looking at the river outside Ledge Hall, the river where he nearly had drowned when he fought the Nephalim on its banks.

"Pull back and show me how far that is from Ledge Hall," he said.

Instantly the Map did so. "And you never complained once," remarked Ilien, remembering Anselm's crotchety magical map and its penchant for moaning and groaning.

"It looks like the nearest entrance to the tunnel is only a couple hours walk from Ledge Hall," Ilien said to his pencil.

The room was silent as Ilien marveled at the Map of the Crossings and its unbelievable abilities. A couple hours walk wasn't bad. A couple hours after they landed and he and Windy would be going home.

"You will take me with you," said his pencil. "You won't leave me here, will you?"

Ilien picked up the pencil off the night stand. "I won't leave you again. I promise."

He refolded the Map and lay down on the bed. His thoughts turned to the Swan. He pictured her paddling happily on the small pond near Farmer Parson's field where Kink would be waiting for her.

"Goodnight, Penelope. Goodnight Kink." With his pencil beside him, Ilien fell quickly asleep.

Chapter XXII

Kale's Secret

Ilien woke the next morning, tired and hungry. His first thought was of the Swan, and he lay in bed feeling sad and lonely. The usually cheery golden hued walls of Hemlock now seemed dull and dreary in the pale light that filtered through the shuttered windows of his room. Part of him couldn't accept that she was gone, but the other part of him, the part that hurt, knew it was true.

He lay in bed until he heard noises outside his door. The others were awake, by the sound of it. He threw off the covers and stretched. The chilly room made him wish for a hot bath and new, clean clothes. He shivered when there came a knock on the door.

"Ilien?" He recognized Jallara's voice. There was a certain lilt in it, as if she were pretending to be motherly, or apologetic. "I have conjured you a nice, hot bath. Yours is the second door on the right. When you are through, please come down to breakfast."

He heard her footsteps receding when she called back, "And you'll find some new, clean clothes. Please wear them."

When he was sure she was gone, Ilien peeked out into the empty hall. Traces of steam escaped from under the door next to his. Thoughts of soap and hot water lifted his spirits a bit, and he tiptoed forward, imagining how good it would feel to soak in something other than his own filth. A smile crossed his lips as he slipped into the steamy room. Ilien closed his eyes and breathed deep the fragrant smell of soap and bath salts. When he opened his eyes, he froze in his tracks. Kale stood before him, a look of utter horror on his misshapen face. Ilien blinked and stepped backward, taken aback by what he saw. The boy stood naked before him, his perfectly chiseled body a sharp contrast to the swollen puffiness of his deformed face. Lean legs, clean now, scrubbed free of the grime and muck of countless days without a bath, stood trembling before him. Arms, small but muscular, hung loose at Kale's side, one lean hand clutching a bar of soap. Ilien's eyes grew wider as Kale's hands flew up to cover what Ilien couldn't stop staring at.

"You-your-your—" Ilien looked at Kale in shock. "You're a girl?"

Kale's eyes hardened at Ilien's words, embarrassment replaced by defiance and anger. "So? What's it to you?" She dropped her hands to her sides again. "Take a long look! Because what you see is what you get!"

She rushed forward and Ilien retreated before her. He stumbled out the door and into the hall.

"Leave me alone!" screeched Kale, as she slammed the door between them.

Ilien stood in the hallway, unable to move. *Kale's a girl? All this time and I never realized that Kale's a girl?* He stared at the door in front of him, expecting to hear crying from within. Instead he heard Kale throwing things about in anger, ranting about whether or not she should use her Breach to knock the tar out of Ilien, or worse.

"Why didn't you tell me?" shouted Ilien, grappling with this new turn of events. "I was just startled, that's all. Really. It's not a big deal that you're a gir—girl."

The door flew open and steam belched out into the hall. "Girl or not, I can outfight you any day of the week!"

Kale leaped into the hallway with Breach in hand, dressed in her old, dirty clothing. Ilien jumped back and dodged a skillfully aimed blow to his head.

"Calm down, Kale!" he shouted. "I'm okay that you're a girl! Honest!"

Kale vented a war cry and swung her Breach in an upward arch, missing Ilien's chin by scant inches.

"Remember your Vow!" cried Ilien as he bolted down the hall. "Whatever you cause to happen will also happen to you!"

By the time Jallara broke them up and sat them both down at the kitchen table, each was sporting an identical black eye.

"I'm still the same person that saved you from those Cyclops," said Kale. "Am I not?"

"I told you, I have no problem with your being a girl." Ilien touched his eye gingerly. "I was just a little surprised."

"And I can still save you from those Cyclops in the future, you know. If I choose to."

Ilien tried not to look at Kale differently. If not for what he'd seen in the bathroom, he still wouldn't know that Kale was a girl. Her bald head was still lumpy and misshapen, like a runted potato. Her oversized eyes, which glared at him now, were still set too far apart. As he searched those eyes, he realized that was precisely the problem. Not only had the Desecration robbed Kale of a normal childhood, it had robbed her of her identity as well.

"And you're still the same person who carried Rose into the stonehall," said Ilien. "Now that was impressive!"

A trace of a smile came slowly to Kale's swollen lips. "So you don't think I'm a freak?"

211

"Of course not." Ilien leaned over the table and locked eyes with Kale. "And don't expect any special treatment, either, now that I know you're a girl and all."

Jallara shook her head. "You of all people, Ilien Woodhill, should know that some appearances are not what they seem." She signed a series of runes in the air. "There's food in the cupboard. Eat and be ready to leave in one hour. And Kale—" She looked her over critically. "Please burn those clothes you're wearing and put on the ones I left you."

Kale left to change, and Ilien prepared breakfast for them. Boiled eggs, oranges and honey bread for himself. Half a loaf of Awefull for Kale. When Kale returned, dressed in new brown pants and a clean red tunic, she nodded her thanks and sat opposite Ilien to eat.

"My real name is Kayla," she said through a mouthful of Awefull. "But everyone called me Kale."

Ilien peeled his orange slowly. "Does Rose know?"

"Of course. Rose knows everything about me. And I know everything about her. We have no secrets." Kale pushed aside her plate. "That's why we have to save her."

Ilien stared at his hands. He didn't have the heart to tell her that he wasn't going through with Jallara's plan, that he wasn't going to save Rose at all. He knew now that the only way to fix this mess called Nadae was to do as the Swan said and go back to the beginning, but that knowledge didn't make it any easier.

"Kayla." As Ilien spoke her true name, a sudden ache grew in his heart. He reached out and grabbed her hand, a gesture he would never have thought of doing just a day before. She tried to pull it away, but Ilien held it tight. "Someday this will all be over and everything will be right. The Desecration will be no more. All of Nadae will be a paradise again and you will live in it, with parents and friends, as it should have been from the beginning."

Kale's eyes were wide with apprehension at being touched.

"I'm sorry that all of this happened because of me," said Ilien. "I promise you this. I'll fix it. I'll fix this whole messed up world."

Kale yanked her hand back. "Don't get all mushy on me just because you know I'm a girl." She stood and straightened her tunic. "Or I may be forced to break my Vow again." She smiled, and the lumps and bumps of her malformed face hunched into a grotesque scene.

Chapter XXIII

Beginning of the End

When Ilien finally did take his bath, the water was cold. He tried conjuring back the heat, but gave up after chasing and extinguishing a dozen floating magical flames that left his fingertips scorched and raw. When he emerged from the bathroom, freshly clothed and clean, the others were waiting for him downstairs.

As they made their way back to the exit-grove, Ilien touched the lump beneath his shirt that was the Map. His pencil was there, too, wriggling about impatiently. His plan, which he had formulated while washing as quickly as he could in the icy bath, was simple. He would go along with Jallara and the others until the proper instant. He would lead Undrei through the Long Dark Road and the Cyclops would slip inside Ledge Hall to take the servant's place. Kale would stay behind in the tunnel while Ilien made his way to the Great Hall where the Onegod sacrificed his servant at dawn. All would proceed as planned, except Ilien would sneak in and open the Crossing in the Great Hall *before* the Onegod brought Undrei there to be sacrificed, and cross back to his own time. Once he got home—well, that was as far as he got before the cold water had driven him out of the tub.

Ilien was so caught up in his own thoughts and plans that before he knew it they were all standing beside Pedustil in the large clearing hemmed in by towering pines. The flat, grey-paper sky hung close above the treetops.

The Gorgul lowered his massive head to Ilien and said, "I'm sorry about Penelope. Take comfort that she talked about you constantly and loved you very much."

Ilien nodded and retreated from the cloud of hot steam that escaped Pedustil's gill flap. The Swan's passing was still fresh in his mind, but now that he knew he'd be going back to the beginning, the sorrow was muted. If everything went as he planned, he would see the Swan again, and everyone else he missed so desperately. If anything, he felt sad for everyone present. If he succeeded in his plan, everyone and everything around him would never come to be.

"Greetings, Pedustil," said Undrei, as he approached the Gorgul. "I trust you're well-rested."

Pedustil bared his massive fangs and puffed a packet of vapor at the Cyclops. "You will be like a fly upon my back, little one."

Undrei's laugh sounded like a snorting cough interrupted by wheezing. "Good to see you, too, my friend."

Pedustil coiled his gigantic tail like a ramp and everyone climbed aboard his back. Jallara led the way, and Ilien was surprised to see that she was coming.

"For some reason, I thought you would be staying here," he told her as they settled themselves in the small of Pedustil's back.

The wizardess lifted her chin. "Even I have a role to play in all this," she said. "I may not be as powerful as you, and I cannot destroy the Onegod, but you will need someone to keep watch outside the Long Dark Road. Besides, I would like to see my daughter when all this is over."

And she would want to see you, too, thought Ilien.

Jallara drew the rune that would take them back outside, and almost without notice, Pedustil found himself knee-deep in mud at the base of the ruined hill just outside the once living pine grove. The night lay heavy and still around them, filled with the croaks of frogs.

"You could have given me some warning," said the Gorgul, pulling a thick leg from the muck with a loud thwuck. Jallara just grinned, and soon they were winging their way above the vast swampland, headed for the Onegod's castle in the mountain.

They flew east toward the Midland Mountains. Jallara calculated that if they flew over the mountains directly to the east, they would they come out on the other side far enough south of Ledge Hall so as not to be seen. Then they could steer farther east and land outside of Asheverry under cover of darkness. From there, it was up to Ilien to find the way into the Long Dark Road. Ilien patted the Map beneath his shirt. *No problem*, he thought.

"Is Asheverry still there?" asked Ilien as he hunkered down beside Kale. Two thousand years was a long time, and he couldn't see how even a castle as formidable as the one at Asheverry could still be standing.

"It's a prison now," said the wizardess. The rush of the wind around them drowned out Jallara's words.

"Did you say it was a prison?" asked Ilien, sitting up.

"Yes," said Jallara, louder. She stood beside Pedustil's tall Breachbone, grasping it to keep herself steady. "After the Onegod defeated the Eastland, he laid waste to all but its greatest city. Asheverry, with its majestic castle, was turned into a prison, a place of torture for those who resisted him the most."

On hearing that, Ilien smiled grimly. He invoked his Heat spell and sat comfortably near Kale, going over his plan in his mind. The Desecration, the disgusting swamps that were once his homeland, the torture chambers that were once Thessien's kingdom, all of it would soon be gone. All of it would never come to be. All he had to do was reach that Crossing and get out of this cursed place once and for all. He closed his eyes and pretended to doze. As far as he was concerned, it would all be over soon.

"Wake up, Ilien," urged Kale. "We are descending."

Ilien woke with a start. He had fallen asleep after all. The sky hung black above them, speckled with stars. Morning was still far off, and from the feel of it they had crossed the mountains and were now flying east toward Asheverry.

Ilien conjured Globe and looked to see Jallara, still standing beside Pedustil's Breachbone, facing the wind. He wondered if she had stood there all night.

"We're close," she said. The silver circlet in her hair glimmered in Globe's pale light. Pedustil's wings beat a steady cadence in the dark. "Pedustil has informed me that the nearest entrance to the Long Dark Road is by the river. We will have no problem landing without being seen. From there it will be a few hours' march to Ledge Hall." She turned to Ilien. "Are you ready?"

Ilien was, but not for what she had in mind. He felt like a traitor, hiding his plans from her. But he kept reminding himself that not only was it for the best, no one would ever know he didn't go through with their plan in the first place. If everything worked out, and it would, he and Windy would cross back to their time and all the pain and suffering in this time would cease to be.

"I'm ready," he answered with a smile. "Is Undrei ready?" He looked at the Cyclops who lay sound asleep and snoring.

Jallara eyes betrayed her worry. "You must remember to strike as soon as Undrei casts the Summon spell. The Onegod will try to undo the incantation immediately, so you will not have much time."

Ilien nodded. Jallara regarded him curiously, and Ilien thought for a moment that his own eyes had given something away. Did the wizardess suspect his intentions? Had she read his mind? She had asked if the Swan had said any last words. Did she know about the Map of the Crossings?

"Don't worry," he said. "I know what to do."

"Good." She turned back to face the wind.

Pedustil landed as silently as he could on the riverbank. Despite the roar of the tumbling water, to Ilien it still sounded as if a hundred horses suddenly fell from the heavens. Ilien breathed a sigh of relief as they disembarked without being discovered. According to Pedustil, most of the Onegod's Cyclops army served their time guarding the borders of the Desecration.

"There are many Cyclops directly outside Ledge Hall, but few venture this far east," relayed Pedustil as his passengers walked down his sloping tail to the rocky ground below. His large, luminescent eyes shined like two green lanterns in the night. "Be careful, though. The Onegod may not use the Long Dark Road, but he does know it is there. You may encounter a guard or two at its end."

A guard or two at its end, thought Ilien. He looked over at Kale, glad suddenly that she had come with them. With Kale's Breach, Undrei's brute size, and his pencil, they would have no problem dealing with a guard or two at the tunnel's end. He brightened Globe and steeled himself for what was to come.

"How long is it until sunrise?" asked Undrei. If the Cyclops was nervous about facing the Onegod, Ilien couldn't tell by the look upon his craggy, one-eyed face. Undrei bore an almost detached expression.

"You will have no difficulty reaching Ledge Hall well before morning," replied Jallara, her own face taught in Globe's wavering light. "You will enter first, Undrei. Ilien, you should wait an hour, no longer, before following him. Go directly to the Great Hall, for your time will be short. You know how to become invisible, don't you?" Ilien nodded. "Good," continued the wizardess. "Once there, you must wait until Undrei casts the Summon spell. Only then can you strike. You'll get only one chance at this, so do not strike too soon."

Jallara turned to Kale. "You must stay in the tunnel. Do not try to help them. Do you understand?"

Kale's lumpy forehead wrinkled with contempt. "I understand," she stated coldly.

"Good." Jallara pulled her wand from beneath her green robes. "I will keep watch at the entrance, in case the Cyclops discover our plan."

Pedustil stretched out his vast, leathery wings as quietly as he could. "And I will not be far away." He blinked, and his eyes dimmed. "Call my name and I will come. My fate is still tied to yours, Ilien Woodhill."

Ilien felt a profound measure of comfort knowing a mountain-sized Gorgul would come to his rescue if need be. He smiled at Pedustil, knowing his ancient friend would never have to risk his life. Soon, everyone would be safe again.

"We should go," said Undrei.

Jallara led them away from the river. The terrain sloped upwards. Large boulders littered the ground and they wove silently between them. They followed close behind the wizardess in single file. The Cyclops brought up the rear, his single eye searching the night for signs of the tunnel entrance. The landscape glowed eerily in Globe's pale moonlight. A hundred yards from where they landed, Jallara stopped before an outcrop of rock that jutted from the side of the hill.

"This is it."

"Are you sure?" asked Ilien, trying to remember what he'd seen on the Map. Over the last few days he had become familiar with hidden entrances to secreted caves. He could see nothing that indicated the Long Dark Road was nearby.

Jallara motioned to Undrei. The Cyclops moved to the outcrop and began excavating rocks and debris with his massive hands until a dark opening grew visible beneath.

"You mustn't forget that you are two thousand years away from home," said Jallara. "All the tunnel entrances are covered by earth and sediment. This one may not be the closest, but it's by far the most accessible." She shot Undrei an appreciative look. "Especially when you have a Giant with you."

Jallara's words were not lost on Undrei. The Cyclops dug with renewed vigor. He had never seen anyone of his race before, but he knew of their savage cruelty. To be called a Giant instead of a Cyclops was an honor. He soon had the entrance to the Long Dark Road cleared of debris.

Ilien peered at the narrow stairway carved into the earth. The shadows tilted and jumped as Globe moved in closer to light the way. Ilien wondered if Undrei would be able to squeeze through such a small opening. He remembered not too long ago, or so it seemed to him, when Anselm nearly got stuck in a stairway very similar to this one.

"Don't worry," said Undrei in response to Ilien's gaze. "I'll fit. No problem." At that, he dropped to his hands and knees and crawled down the stairs into the darkness below.

"Remember, Ilien," said Jallara. "When you reach Ledge Hall, there may be guards watching the entrance. After you dispatch them, wait one hour, then follow Undrei. You should meet no one on your way to the Great Hall. Once there—"

"Wait until the Onegod has been fully summoned before I strike," said Ilien, nodding.

The wizardess seemed about to say something more, but she turned to Kale. "If it was not for you, young Watcher, we would all still be doomed. Your courage and strength brought Ilien this far, which has given us hope. Your people will sing songs of you for generations to come."

"Yeah, yeah," mumbled Kale. "But I still have to wait for Ilien at the end of the tunnel." She stuck her tongue out at Ilien, smiled sweetly at Jallara, then followed Undrei down the stairs, her Breach leading the way.

Ilien motioned Globe to follow Kale. "Goodbye, Jallara," he said. Then catching a wondering look in the wizardess' eyes, he added, "In case something happens. If we don't make it out of there, I mean."

Jallara laid a hand on his shoulder. The darkness was heavy between them as Globe bobbed halfway down the stairs. Her eyes shined dully in the gloom. "I believe in you, Ilien Woodhill. I know who you are."

Ilien turned and followed Globe. He knew who he was, too. And he knew what he had to do.

Down below, Undrei stood wiping the dirt from his pants. Off to one side, Kale drew lines with the tip of his Breach in the thick layer of dust that covered the tunnel floor. The tunnel was huge. Built by the Giants, it stretched thirty feet wide and was high enough for Undrei to stand erect with room to spare. The tunnel was also old. Rubble littered the floor in several areas, debris from the crumbling walls and ceiling. Ilien hoped the way to Ledge Hall stood open. There had been pitfalls in the tunnel back when Ilien

221

first traveled it, nearly two thousand years ago. Things could only be worse now.

"I'll lead the way," said Ilien, dimming Globe so her light shone only at their feet. "Kale, I want you behind me. Undrei will bring up the rear." Ilien's voice echoed loudly around them. "And no talking. If there are guards up ahead, we don't want to warn them we're coming."

Undrei shuffled his booted feet. A stream of dust fell from the ceiling and snaked its way to the tunnel floor.

"And try to walk lightly," said Ilien, eyeing the Cyclops. Undrei squinted his one eye in apology.

They marched as quickly as they could along the sloping tunnel. The air lay thick with dust and it filled their mouths and nostrils. Several times they stopped to drink some water from a skin Undrei carried. Twice Ilien fell into a fit of coughing so severe that they huddled around him, hoping the noise didn't carry too far into the dark. Ilien kept a watchful eye on the ground, recalling all too well the hole he'd fallen into the last time he traveled the Long Dark Road. He remembered the monstrous snake, too, the Evil's servant, and how the Grovelstone had destroyed it. He suddenly wished he still had that magical yellow stone from the banks of the river Dorund, the river that flows through the land of the dead. It was the one thing the Evil had feared.

The tunnel sloped steadily upward as they made their way toward Ledge Hall. They had no way of knowing exactly when the tunnel would end. From the Map of the Crossings, Ilien determined they had to march perhaps ten miles. There the tunnel ended at a great set of stone doors. Through those doors was Ledge Hall and the Onegod. Through those doors he would find Windy and the Crossing that would take them back home.

"Stop," whispered Kale, as she grabbed Ilien by the arm.

She sniffed the air. "Don't you smell that?"

Undrei lifted his head. The holes he counted as nostrils flared open but his single eye looked doubtful.

Ilien wrinkled his nose. Perhaps his senses weren't as sharp as Kale's. Or perhaps his nostrils were too full of dust. He could smell nothing either, except the dank odor of ancient rock overgrown with centuries of black, slimy mold.

"I don't smell a thing," he said, pulling away from Kale's grasp. "Keep your voice down and follow me."

Ilien walked on, mindful now of any smells he might encounter, recalling the giant snake and its sour stench. Kale's face was pinched in disgust. Then Ilien smelled it, too. It was nothing like the sickly scent of the Evil's serpentine servant. The smell of rotting corpses drifted to them from ahead.

Ilien raised a hand, but the others had already stopped. He sent Globe out farther into the tunnel, but she illuminated nothing except more of the same—dust, rocks and crumbling walls. There was nothing to do but grab their noses and march on. Ilien brought Globe back to his side, dimmed her light even more, and led the way forward.

A hundred yards up the tunnel, the stench grew so sickening that Ilien stopped and gagged. Undrei shoved a meaty finger into each nostril. Kale held her Breach defensively before her.

Ilien brightened Globe and fell back at what he saw. The tunnel lay littered with the crumpled and rotting bodies of hundreds of Cyclops, all in various states of decay. The nearest were nothing but skeletal husks, withered piles of bones and ragged clothing that were once giant Cyclops. Others looked like cracking leathered hides draped over mounds of puffy, red flesh. Ilien stumbled forward, his hand over his mouth. The others followed, trying to avert their eyes from the horror around them. The worst corpses lay farther along the tunnel. These were freshly slain bodies, their bloody one-eyed faces staring blankly into the darkness.

Ilien began to run, all thought of caution gone. He had to escape the corridor of bodies. Kale and Undrei staggered close behind him. They raced through the tunnel, Globe lighting the way. Still the bodies rolled on in a horrific, vast carpet of flesh. They ran to escape the freshest kills, where caked blood pooled around corpses that looked as if they might stand up at any moment. Ilien wanted to close his eyes but couldn't for fear of tripping. He lurched on, leaping over bodies and praying for an end to the nightmare they had stumbled upon.

At last, the stench began to lessen. They could see no more bodies ahead of them. They had made it through the carnage, but they continued to run to put some distance between them and the open graveyard. Several minutes later, they stopped, panting and gagging in the small circle of Globe's reassuring light.

"Now we know what the Onegod does with his slain servants," Undrei uttered grimly.

Ilien clutched his pencil in his pocket. He wanted to turn and rain fire down the tunnel, incinerating all that lay behind them, but he knew he couldn't. Instead, he vowed to save his outrage. When he returned home, he knew who to let it out upon.

"How much farther?" asked Kale. She dug her Breach into the dirt, her swollen lips pursed in revulsion.

Ilien realized they had run far to escape the Onegod's gruesome burial chamber, and a sudden panic surged through him. He raised a finger to his lips and then pointed ahead of them. There, dimly lit by Globe's wavering light, they beheld the two stone doors to Ledge Hall.

Chapter XXIV

Windy

The doors were closed, which was both a blessing and a curse. It meant there were no guards to deal with, but it also meant they could not get into Ledge Hall. The doors opened only from within.

Ilien breathed a sigh of relief, then cursed. "Now what?" He remembered how Bulcrist had sealed the Swan into the tunnel of the Long Dark Road after his watchdogs had tried to kill her. These were the very doors Penelope had broken her wing trying to open.

Undrei examined the two stone slabs, testing them with his shoulder. "I think I can move them," he said. "Stand back."

The Cyclops threw himself forward like a battering ram. The force of the blow shook the dust from the surrounding walls. The doors groaned under the assault, but did not move. Undrei's craggy face twisted in pain with the strain of his effort. The muscles of his neck and shoulders bulged beneath his shirt and his eye moved wildly back and forth as he struggled to force open the doors. Finally they moved. By degrees the two stone slabs grated forward on unseen hinges. The battle was fought an inch at a time, yet Undrei never stopped. His thick, bandy legs claimed first one step, then another, as he marched the doors ajar. Beyond, they saw nothing but blackness, split down its center by the growing shaft of Globe's luminescence.

225

The Cyclops fell to his knees, spent of all strength, but the doors stood open before him. He had gained them access to the cellars of Ledge Hall.

Ilien sensed a whisper of movement from within and heard the faint clink of metal. Kale froze, her misshapen face taut with fear. With a trembling hand, Ilien drew his Light rune. The room beyond jumped with magical light. Kale gasped and fell back, her Breach like stone in her grasp. Undrei staggered to his feet. Past the double stone doors, a dozen Cyclops crouched ready to attack, their swords unsheathed. In their midst stood an old man in grey robes.

Kale sprang forward. "The Onegod has found us! Behind me, Ilien!"

"Father!" shouted Ilien. "Father! No!"

The Onegod raised Gallund's silver wand and the Cyclops charged.

Ilien drew the Fire rune. "Illubid!" he cried. "Illubid ador!"

The room erupted in flames, engulfing all but the closest attackers in a torrent of blue-green fire. Three Cyclops crashed into Undrei, knocking him from his feet as the remaining Cyclops fell writhing to the floor in the center of the inferno. The Onegod stood unfazed.

Ilien drew forth his pencil. "Propel!" he shouted, leveling it at Gallund. The force of his spell knocked the Onegod back farther into the room.

"Behind me!" screamed Kale. She held her Breach before her as the three remaining Cyclops wrestled Undrei to the ground. One drew its sword and raised it to strike, intent of beheading Undrei where he kneeled.

"Propel!" shouted Ilien once more.

The Cyclops' sword flew from its grasp and clattered against the wall. Kale moved quickly to stop the Cyclops from retrieving it but the Cyclops rushed her, brawny arms swinging wildly. A vicious blow struck the tip of Kale's Breach and knocked it aside. With a snap of her wrists, Kale brought her Breach around again, blocking her attacker's advance. The Cyclops rained a flurry of crushing blows, but none found its mark. Impenetrable as a stone, Kale held the monster at bay.

Undrei drove to his feet, battering his two opponents aside. Seizing one by the shoulders, he smashed its head against the wall and knocked it unconscious. As he spun on the other, a sword sliced through the air in front of him. He stepped back, blood seeping through his shirt. His opponent rushed him and he fell to one knee, grasped the Cyclops by the arm and flung it off its feet. When the Cyclops leaped up, it found its sword had been pirated. With a lightning blow, Undrei severed its head from its neck.

Unable to reach Kale, the last Cyclops turned and rushed at Ilien. Overwhelmed, Ilien stumbled to the floor. Undrei lunged to his aid but the Cyclops swept past him, fist raised, determined to crush the life from its enemy. Ilien lifted his pencil—too late. He rolled to escape the onslaught as the Cyclops drove its fist down like a hammer.

The fist never struck. The Cyclops fell forward with a cry, stumbled over Ilien and crashed to the floor unconscious. Ilien clambered unsteadily to his feet. A crimson stream coursed from the Cyclops' head. Kale's Breach lay beside it, covered in blood.

Ilien rushed over to her crumpled form. "Kale, no!"

Beyond the stone doors, the roiling flames vanished and the old man raced out, trailing a column of smoke. His sunken, grey face, the face of Gallund, was twisted with hatred. Eyes black as coal bored into Ilien's. Ilien fell back, blinded, as the Onegod screamed forth his spell.

"Balaka borgatum!"

Undrei leaped forward. He seized the Onegod's outstretched hand, heaved him off his feet, and swung him into the wall with a sickening crunch. The Onegod's wand blasted forth a volley of black missiles and Undrei shuddered and fell to his knees. Black bolts of power lanced through his body and issued from his back, hammering into the ceiling above. With a final effort, Undrei reared up and bludgeoned his fist into the Onegod's forehead. The outpouring of missiles stopped. The old man lay still. For a moment Undrei stared at him in triumph, then collapsed with a cry.

The tunnel grew quiet as Ilien hovered over Kale. The carnage of shattered bodies and fallen friends lay around him. Undrei was dead, Kale mortally wounded, a wicked gash across the side of her head. Though a vessel of the Onegod, Gallund, too, was gone. Their plan had failed. The Onegod had known they were coming from the start. Now he knew Ilien was there, alone and defeated, and he would send reenforcements. More Cyclops would come.

"Restori somana, restori siruz."

Ilien's voice sounded frail as he incanted the Healing spell. He touched the lumps on Kale's forehead and stroked her malformed face. The magic began to work. The open wound on the side of her head began to close. The bruising that had spread to her temple faded and Kale gasped in air. In Globe's pale light, Ilien could plainly see the pretty girl that hid beneath the hunched face and crooked eyes. She was beautiful, or would have been if this world and its Onegod had never existed. He saw past the runted head and swollen lips, the cat-like teeth that showed when she grinned. Ilien bent and kissed her gently on the forehead. He knew what he had to do, and he had to do it quickly. He had to free Windy and get to the Crossing. The element of surprise was gone.

The Onegod knew exactly where he was and where he would go. There was no time to lose.

With Globe in the lead, Ilien raced through the doors. The room beyond lay littered with burned and smoking Cyclops. He ran to the stairs at the room's far end. Leaping them two at a time, he left the grisly slaughter behind.

Up he climbed, wishing he had Manna to quicken his steps. The heavy air began to lighten as the sickly smell of the smoke from below faded. The stone stairs beneath his feet grew smoother, and just when Ilien believed he could climb no farther, the stairs stopped at a polished stone landing. Double doors stood before him, intricately carved with runes.

He crashed through the doors and stumbled into a hallway with smooth, polished walls hung with ornate drapery and oil paintings. Ledge Hall proper, as Bulcrist had called it. Ilien knew where to go. He sprinted to his left.

At the far end of the hall, a Cyclops block his way. With a word, Ilien sent torrents of blue-green flames racing ahead. The Cyclops fell amidst the fiery onslaught. Ilien leaped the smoking body without slowing, charged up another set of stairs and burst through double doors. The corridor here was wide, with doors along its length on either side. Two more Cyclops blocked his way.

"Illubid ador!" he shouted, raising his pencil. Flames jettisoned along the length of the corridor, struck the floor before the Cyclops and blasted them off their feet. Ilien ran past their lifeless forms.

The hallway branched left. Ilien counted three more door on his right, stopped, and looked back at the empty hallway. This was it. The door to Windy's room. He turned the knob, but it was locked.

"Propel." The door shuddered. The lock broke asunder

and Ilien burst into the room.

Windy was gone.

Chained to the far wall, Rose lay curled upon the floor. Ilien ran to her. He shattered her chains with his spell and rolled her gently onto her back. The inner wounds she had sustained back at the stonehall remained. She was unresponsive, her breathing shallow. Ilien drew the Healing rune and whispered, "Restori somana, restori siruz."

Rose stirred as color flushed back into her cheeks. Ilien repeated the Healing spell and guided more runes to her body. She coughed and took a deep breath. Her eyes fluttered open and she gazed blankly at Ilien.

"Rose," he said. "Wake up." He drew one last rune and let it melt into Rose's forehead. "Windy," he said. "Where is she? Have you seen her? The girl I crossed with. Have you seen her?"

"Ilien," whispered Rose. "It's you."

Ilien laid a hand on her arm. "Don't worry. Kale's safe."

Rose blinked and a tear rolled down her face. "Ilien. It's you," she said. "I thought about you all the time. I waited for you and you came at last."

Ilien stroked her hair. "Yes, we came for you. Everything will be alright." He looked to the door. There wasn't much time. Windy had to be in another room.

"I'm right here," said Rose. "I'm right here, Ilien."

Ilien stood. "You're alright now," he said. "I have to find Windy, then everything will be alright." He strode to the door.

"Ilien. It's me."

Ilien froze. Behind him, Rose whispered, "It's me, Ilien. It's me, Windy."

Ilien felt the strength leave his legs. He turned, his mind reeling. What did she say?

"It's me," Rose said weakly, tears streaming down her face. "It's me, Ilien."

It was impossible. Ilien stood frozen, staring at the woman before him.

Rose tried to sit up, but couldn't. "The crystal," she said. "The crystal that shined like a Rose. I left it for you in the stonehall. It's really me, Ilien."

Ilien studied Rose carefully. The wavy brown hair. The high cheek bones. He peered at her ragged clothing. The green tunic she wore was worn and faded, frayed from years of use. Like him, Rose had crossed here from another world. Like him, she had been seeking help from the wizardesses. But that was thirty years ago.

Rose blinked away tears. "Gallund told me not to fight its pull," she said. "He told me, but something happened. Someone surprised us and I resisted. I crossed. Only, I arrived here thirty years before you, Ilien. Thirty years."

She curled into a ball and began to weep again. "Oh, Ilien. I waited so long," she sobbed.

Ilien knelt beside her. "Is it really you?" He pulled back the long hair from her face. She gazed up at him, and he knew then that it was Windy. He hugged her fiercely, his mind turning in circles.

"I can't believe it!" He straightened suddenly, his heart threatening to explode in his chest. "We have to leave. There is a Crossing. You must come with me! There's no time to lose!"

Ilien leaped to his feet and tried to help her up.

Rose pulled from his grasp. "I can't go, Ilien."

"You have to. It's the only way." Ilien reached for her. "Don't you see, if we go back to the beginning we can set everything right again. It'll be like none of this ever happened."

"No, Ilien. If you go back you'll be young. If I go back—"

"It doesn't matter," said Ilien. "You can't stay here. I won't leave you behind!"

Windy's face grew calm. She let out a breath and pulled Ilien close. "Magic cannot heal what ails me. Only you can."

Ilien looked toward the open door. He heard the sound of boots outside.

"Go back," said Windy. "Go back and stop me from crossing."

Ilien grabbed her hand. "No, Windy. Come with me." He didn't have the heart to tell her that he couldn't stop her from crossing, that if he tried, he would die.

"Please, Ilien. It's my only hope."

A Cyclops burst through the doorway, followed by three others. Windy raised her hand. In it she held her broken shackles.

"Propel," she whispered.

The lead Cyclops fell dead to the floor, the shackles embedded in its skull. With a fierce word, Ilien incinerated the others where they stood. He turned back to Windy. Rancid smoke billowed around the two of them.

"Go," she said, turning her tear-streaked face from his. "Go back and stop me from crossing. Stop me from living this life."

Shouts issued from the hall outside. Boots pounded on the stone floor. Ilien clenched his fists, then stooped and hugged Windy once more. A part of him seemed to drain away as he pulled reluctantly away from her. He realized it was his heart. "I love you."

He ran from the room streaming tears and fire in his anguish. He filled the halls with flames, shattering every door to pieces in his rage. Tapestries and wall paintings ignited.

Cyclops ran screaming before him, clothes ablaze, swords flying from their flailing hands. Still Ilien poured forth his destruction as blackness filled him. Nothing would stop him from reaching the Crossing. Nothing.

When Ilien reached the door to the great, gem-encrusted Hall, his eyes were as dark as night. With a nudge of his pencil the double doors exploded into the room beyond, filling the air with deadly splinters. Ilien waded through the wreckage and into the Great Hall with Globe dancing madly above him.

"Revel bevel metor annoy!" The echo of his incantation boomed like thunder in the Hall. Globe raced to the center of the room where a circular, black hole began to grow. The Crossing spread quickly like an open hand of darkness, blotting out everything it touched. Ilien strode forward, his pencil raised high. "Pentar, Entar, Figaru, Pari!"

Sudden motion spun Ilien about. A tall figure bore down upon him and an explosion of pain tore through his body, obliterating his rage. He fell to his knees, raw, exposed, wracked by an agony far greater than even the Desecration's savage assault. He clutched his pencil and tried to fight it, strove to repel the power that so quickly had overwhelmed him. His pencil screamed and writhed in his palm. His vision began to recede. The world filled with night as his senses began to leave him. He toppled to the floor and lay gasping before his attacker.

"You should have killed me when you had the chance," said the figure before him.

The coursing pain withdrew. Fear cleared Ilien's wits and he propped himself painfully up. He knew the silky voice, recognized the long cloak and streaming black hair.

"You are not Tannon Bulcrist," he said through clenched teeth.

Globe streaked toward Bulcrist, burning like a dazzling sun. Bulcrist raised a hand. She vanished before he could cast his spell, and he smiled in the darkness. "Charming little toy you have," he said. "Quite charming."

Ilien drew the light Rune and the chamber jumped with bright light.

"You are nothing!" he shouted. "You have no form so you take the form of others. You are not Tannon Bulcrist!"

Bulcrist strode toward Ilien, his amusement gone. His long legs were clothed in tight-fitting black pants, and his feet were shod in heavy black boots. His streaming black hair, now dirty and matted, framed a mummified face that bore little resemblance to the once handsome NiDemon.

"You will call me Onegod!" he shouted, his taut face filled with hatred. "For that is what I am!" Bulcrist's head jerked up as he suddenly gazed past Ilien.

Ilien slowly stood. He felt the presence of the Crossing behind him, tugging at his mind. Bulcrist's black eyes grew wide as he studied the open portal, adding deep shadows to his sunken cheeks.

"So that is what you came for," he said, pinning Ilien with a blinding glare. "I thought you sought the girl, but you looked for your own escape instead. How weak of you. How pitiful. And they call you the Creator."

Ilien forced himself to meet Bulcrist's gaze, even as his sight was leeched away. "I came here to destroy you," he said. "Now I know that destroying Evil is impossible."

Bulcrist's eyes narrowed, his parchment skin cracking at the corners. Ilien felt his sight slowly returning. "It is true," said the Onegod. No one can destroy me. Not the Creator. Not some little boy who thinks he is being profound. I am more powerful than both of you. It is I who made you who you are. It is I who chose who you would become. My designs have prevailed from the start. It is I who am the Creator. You are the Nothing."

"No one gets to choose for another," said Ilien. "Choice is all one truly has. You are only a choice, nothing more."

Bulcrist advanced on Ilien. The blackness beneath his eyes writhed and twisted like roiling smoke. Ilien held his ground and Bulcrist stopped. "You cannot hurt me," said Ilien. "I choose to let you be."

Bulcrist quivered with rage. "Then you choose death. If you will not destroy me then you will be destroyed!" He backhanded Ilien across the face and Ilien tumbled to the floor, clutching the bright welt the bony hand left. "As before, your choices go awry, little boy."

Bulcrist raised his hands and shadows gathered to his palms. The shadows spread down his skeletal arms and swept through his body, cloaking him in utter darkness. He loomed over Ilien like a pillar of night.

"You are more foolish than I had hoped. All that you have created, all you have cherished, you have abandoned. Your favored Nomadin were left alone to fulfill your vision, and see how they have repaid you. Your precious Laws rule over nothing. Even as a mortal, you deserted this world and its people, left them when they needed you most. Now they call you Necromancer. You speak of choice when the only thing you have ever chosen is failure."

Ilien cowered before the Onegod, but in his heart a flame of anger sprang forth.

"I am still here!" he shouted, pointing his pencil at the Onegod's chest. "After all of your plans, after all you have done to stop me, I am still here! You are the one who has failed!"

The Onegod's black form swelled larger. "I will soon remedy that!" A black bolt of power sprang from his hands.

It struck Ilien's pencil and clove it in two, cutting short its scream of terror and pain.

"No!" cried Ilien, clutching what remained of his wand in a bloody hand. A torrent of silver light gushed from the broken wand and blasted into the ceiling. Great chunks of stone came crashing down from above, shattering on the floor behind the Onegod. A cloud of dust filled the Hall and Ilien leaped to his feet. The open maw of the Crossing hovered before him. He reached it in a single bound and jumped into the blackness.

Chapter XXV

The Onegod

Ilien fell through the emptiness like a stone through the abyss. A biting cold smote the air from his lungs. His body throbbed with pain as he flew through the void, and his mind filled with a swarm of bright lights as he fought to remain conscious. Just before he succumbed to the deadly blackness, he tumbled into light and spilled headlong onto a polished stone floor.

He gasped for breath and rolled to his side. Gleaming walls of fiery carnelian rose to a high-arched ceiling of blue and white jasper. The unearthly light from a Nihilic spell lit the air. He was still in the great, gem encrusted main room of Ledge Hall, but he was not alone. Bulcrist stood before him, flanked by a company of old men. Ilien scrambled away from him, then saw that his face was smooth and lean, his hair long and flowing. He was back at the beginning. This was not the Onegod. Not yet. The NiDemon's dark eyes clouded with sudden fear and he stepped back as if bitten. The old men held their ground, their wands pointed menacingly at Ilien.

"It's the boy!" cried Bulcrist. "He's come to destroy you!"

A murmur passed through the old men. Some held their wands at their side. Others exchanged quick glances. Their faces were grim, not sunken, their eyes shaded with wariness not shadowed with Evil. They were the Nomadin, not

237

servants of the Onegod. Ilien climbed to his feet, stashing the broken remnants of his pencil in his pocket.

"What are you waiting for?" shouted Bulcrist. His eyes grew black and his face livid. "Strike him! Strike him now!"

"You are not yourself, Bulcrist," said Ilien as he stood before the NiDemon. "But neither are you Evil yet."

Bulcrist's hands knotted to fists. "You would have the world think you are the savior when it is you who will be its undoing!"

Ilien took a step forward and Bulcrist gave way before him "I know your plans. I have seen the world you long to create. You called the Nomadin here to test them. When they pass your test, you will bide your time and stoke the flames of war for your own gain. You are a shadow, veiling the eyes of the Nomadin and men alike. But a shadow is all you are."

In unison the Nomadin turned to Bulcrist. A wizened old man clad in crimson robes emerged from the throng. He held a long blue wand.

"What trickery is this, Bulcrist? You show us powers the like we have not seen. You proclaim yourself the forbidden Nomadin child, the Creator reborn, yet you stand in fear of this boy?"

"I *am* the Creator reborn!" exclaimed Bulcrist. "Do you doubt my abilities, Inisad? Have you not seen what I can do? Did I not tell you that the Evil which divided the Nomadin lives on? Do not be fooled by appearances, by those who are not what they seem. The boy has come to kill you before you realize the truth! He is the Evil of old. He must be destroyed!"

"If you were truly the Creator," said Ilien, "you would know that Evil cannot be destroyed."

"Yes!" said Inisad, pointing his blue wand at Bulcrist. "The boy is right. To destroy Evil is to create more of it."

The other Nomadin nodded and muttered their assent. "You would know that if you were the Creator."

Bulcrist glared at Ilien, but Ilien did not look away. "Evil is a choice, nothing more," said Ilien. "It is not too late to choose, Tannon Bulcrist."

The great Hall filled with silence. Bulcrist's face flushed the color of Inisad's robes. His knuckles flashed white at his side. The blackness behind his eyes withdrew and his shoulders slumped forward. He sank to his knees before the Nomadin as a tremor passed through him.

"What's happening to me?"

The Great Hall dimmed and the Nomadin pressed forward, gathering around Bulcrist, their wands at the ready. Ilien felt a numbing chill on the back of his neck. A sudden dread swept through him. He turned to the still-open Crossing behind him. In its black opening, darker than the surrounding void, the Onegod emerged.

"It's an ambush!" cried Inisad.

Ilien staggered back, reaching instinctively for his pencil. Ambush at the Crossing! This was the ambush Gallund had warned him about! This was the Crossing where he would die!

Like a stroke of black lightning, the Onegod's dark shape streaked through the air and hurtled into Bulcrist's prone form. The NiDemon sprung upright like a snare. His arms flew out and his head snapped back as the shadow of the Onegod coursed into him like a vile wine filling a goblet.

The Nomadin attacked as one, their wands pouring fire from all directions upon Bulcrist's tortured form. Flames engulfed the NiDemon in a raging conflagration of emerald green magic. Within the tumult, Bulcrist stood tall. He lifted his arms and biting laughter rose above the din of fire and flame. He turned upon the Nomadin, unfazed by their assault.

"I am more powerful than ever!"

In desperation, the Nomadin intensified the onslaught, their wands blasting forth torrents of multicolored energy that crawled up the walls and laid waste to the ceiling above. Ilien waded forward. "Stop! This is what he wants! You cannot destroy him!"

An explosion of molten night blasted the Nomadin off their feet and shattered their enveloping flames, snuffing their kaleidoscope of magic and leaving swirling black smoke in its place. The Onegod turned on Ilien, blinding him with his leering gaze.

"You die here! You will never become the Creator! Never!"

Ilien raised the stump of his wand and deflected the barrage of writhing black energy that streaked from Bulcrist's hand. The force of the blow staggered him backward and punched the air from his lungs. His ears rang loudly and he tasted blood in his mouth. The Onegod was too powerful. Ilien knew he wouldn't survive the next assault. Half blind, he turned and fled. Behind him, the Nomadin regained their feet. The Onegod turned to deal with them, momentarily forgetting about Ilien. The door at the far end of the Hall stood ajar. Ilien bounded down the stairs toward the cellars of Ledge Hall.

The air grew quickly colder as he hurtled down the wide stone stairway, staggering at each broad landing, his broken pencil held white-knuckled in his hand. His footfalls boomed around him, reverberating in the dank and musty air. He didn't know if the Onegod was following. All he knew was that he had to get out. He was overmatched. The Onegod's power was too overwhelming. If the combined might of the Nomadin was not enough to stop him, then what could he do? Creator or not, he was just a boy. The Swan had foreseen his failure. Gallund had warned him not to return. His only hope was to flee before he proved the book correct.

A bright green flash lit the stairs above and a thunderclap shattered the air, sending Ilien crashing to the floor. Rocks and debris rained down, followed by shouts, a stab of emerald light and a chorus of boots upon the stairs. Ilien regained his feet. A blast of black plasma brittled the stone wall behind him. He leaped down the stairs as another rifled past him. The Onegod cursed from above.

"Illubid!" cried Ilien, as he reached the final landing. A flame jumped to life above his head. This was the lowest level of Ledge Hall, abandoned and unused, carved from the bedrock of the mountains and littered with debris and refuse. It wasn't far to the ancient entrance hall and the great golden doors that led outside.

He pushed through the doors before him. The room beyond was cavernous and his spell did little to light the way. He stumbled on a rock and spilled to the floor. The room filled with bright, yellow light as Globe sprang to life beside him.

"Hurry!" she cried. "He's coming!" She raced across the room and Ilien chased after her.

Left and right, forward then left again, Globe led the way through the rubble-strewn rooms. The boom of closing doors resounded behind him in the blackness. Distant shouts followed. They put on a burst of speed and crashed through a set of double doors.

"This is it!" said Ilien. "The entrance hall!" A large stone door stood ajar to their right where the trickling of water could be heard. At the far end of the hall, the massive double doors that led outside, carved of golden marrow from the trees of the Drowsy Wood, stood closed. "Come on!"

Halfway across the room, Globe disappeared. Ilien's foot

struck a stone and he tumbled in the dark, scuffing the skin from both his hands and striking his head violently on the stone floor. Bright specks flocked and swarmed before his eyes. Howling laughter filled the air and a door boomed shut in the blackness behind him.

"Going somewhere?" The Onegod's disembodied voice reverberated in the dark, coming from every direction at once. Ilien moaned and rolled to his side, nursing his wounded head. "You can run from me no longer," said the Onegod. "I will finish what I could not in the tunnels of the Long Dark Road. I will destroy you and then I will be the Creator. I will remake everything as it should be, as it should have been."

"I've seen the world of your making," said Ilien as his head cleared, the biting pain in his skull turning to a dull throb. He struggled to his knees, one hand raised before his eyes, the other clutching his shattered pencil. Though the darkness was absolute, he could still feel the blinding power of the Onegod towering over him. "You created nothing but pain and suffering."

"Pain and suffering are creations, nonetheless," said the Onegod. "Just as I was created by you, so they are created by me."

Ilien climbed to his feet. "You are wrong. Evil is not a creation. It is a choice. You are a choice."

A clamor of muffled shouts startled Ilien. The Nomadin pounded on the doors to the room, unable to breach the Sealing spell the Onegod had placed upon them.

"It is a choice many have chosen," said the Onegod.

Ilien sensed the Evil drawing nearer, preparing for a final strike. "The only true creation is choice," said Ilien, standing his ground. "Without the freedom to choose, there is only destruction. The true Creator knows this."

"I grow weary of this," said the Onegod, raising his hands above his head.

Ilien fell back to his knees and raised his lifeless pencil, intent on deflecting the barrage of black power that would come at any moment. Suddenly, an image of Bulcrist kneeling before him flashed through his mind. He saw Bulcrist cowering in the scorched grass outside the exit to the Long Dark Road.

You will return to Ledge Hall and live out the rest of your days alone.

Ilien knew then what he had to do.

The room suddenly exploded with bright, yellow light, blinding Ilien as thoroughly as the Evil presence before him. Globe shined like a blazing sun between the Onegod and Ilien. She swelled with power, burning with a blue-white radiance, then burst apart in a cloud of shimmering silver dust. Ilien gasped. In her place stood the glowing form of a slender, young woman. Her flowing silver robes rippled with an inner light, and her long gilded wand burned with golden magic. With a wave of her hand, the doors at either end of the room crashed open. Early morning sunlight streamed in through the wide golden doors behind Ilien, and the Nomadin surged into the room behind the Onegod.

"Flee, Ilien!" cried the woman in a voice that sounded like Globe's.

The Onegod shrieked in fury, striking the slender woman who stood in his way with soaring fists of jet black power. The Stygian magic punched through the woman's defenses, and she cried out in pain. Behind the Onegod, the Nomadin poured forth what magic they had left, bludgeoning his exposed back with bolts of green and gold sorcery that turned aside like arrows on stone.

Ilien stood frozen. Behind him, the doors to freedom and

243

escape lay open. He could flee, but how far would he get? Before him, the Nomadin, and the woman who had been Globe, fought uselessly against an Evil that could not be destroyed. The Nomadin, that group of old men who had made his life a living nightmare, and the woman—the woman who had been Globe, but who Ilien now knew had been none other than Gilindilin all along.

Gilindilin. His Nomadin mother.

"Stop," he said, softly, nearly choking on the word in the twin realizations that not only had Gilindilin been with him all the while, but now she was going to die before he would ever get to know her. His mother, the old men and himself, would all soon be dead. The Onegod would turn Nadae into the world Kale had lived in, would live in still, only sooner than later.

"Stop," he said again, no louder than before. He walked forward, and no one heeded him. Gilindilin had encased herself in a waning cocoon of golden magic that deflected the Onegod's relentless attacks, spraying onyx bolts of magic about the room like deadly arrows. The Nomadin were all but spent as they clustered in a tight knot looking frantic and fearful. The Onegod stood locked in his rage, releasing his magical torrent upon Gilindilin, not noticing that Ilien approached, the stub of a pencil held loosely at his side.

Ilien reached out and touched the Onegod's arm. A spell whispered through Ilien's mind, a single word, and he felt the Onegod's power intensify. "Stop," he said, and fell to his knees before Bulcrist. "Please. Stop."

The Onegod ceased his attack and looked at Ilien quizzically. The golden shield that protected Gilindilin disappeared, and she fell to the floor, spent. She looked up weakly, trying in vain to raise her wand.

The Onegod smiled Bulcrist's oily smile. "You wish for

mercy," he said, staring down at Ilien, "but I am not merciful."

Ilien released Bulcrist's arm and bowed his head, laying his broken wand at the Onegod's feet. "Not mercy," he said. "A choice."

"What are you doing?" cried Gilindilin. "He'll kill you!"

"He is the Creator," said Ilien. "He can kill me whenever he chooses. I wish only to make a choice before I die."

"So you admit it," said the Onegod, a burgeoning smile crossing Bulcrist's face. "You admit I am the Creator!"

"Yes," answered Ilien. "You are the Creator."

"And you are the Nothing," said the Onegod.

Ilien lowered his head, placing his hands on Bulcrist's boots. Gilindilin's wand dropped from her grasp. The Nomadin seemed to deflate behind the Onegod.

"I am the Nothing," said Ilien. "You are the Creator."

Bulcrist was so pleased by Ilien's words that he laughed. "You said I created nothing." He chuckled at the implication. "What else did you say? The only true creation is choice?"

Ilien looked up and peered into the Onegod's blinding gaze. "Yes. The true Creator knows this. A choice before you destroy me, that's all I ask."

Bulcrist glanced behind him at the huddled Nomadin as he weighed Ilien's words. "Very well," he said. "I suppose you wish to choose how you will die."

"No," said Ilien. "Not how, but where."

The Onegod looked confused, and Ilien could see that his confusion was quickly changing to impatience.

"Not in front of my mother," Ilien said, hurriedly. "Outside. I wish to die outside. That is my choice."

Gilindilin cried out but Ilien stilled her with a weighted glance. "The true Creator knows that choice is the most precious of all creations."

The Onegod studied Ilien, as if trying to determine the true meaning behind his words. "So be it. You will die outside. What does it matter as long as you are dead just the same."

Ilien climbed slowly to his feet.

"Tut, tut," said the Onegod, raising a long finger. "You won't be needing that, even if it is worthless." He kicked Ilien's ruined pencil away. It skidded across the stone floor and landed in a pile of rubble. "Lead the way, Ilien Woodhill."

Ilien gave one last look at the Nomadin, who stared back at him in shocked confusion. Gilindilin remained motionless, glowing faintly as if she might at any moment morph back into Globe. Without a word, he moved toward the open doors and the sunshine outside.

"I will kill you slowly," the Onegod said under Bulcrist's breath. "There is a high price to pay for choice."

Ilien saw the river through the open golden doors. Early morning sunlight dappled its surface and lit the rocky landscape in shades of grey and yellow. "That's what makes it so precious," he whispered.

When Ilien reached the doors, he stopped. To either side of the entrance, carved from the hard rock of the cliff, rose two massive pillars intricately etched from top to bottom with a spiraling design that shimmered in the slanting sun. Broad stairs led down to the river's edge. He breathed in the clean air that came off the river. The roar of the tumbling water sounded like the never ending rumble of distant thunder. The warm morning sun soaked into his skin, chilled from the damp confines of lower Ledge Hall.

"Move!" said the Onegod, and he pushed Ilien forward. Ilien's foot caught on the stone and he tumbled down the stairs, bouncing off each step until he lay staring up at the

Onegod from the bottom—staring up and smiling.

"You are as clumsy as you are witless," barked the Onegod from the top of the stairs. Bulcrist's black robes fluttered in a gust of wind that attempted to enter Ledge Hall, and the Onegod straightened them impatiently. "It's time to pay for your precious choice."

Ilien tensed as the Onegod stepped out upon the stairs. Bulcrist's boots rang on the stone as he descended them one by one. His face was smeared with contempt as he raised his hands above his head. Ilien's heart raced. How could it be? How could he have been wrong? He had been so certain.

Halfway down the stairs, the Onegod stopped. The hatred drained from his face, leaving it pale and drawn. His black eyes flew wide with surprise as he dropped his hands to his side and clutched at the air. Something was wrong.

Ilien rose to his feet, his cheeks hot and itchy, his own hands bony fists at his sides. He was right after all. "I warned you, Tannon Bulcrist. You were to return to Ledge Hall and never set foot outside its gates again."

The Onegod's panicked face turned defiant, and he raised his arms once more. But no magic came. A shimmering rune, a red phantom against the black of Bulcrist's robes, grew visible in the center of the Onegod's chest. It was the rune Ilien had placed on Bulcrist as he knelt in the scorched grass outside the exit to the Long Dark Road.

"If ever you set foot outside its gates, the rune I placed upon you will strike you dead," said Ilien, stepping forward.

The Onegod reached for the rune as if to pull it off him. He tore his robes to pieces in a frenzy of panic and terror. Soon, he stood naked and shivering with pain before Ilien, the burning red rune like a brand upon his chest.

"You cannot destroy Evil," groaned the Onegod through Bulcrist's shiny white teeth.

NECROMANCER

"I did not destroy you," said Ilien, his face solemn. "I gave you a choice. You chose wrong."

The Onegod turned to flee up the stairs, but Gilindilin and the Nomadin issued from the golden doors and stood squinting in astonishment at the sight before them. He turned back to Ilien, his face a livid pool of terror and pain. The crimson rune on his chest looked like bloody claw marks.

"You will never destroy all of me!" shouted the Onegod. He clutched at Bulcrist's head, eyes bulging as if something wanted desperately to escape his skull through his eye sockets. He doubled over, screeched in agony, then fell upon the stairs. Like a slithering snake, Bulcrist's body slid limply down the steps, coming to a rest in front of Ilien.

Ilien jumped back, fearful of the shadow that would rise from the Onegod's slain shell. Bulcrist lay still. The dark spirit of the Onegod did not appear. The Summon spell had worked. The Evil was gone, not entirely gone, but gone from Nadae.

"Ilien!" cried Gilindilin. She rushed down the stairs, her silver robes trailing out behind her. As if unsatisfied with her own mortal speed, she morphed into Globe and streaked to Ilien like a small shooting star. She stopped before him, radiating brightly. Ilien cupped both hands beneath her.

"Mother?"

All at once, Globe burst into Gilindilin again and she stood hesitantly before him. "Yes. It's me, Ilien."

Ilien peered at her doubtfully. Her silver eyes shined brightly, shimmering in the sunlight like twin, iridescent Globes.

"But how?" he asked.

"I've been with you from the beginning," she said. "I never could bring myself to leave you."

"Globe?"

Gilindilin laughed. "Do you know how much I hated being called that these past few months?" She reached out and placed her hand on Ilien's shoulder. Her face softened as she peered at him expectantly.

Ilien thought back to the night he first conjured that pesky little globe of light, back when he was just a normal boy from a normal town in a normal time. He recalled how she had a mind of her own and followed him downstairs after he told her to fade. Only after Gallund had pointed his wand at her did she obey.

"Gallund knew all along," he said.

"Yes." Gilindilin laughed again. "I couldn't stop myself from irritating him any opportunity I could. He's so easy to irritate."

Her hand still rested on his shoulder, and Ilien reached out and hugged her. When he pulled away, Gilindilin held him at arms length.

"You have grown, Ilien. You have changed. You know who you are now, don't you?"

Ilien nodded, then glanced behind her. The Nomadin filed down the stairs toward them. Ilien regarded the old men solemnly, his face forbidding. "My birth mother," he said, pulling away from Gilindilin. "Where is she? Where have you taken her?"

Inisad, the Nomadin leader, spoke up, his voice full of caution, his eyes respectful. "She is gone."

"Gone!" Ilien stepped forward angrily, but Gilindilin stopped him.

"Yes," said Inisad, looking back at his Nomadin brethren. "We took her south. Please understand, we treated her well." He swallowed as he searched for his words. Ilien realized that the Nomadin were afraid of him. "One moment she was standing beside me and the next she was gone."

"I don't believe you!" said Ilien, struggling to free himself from Gilindilin's grip. The wizardess held him tight.

"It's true," she said.

Ilien didn't hear her at first, but then stepped back in confusion. "How do you know it's true? You couldn't possibly know. Unless—"

Gilindilin smiled coyly. "Like I said, I never could bring myself to leave you."

Ilien studied her, looking for signs that what she was implying was true. "You can't be her. The Swan said I was twice-born. She said—"

"Twice born you were, Ilien," said Gilindilin. "By me."

Ilien's jaw dropped open.

Gilindilin squeezed Ilien's hand. "I couldn't bear the thought of someone else raising you. So I disguised myself with magic, and—" She pulled the golden wand from beneath her silver robes and held it above her head.

Ilien's eyes widened as Gilindilin slowly changed into his mother—his mother back in Southford.

His birth mother.

Ilien nearly fainted. Gilindilin gathered him into her arms. "I've missed you, Ilien. Though I've always been with you, I've missed you so much."

Ilien fell into her embrace, his heart beating wildly. His mom was safe. "Mommy," he whispered, suddenly the little boy he always desperately wished he could be.

Reality crashed back upon him. The little boy would have to wait. "Windy!" he cried, holding his mother at arm's length. "The Crossing! I have to stop her from crossing!"

His mind reeled with the impossibility of it. The Crossing lay in the Damp Oaks. It was too far away to ever get there in time. He looked in panic at the sun, still low in the sky, but climbing. It was not yet mid-morning. Back in the Damp Oaks, he and Windy would still be preparing for their journey. They hadn't yet Crossed. But they soon would. He would never get there in time. Windy would cross and spend thirty years in that godforsaken land waiting for him. She would die.

"Windy," he whispered, hanging his head. "I'm sorry."

"Look!" cried Inisad, pointing to the sky.

Ilien knuckled the tears from his eyes. A lone cloud hung in the pale morning sky. But this cloud didn't just hover there as it should have.

"Pedustil!" cried Ilien. "Pedustil! You've come!"

The sound of a steam engine crashing off its tracks split the air and the Gorgul landed beside the river, kicking up rocks and debris. Ilien rushed into the rising dust cloud where Pedustil sat flicking his tail back and forth in agitation.

"I heard you call me," said the Gorgul, eyeing the Nomadin on the steps and baring his icy fangs. "I heard you in my mind."

Ilien threw his arms around the Gorgul's long reptilian neck, glad his old friend was no longer the size of a small mountain. "Fly me to the Damp Oaks! We have to stop Windy from crossing!"

The Gorgul stepped toward the Nomadin, who clamored back on the stairs like a flock of frightened geese. "I heard you in my mind," he growled. "But how can you be here when I just left you in the forest?"

"Never mind that!" shouted Ilien, as he climbed aboard the Gorgul. "There's no time to explain. Fly!"

Pedustil shot a jet of steam at the retreating old men, then turned to leave.

"Wait!" shouted Ilien. He faced the Nomadin, raised his hand and shouted, "Propel!"

The Nomadin fell back, raising their arms above their heads. From between the great, golden doors there came a swiftly flying object that streaked toward Ilien.

"I said I wouldn't ever leave you again," said Ilien, catching his pencil and holding it gently. "And I meant it." He laid his slain friend gently in his shirt pocket.

Chapter XXVI

The Beginning

Gallund nodded to Anselm and raised his hands once more. "Now for the words of Opening."

"Wait," said Ilien. "Why did the wizardesses leave Nadae, anyhow?"

Gallund left his hands suspended in mid air, and winced.

"What?" asked Ilien. He looked around at the others. Thessien tightened his grip on his sword. The Swan grimaced, and the feathers upon her neck bristled. Anselm looked puzzled.

"It's them you're afraid of," concluded Ilien, "not some foul creature from another world. It's them. I don't believe it!"

Windy put her hands to her hips. "You did something to make them leave, didn't you? Didn't you!"

Gallund lowered his hands, a grimace upon his face. "Nonsense. The wizardesses left Nadae of their own accord. They understood the dangers of Reknamarken's prophesy. They knew it was the only way to prevent it from coming true."

Ilien shook his head in disbelief. "You forced them to go. You were so afraid of fulfilling the Prophesy that you made them leave."

Windy could hardly contain herself. She stormed about between the trees, throwing her hands in the air. "You men are unbelievable!"

"Now hold on there," said Gallund.

The princess spun on him. "It takes two to tango, you know. Why do men think they're so high and mighty that they can throw their weight around and make women do whatever they wish? So the Necromancer prophesied that a Nomadin child would free him from his prison. So what! So what if having a child would doom the world to destruction. Why condemn the women to exile? Why force the wizardesses to leave? If you were all such tough men then it should have been you, not them, that left. It's just so typical!"

"The wizardesses abandoned the wizards," said the Swan. "Not the other way around."

Silence fell about the small clearing.

"I don't believe you," said Windy. Her voice sounded small.

The Swan sat down, her feet disappearing beneath her feathery body. "It's true. They left on their own accord, as Gallund says. It was their idea."

Windy turned to Gallund.

"We didn't want them to go," said the wizard. "But they insisted it was the only way. So they left." He gazed at the black entryway of the Crossing, the closed door behind which the wizardesses could be found. "They just left."

Thessien lifted his head suddenly and searched the woods with his eyes.

"What is it?" asked Gallund.

"Where is Pedustil?"

Gallund shook his head in annoyance. "How should I know? Now stand back. Stand back everyone. I'm opening the Crossing."

The wizard raised his hands once more. "Pentar, Entar, Figaru, Pari!"

The darkness of the Crossing paled. A grey pall spread from its center, pressing back the black void. Like a swirling whirlpool, the Crossing began to roil, fast and faster, casting out dizzying eddies of rippling magic. Ilien found himself strangely drawn to it, as if the Crossing was truly a whirlpool seeking to drag him forward, pulling at his mind and body.

"Ilien will go first," said Gallund. "Then you, Windy. In quick succession. I will bring up the rear."

Ilien adjusted the pack upon his back and stepped a pace forward.

"Get ready, Ilien," warned the wizard. "Follow him quickly, Windy. Ready! Now go!"

Ilien felt the world drop from beneath him.

"No! Stop!"

He heard the startled cry, but it was too late. Blackness descended upon him like a net and yanked him off his feet. He remembered Gallund's words and did not fight the pull of the Crossing. He turned in somersaults as an invisible hand flung him down and around, down and around. He couldn't see. He couldn't hear. Nauseating vertigo overwhelmed him. Then came a jerk so violent that his very thoughts went blank, as if they were knocked from his mind by the force of the blow. Specks of light filled his vision, phantom stars that told him he was close to blacking out. He sped through the nothing around him like an arrow from a string. The startled cry returned.

"No! Stop!"

It sounded like his own voice ringing in his ears. Lightning crashed over him and he knew no more.

Pedustil crashed through the trees, shattering boughs and cracking trunks as he swooped down upon the small clearing. Ilien bounced about like a ball upon his back, holding fast to the small fin that would some day grow into a full-sized Breach. Below, he saw himself step into the Crossing.

"No! Stop!" he shouted again.

Gallund and Thessien stood at the ready before the roiling black hole of the Crossing. The Swan and Anselm looked up at his shout, eyes wide, mouths agape at seeing Ilien upon Pedustil hurtling toward them. But it was Windy Ilien saw stepping toward the maw of the Crossing, her pack strapped low upon her back. Windy! That boisterous, impetuous girl who Ilien now knew he loved most, worried about most. That girl who had captured his heart.

"Windy!" he shouted. She didn't hear him. She stepped toward the Crossing. She was going to cross! He couldn't stop her!

"Rose!" he screamed.

She stopped and spun around, looking up with wonder and surprise in her eyes. Pedustil dove quickly toward the ground.

"Ilien?"

Pedustil's right wing struck a tree. He crashed to the earth in a violent tumble of clawed limbs and exploding vapor. End over end he sailed, tearing up great ribbons of earth before landing unmoving on his back.

"Ilien!" Windy ran to Pedustil, her pack flying from her back. "Oh my god! Ilien!"

Pedustil moaned and flopped his great, scaled head to the side. Steam leaked from his gill flaps in a slow, steady stream. He lay on his back, legs and arms splayed outward.

"Where's Ilien!" screamed Windy. She scrambled around the Gorgul, looking for him. "Get up!" she cried, kicking the Gorgul in the side. "Get up! He's under you!"

The Swan flew toward Pedustil, wings flapping wildly, honking and screeching. "You're crushing him!"

"Get up, you fool lizard!" shouted Gallund. "Get up!" Anselm strode forward and heaved the Gorgul onto his side. Only Thessien remained calm, peering up into the tree above Pedustil.

"I didn't know you all cared so much," said Ilien from a bough overhead.

Gallund scowled and mumbled something inaudible under his breath. Anselm and the Swan breathed a simultaneous sigh of relief. Windy glared up at him, her hands upon her hips. There were tears in her eyes.

"You stupid boy! I thought you were killed! Of all the idiotic tricks to play—"

Ilien incanted his Flying spell and floated lazily down to Windy, a grin upon his lips. Before she could argue with him further, he threw his arms around her and hugged her fiercely. She stood dumbfounded, her arms pinned at her side, her face red.

"Windy," he said. "Oh, Windy. It's good to see you. It's so very good to see you."

Ilien held her in silence for a long moment, then felt a feathery tap upon his shoulder. He spun and embraced the Swan, burying his face into her downy bosom. Whatever she was going to say was forgotten. A look of relief and wonder spread across her quilled face and she lowered her head, wrapping her long, slender neck closer to Ilien.

"It worked," said Ilien. "It all worked out."

"What worked out?" asked Anselm, his stony countenance bent with confusion.

Ilien fixed the Giant with a sudden, tearful gaze. No off-center, watery eye. No scarred face. No lipless mouth. Anselm was a Giant, not a Cyclops. A broad smile spread across Ilien's face as he realized that now there never would be a Cyclops race.

"Father!" he cried, and ran to hug the wizard. Gallund seemed taken aback by the sudden onslaught of affection. But soon he stood squeezing his son with a crooked smile upon his wizened face.

"You're handsome again," laughed Ilien.

Gallund reached up and stroked his whiskered chin. Peanuts dropped from his open hand.

"It's finished," said Ilien, pulling away from the wizard and addressing the others. "The Evil is gone. Bulcrist is dead. The Nomadin are no longer our enemies." He had done it. He had set things right. Everything was as it should be. He had his friends back. He had his entire world back.

He had done it.

He suddenly felt the broken stub of his pencil through his shirt. He pulled it out, his joy forgotten.

"Oh no," gasped Windy.

Ilien hung his head. Well, not all of his friends.

"That's disgusting!"

Ilien looked up, his heart skipping a beat.

"Tell me that's not what I think it is!"

Ilien blinked, then his face exploded with delight. Gallund held Ilien's wriggling pencil in one hand. "That's right!" exclaimed Ilien. "Gallund kept you here. You never crossed! You're still alive!" He leaped forward and snatched the pencil from the wizard's grasp. Peanuts flew everywhere.

"Gross! Get it away from me! Help!" cried the pencil.

Ilien realized he still held the dead pencil stub in his other hand. He winced and stuffed it in his back pocket.

"Was that me?" screeched his pencil in horror, and with a plaintiff cry, it passed out.

"But how?" asked Thessien. He regarded the Crossing in the center of the clearing, its swirling black void still churning slowly in circles. "How is this all possible?"

"It's a long story," said Ilien. "A long, long story. But trust me, it's finally over." He gazed around him at the lush green forest, remembering the Desecration that had blighted the land, the flat, bleak greyness devoid of all life that had stretched as far as the eye could see. "This place is a paradise," he said, a smile splitting his face. "It's finally all over."

The Swan shook her tail feathers and slowly sat down, her webbed feet disappearing beneath her. "Not quite," she said.

Windy reached out and grabbed Ilien's hand. "What now?"

"There is one final choice to be made." The Swan turned her black marble eyes on Ilien. "Remember what you told me, Ilien, long before you became a man."

"But he's not a man," said Windy. She squeezed Ilien's hand and blushed. "Not yet, I mean."

"Paradise is nothing without freedom," recited Ilien, remembering what the Swan had told him as she had floated away on the glassy lake. "Choice is all we have."

"Yes," said the Swan. "And the final choice is yours to make. You told me that, too, that the choice would be yours when the time came."

"When what time came?" asked Windy, suddenly nervous again.

"He must decide who he truly is," said the Swan, never taking his eyes from Ilien. "He has to make a choice. Does he become the Creator again, or choose to remain as he is?"

Ilien felt a sudden surge of energy rush through him, like an unsummoned spell that hovered on the tip of his tongue.

"Ilien, what is it?" asked Windy.

She still held his hand, but Ilien couldn't feel it. The magic that imbued his body drowned his senses in a wave of dizzying mental images. He squeezed his eyes shut, and though he didn't know it, his body began to glow, casting his shadow thin and wavering beneath him. Pictures flashed through his mind. His mother's face. His bedroom back home. His two story farm house. Stan and Peaty. He saw himself cheating on his geometry test, walking home from school, lying out by the stream behind his house, fishing in Parson's pond. Sounds came next. His mom singing to him in the night, that creaky fifth step he always avoided, the raucous calls of the crows on Parson's Hill, the cry of a baby. He felt soft hands upon his skin, cold water on his legs, hot wind on his neck, bark against his back. Emotions flooded through him. Laughter, hatred, shame, joy, confusion, embarrassment, rage, empathy, love. He was losing himself.

Losing himself? Or discovering who he truly was?

Windy threw her arms around his glowing form. "Stay with us, Ilien. Stay with us."

She put her lips to his ear. "Stay with me."

Chapter XXVII

Ilien's Choice

"How are they biting?"

Ilien sat up so quickly that his fishing pole jumped from his lap and fell with a splash into the water. He blinked and looked around in confusion, caught between dreaming and waking. He sat on a wide, flat rock near a calm pool of water. Ripples raced across its surface, the result of his lost pole. Beyond the pool, a sloping field ran up to meet a thin line of trees. The afternoon sun warmed his skin.

He knew this place. The flat rock, the pool of water, the grassy field speckled with tiny white flowers. An imposing grey barn towered over a small white farmhouse. It was a scene from out of a recurring dream. Or nightmare.

"I said, how are they biting?"

Ilien gazed up at the person standing over him. The sun hung poised behind their head, blocking out the face that stared back at him. He blinked, and his breath caught momentarily in his throat.

"Ilien Woodhill! Are you going to answer me or are you going to sit there like a stupid cow and stare off into space?"

Windy bent and picked up a stone at her feet. A perfect skipping stone. "It doesn't look like you even care if they're biting," she said with a laugh, and tossed the stone into the center of the pool. A widening ring of ripples expanded toward the shore. "Asleep while fishing. So typical. So typically Ilien."

Ilien grinned up at her. "There's still a lot of daylight left, you know. Care to join me?"

Windy looked back in the direction of Farmer Parson's house. "If Mrs. Parson catches us back here, she'll sic her dogs on us."

Ilien reached up and pulled Windy down into the grass. "Then we'd better hide!"

Chapter XXVIII

The End

The young girl sits on the old stone wall, watching a squirrel skitter from the moss-covered rocks to the trunk of the oak tree her grandfather planted. The sky is scudded with pink and gold clouds, reflecting the last rays of sunlight after a long, warm day. The seesaw peaks of the distant snow-capped mountains look like cones of vanilla ice cream, her favorite flavor.

She sighs and thinks about the boy from school, the short boy with the long, dark hair and piercing brown eyes, eyes that seem to look into her. She thinks of him and smiles. Owen. She whispers his name and reaches up and touches her forehead, a habit of hers whenever she gets nervous. Thinking of Owen makes her nervous. Owen thinks she is pretty. That's what Emily Pandrake said.

It is getting late and she knows her mother will be calling for her to come in soon. There is homework to do, and chores to finish, then bed. Just like that, the day will be over, and a new one will begin. *Why is everything so boring and monotonous? At this rate, summer vacation will never get here quick enough.*

Somewhere behind her, the front door to her house bangs shut. That will be her mother, searching for her. Her father is probably inside, reading the paper. As usual.

"Kayla! Time to come in! Kayla!"

Yup, that's her mom. Right on cue. "Coming mom!"

About the Author

Shawn P. Cormier was born in 1967, and grew up in the rural town of Southbridge, Massachusetts. He has been scribbling down stories since the fifth grade, and earned his degree in Creative Writing from Long Island University, Southampton Campus. He published his first novel, Nomadin, in 2003. Its sequel, NiDemon, was published two years later. When not writing, he can be found in his family's jewelry store, repairing jewelry and studying gems. If not there, check the local tennis courts. He currently resides in southern Massachusetts with his wife and two children.

Author's Note

Twenty years and more than a million words after it began, Ilien's story has finally been told. Though the first book in the series, Nomadin, was published in 2003, and the final word count of the finished trilogy is just shy of 240,000 words, there is no doubt in my mind that it took twenty years and a million words to tell. I didn't know it then, but 1987 was the year Ilien was born. It was also the day my life changed. The small boy with the big heart would haunt my thoughts for another fourteen years before I listened to him and started recording his deeds. If you are a writer at heart, you know what I mean.

"What now?" I'm often asked. "What will you do? Will you continue to write?" It's like asking a marathon runner if he'll ever race again as he's laying in a pool of sweat at the finish line. Of course he'll run again. He'll be better than he ever was. He'll rest. He'll regain his strength then begin his training for the next race.

A writer, like a marathon runner, is compelled to do what they do because they can do nothing else that makes them feel so complete. I believe this is true of all writers whether they write fantasy, science fiction, horror, mystery, contemporary fiction, chick-lit, poetry or good old non-fiction.

Thank you for sticking with me through Ilien's adventure. His tale was worth telling. In a world where there are so many choices available to us, it is ever-more important to remember those famous words: Be, then do, then have!